Sutherland Downs

80003557578

Sutherland Downs

Peter McKelvie

W F HOWES LTD

This large print edition published in 2022 by
W F Howes Ltd
Unit 5, St George's House, Rearsby Business Park,
Gaddesby Lane, Rearsby, Leicester LE7 4YH

1 3 5 7 9 10 8 6 4 2

First published in the United Kingdom in 2020

Copyright © Peter McKelvie, 2020

The right of Peter McKelvie to be identified as
the author of this work has been asserted by him
in accordance with the Copyright, Designs and
Patents Act, 1988.

All rights reserved

A CIP catalogue record for this book is available
from the British Library

ISBN 978 1 00409 658 9

Typeset by Palimpsest Book Production Limited,
Falkirk, Stirlingshire

Printed and bound by
T J Books in the UK

Northamptonshire
County Council

W F HOWES

I'd like to dedicate this book to my mum and dad, who courageously moved us from the city into the country and onto a farm when I was just eleven years old. Later, my father organised an opportunity for me to travel away with a shearing team as a wool presser for a month-long contract. I moved back to the city in my early twenties, but my time in the country and as a jackeroo for a few years remains some of the most influential of my life.

PROLOGUE

'Thank you, Mr Cookie, you are very kind'
'Please Girlie, please, it's just Cookie. Cookie ain't me real name. It's just me nickname . . . cause I'm the Cook . . . yer see?. Me real names Howard, but any man calls me that'll get his neck rung like a bloody chook. I don't know what me old Ma and Pa was thinking when they called me that.' Cookie was smiling at Maysa.

'Well Cookie,' Bob Jackson looked earnestly at Cookie and with a measure of genuine concern. 'You look after this young lady, mate. She's had a bloody rough trot of late, and the last thing she needs is one of these no good for nothin' layabouts poking their nose around her. You've got my permission to run em off with a clip under the ear, and quick bloody smart too.'

Bob turned to Maysa and fixed her in a solemn gaze.

'Well Luv, it's up to you now. You take care of yerself, keep yer head down and work hard. Show me a young sheila like you can cut it out here, ok?' He looked uncertain. In a short time, he had grown quite fond of Maysa, and he had her best interests at heart, but in truth, he was anxious.

1

With that, Maysa stepped forward quickly, and with a hand on each of Bob's arms, she kissed his cheek.

'Thank you, Bob, very much . . . for everything. I will not let you down. You will see. I will make the best bloody damn fair dinkum Cookie-hand you ever had.'

Completely taken aback and embarrassed by the kiss and the confusing description, Bob stuttered.

'Yes, b, bye girl.' He turned to shake hands very formally with Cookie. He had rarely shaken hands with Cookie in 20 years of working together. Usually, Cookie got some form of goodbye punctuated by 'you old fat bastard.'

Cookie was equally embarrassed by the formalities and the feminine presence. He stepped forward awkwardly to take Bob's hand.

'Ah, yes Bob, safe trip, we'll see you in a couple of weeks then.'

And so began the shearing contract and a new life for Maysa.

CHAPTER ONE

'Duck on the pond,' came the cry from inside the big old corrugated iron shed, baking in the hot sun. The words were muffled by the din of bleating sheep, of shearing plant with long leather belts sliding over pulleys, slapping together like slow rhythmic applause, and the chattering of shears as they were pushed through the wool.

It was 9:20 in the morning and already uncomfortably hot. The smell of eucalyptus was beginning to burn in her nostrils as Maysa delivered the morning tea to the shearing shed. She stood outside on the wooden landing with a basket of sandwiches and scones, waiting to be noticed by a roustabout.

Driving the shears through the long blow, a cut along the spine of the sheep, the shearer with the jet-black oily hair, muscular arms and shoulders shiny with sweat, looked up and toward the door hungrily. His hunger extended from morning tea to the pretty young girl with the baskets, talking to the roustabout.

As tradition dictated, women were mostly

forbidden from entering the shearing shed during working hours. The men were alerted when someone, noticing a woman entering the shed, would call 'duck on the pond.' It was expected the crew would mind their language and behave respectfully. In truth, it was much preferred that the sheilas just kept clear of the shed. But this young lady was no duck, she was a swan, and she caught the eye of all the good and the not so good men in the shed.

'I'll take that missus,' Dean mumbled self-consciously. He wasn't used to speaking to women and certainly not to any as strikingly good looking as this one.

He was the youngest of the roustabouts and was tall, thin and shy. He wore the unofficial uniform of roustabouts, a blue singlet, khaki shorts and shearers moccasins. The moccasins were made from sheepskin fashioned into a boot with no separate sole and laced with leather straps. Dean's blue singlet was flecked white with wool pieces and wet with sweat, and his shorts were stained dark by wool grease.

'Thank you, Dean, enjoy your morning tea, and please call me Maysa.'

Maysa turned and strolled down the shearing shed steps slowly, enjoying the few minutes of peace before she and Cookie began the preparation of lunch in the hot furnace that was the kitchen. She found herself quickly developing an affection for this harsh country, its rich red soil,

4

beautiful old gnarled gum trees, and the occasional clumps of green grass that tried in vain to soften the landscape. It had been two years in Australia, and until now, all of it in Melbourne, which was a complete contrast to this outback setting.

Walking between the shearing shed and the kitchen, Maysa faintly heard the now familiar sound of the working dogs barking and sheep calling. She stopped under the shade of an old gum tree to look out at the paddocks and watch the next mob arriving at the yards. Each day, more sheep were driven into the yards by the shed in readiness for shearing. Lambs were drafted off the ewes and kept in a separate paddock, resulting in a constant din of mothers calling for babies and vice versa. Late in the afternoon, as many sheep as possible would be packed in under the floor of the shed for the night, ensuring the shearers had dry sheep to begin the next day. The shearers refused to shear wet sheep. It was uncomfortable to work in wet, heavy clothing. And the graziers didn't want their sheep shorn wet because it could result in mildew in the wool. None the less, it hadn't rained for weeks, so there were no threats of a stop-work. The shearing was progressing according to the schedule.

In the distance, out in the paddock, moving between the old river gums was a mob of sheep, identified by a rising cloud of red dust. Maysa watched three horsemen coming into view. An occasional dog appeared at the flanks of the mob, barking furiously and biting at the ankles of any sheep that dared to stray too far from the mob, returning them at a gallop.

The horseman's cries were becoming audible now, with shouts of, 'steady, sit down you bloody mongrel,' and, 'get up, come on, get up.'

It was the very foreign daily routine that Maysa found both fascinating and strangely comfortable.

She watched as one of the horsemen broke away and rode ahead of the mob to the yards, dismounting in one fluid motion and opening the gate for the incoming sheep. Two dogs followed dutifully behind him. They ran what Maysa considered to be dangerously close to the back hooves of the horse and she watched with some concern. The horseman mounted his horse again and reined it around in Maysa's direction. He was looking directly at her, no more than one hundred and fifty yards away now. He waved tentatively at Maysa, who turned to look behind her to be sure it was she he was waving at. Shyly, she raised a hand and returned the salutation. With that, the horseman spurred his horse into a canter and rode straight toward her.

Maysa was startled. She immediately began nervously brushing her cotton dress out flat. She wiped the sweat from her forehead with the back of her hand, then wiped her hands on her apron. Apart from a good dusting of self-raising flour, she felt she looked quite presentable. Certainly, presentable enough for this outback setting.

Having not met any of the stockmen so far, she was pleasantly surprised to see as he got nearer that he was young, possibly only a few years older than she was. She could also see he was very good looking as his face emerged from under the shade of his broad-brimmed Akubra hat. He was quite a contrast to the shearers and roustabouts, who were a very rough sawn group, and who had not enough manners between the dozen of them to make one gentleman.

'G'day, how yer going?' he enquired, reigning the horse into an abrupt halt only a few yards from Maysa. Although having had little to do with horses, she nervously stood her ground, but only because an old wire fence separated her from the stock horse. A small cloud of dust followed the cantering horse into its halt and drifted over Maysa, who try as she might, could not help but cough a little.

'Oh, sorry.' The young stockman's face flushed a little as he looked at Maysa. She had long dark hair, tied back loosely, blue eyes and olive skin. This was the first time he had seen her any closer than from the yards. To Maysa, his face was an open book. She was nothing if not modest, but she was aware she was blessed with a pretty face, and she could see the impact in his eyes. Typically though, her modesty persuaded her that his reaction was just the result of her being the only young lady for miles in any direction.

'That's alright,' replied Maysa. 'You can see I am already filthy.' She smiled an easy smile.

A hot wet tongue licked at Maysa's shin. She stepped backward with a start.

'Si' down, you bloody idiot.' The Stockman yelled rather too enthusiastically at one of the sheepdogs, who was craning through the fence to sniff and lick at Maysa's leg. 'Geezus, . . . sorry again.'

'It's fine, honestly. He is just saying hello.' Maysa assured the stockman with a broad smile as she leant down to pat the dog through the fence. It was quickly joined by the second dog, eager to have its share of this rare show of affection. 'What are their names?'

'Billy and Barney. A pair of bloody ratbags if ever there were. Abbot and Costello, I call 'em. They're loving you to bits now. Don't encourage them, you'll never get rid of them.'

'They are lovely, and so pleased to see me.' Maysa happily continued patting the excited hounds. She had no idea who Abbot and Costello were but smiled regardless and paused for a moment waiting for the stockman to speak.

'I'm Tom, by the way. I am one of the jackaroos here. I've seen you taking smoko up to the shed a couple of times and thought I'd come and say G'day. If that's alright?'

'That's very nice of you. I'm Maysa. I work in the kitchen with Cookie.'

8

He was quietly watching her, almost staring, so she continued a little self-consciously.

'Does your family own the station, Tom?' Maysa squinted and shaded her eyes from the sun. It had settled annoyingly into position behind and only half eclipsed by Tom's head.

He dismounted and walked over to the fence and leant on an old weathered timber post near to Maysa to get some shade while holding the reins to his horse at his side.

'No, I'm just a Jackaroo here. Where are you from Maysa?'

'I am from Melbourne. Carlton. I'm just here for the shearing contract.'

Tom smiled. 'I don't think you were born in Melbourne, were you? You look.' He hesitated for a moment as if to rephrase what he was trying to say. 'Well, your accent, it's intriguing.'

'Ah, my accent. I am trying . . . no, I'm trying . . . to make it less noticeable.' Maysa blushed. 'You are very right. I came here from India. My father was Irish, and my mother was Indian, actually. I am . . . how would you say . . . a melting pot.' Maysa hammed up her accent for effect. 'A strange and unusual combination. I have only been in Australia for two years.'

Tom's horse stepped forward and rested her forehead affectionately against Tom's back. She sought what little shade she could and swished her tail to deter the bush flies that were gathering by the hundred on her rump.

9

'So what are you doing here then? Up here in the Aussie bush with a shearing team?' Maysa's facial expression changed from a happy smile to sad and reflective. She could see Tom immediately regretted asking the question.

Looking down and brushing more flour from her apron, Maysa spoke quietly.

'My brother found me this job with Bob Jackson, the shearing contractor. My brother works at the wharf in Melbourne with Bob's son David, and they kindly offered me this job when they heard about my father . . . he died just two months ago. My brother and I had to move out of our family home. We couldn't pay the rent. He moved into Bob's house. I had to go somewhere where I could get a job and somewhere to live. It is very difficult to get a good job when you're a woman. It is even worse if you have an accent or look a little different as I do. So when Bob asked me if I could cook and if I would like to see Australia, I said, why not. It seemed too good to be true. I really had no idea what I was saying yes to, of course.'

They stood in silence for a moment, reflecting, Maysa on her personal grief.

'That's amazing! I have never seen a cook that looks like you before.' Tom smiled, obviously trying to break the tension and speaking with enthusiasm. 'Old Cookie's about as good looking as they get out here, and you're sure a step up from him. A big step.' Maysa smiled in return, shaking the

10

momentary dark cloud that had settled over her. She still looked a little down. Tom persisted.

'Well, I know what it's like to lose someone you love, so I kinda understand what yer' going through. If you need someone to talk to, I'd be happy to have a chinwag anytime.'

'Fairdinkum, you Aussies say strange things! Chinwag?' They laughed at Maysa's mock Australian accent.

The conversation paused momentarily. As it did, Tom's horse nudged him in the back impatiently. He was flung forward into the fence against Maysa. She caught him with two flat hands on his chest as he arched himself over the top wire, not able to avoid a scratch on his stomach as his shirt got tangled in the barbs. They were both embarrassed but felt a rush of excitement with the contact.

'Shit, bloody horse.' He cursed, Maysa laughed.

'She loves you Tom, and I think she's jealous of you talking to a strange girl.'

An unwelcome shout came from the sheep yards.

'Hey lover boy, we do have work to do today, you know.'

'That's bloody Paddy, the lead hand.' Tom was embarrassed by Paddy's comment. He's kinda my boss. He's a smart arse that fella. He's a bit odd too. I better get a move on.' He struggled to pull away from the fence. His shirt was hooked tight.

'Jesus, I can't get this bloody shirt untangled.'

Tom mumbled. 'I'll have to rip it.' His struggles only served to further ensnare him on the barbed wire.

'Wait, let me try,' Maysa offered. As she wrestled with the tangled and torn shirt, her fingers brushed against his stomach, and his face flushed red again.

There was another shout, now from the door of the kitchen. Maysa's boss was standing in the red dust, yelling across the yard at her.

'Maysa, hurry up and get over here, will yer. These bloody potaters aren't gunna peel emselves are they.' He turned and waddled back into the old tin shed, mumbling and cursing under his breath.

'Better go 'ey.' Finally freed, Tom climbed up into the saddle. 'Was good to meet you Maysa.' In a shy voice, he added, 'would like to chat to you again sometime if you'd like to?'

Shielding her face from the sun and still smiling, Maysa replied.

'I would like that very much.'

As Tom began to ride off, Maysa waved after him and called as an afterthought, 'I could mend your shirt if you bring it to me.'

Tom rode off without answering, and Maysa wondered if he had heard her.

CHAPTER TWO

The shearers quarters, in a fenced-off compound, comprised of a few simple corrugated huts set some three hundred yards away from the shearing shed. A few ancient gums provided a little shade.

Each of the shearer's sleeping huts had four doors to four individual rooms. Each room had nothing other than two steel-framed stretcher beds, a thin mattress that barely countered the discomfort of sprung wires below, a grey blanket, and a single light globe hanging by an electric wire from the ceiling. Each light had an on and off pull cord.

A small shed stood at one end of the compound, covering a long drop toilet. It was merely a deep hole in the ground with a wooden seat perched precariously over it. The only light in the shed was from the sun or moon shine streaming through the loose tin on the walls and roof, swinging in the breeze, or the knotholes in the timber door. A handful of lime from a bucket, thrown down the hole after use, killed the smell of waste and discouraged flies and vermin. A pile of old newspapers, torn in strips and hanging from a wire hook, acted as toilet paper.

Four people could stand side by side on a rough concrete floor showering in another old tin shed known as the shower block. Water was pumped from a nearby river and heated in a tank by a wood fire lit by one of the roustabouts at afternoon tea time each day. It housed a row of troughs for washing before meals, cold wash starts each morning and laundering clothes over the weekend. Clothes were hung on plain wire lines strung between trees. They were typically brimming with blue singlets, blue underpants, blue socks and denim double-fronted shearers pants by lunchtime each Saturday.

A small dam, a short walk from the compound, provided some of the little entertainment offered the shearers on the weekend by way of trapping yabbies. These were cooked on the campfire and washed down with an unhealthy volume of luke-warm beer. Other sport included chasing and shooting wild pigs, kangaroos and even the occasional emu over the weekend.

The kitchen was a tin shed set amongst the shearer's quarters. The roof and walls were corrugated iron. Inside, a large fan circulated the hot air around the room, creating nothing more than the impression it was cooling the occupants. A slow combustion wood stove sat in one corner and contributed to the hot and oppressive environment. A length of water pipe running between walls, with butcher's hooks hanging from it, held a series of old cooking pots, fry pans, saucepans and various ladles. More than once, Maysa had seen her boss, Cookie, walk headfirst into a pot as the afternoon wore on, and he became more intoxicated. The bumps and crashes were always accompanied by a new set of expletives. They meant nothing to Maysa but for the tone. She found herself frequently turning away to hide her smile.

In the middle of a room was an old timber table, worn through the pale green painted top to the raw wood. On it lay knives, a large pot of potatoes and cutting boards.

Along one wall was a set of pantry shelves. They held sacks of potatoes, onions, boxes of cereal, flour, sugar, salt, sauces, bottled fruit and many more basic foods. In another corner sat the icebox, which typically had little in it.

As Maysa neared the kitchen, Cookie appeared in the doorway, his substantial frame filling it entirely.

'Take yer bloody time, why don't yer. Do you want me to do the bloody lot meself? It's as hot as bloody hell back there.' He grumbled, pointing back over his shoulder into the dim interior of the kitchen with his thumb.

'Be a good girl and go fetch me a sherbet, will yer Luv.' He spoke in a more pleasant tone now. Cookie was in his late fifties but looked much older. He was excessively overweight. He wore a white singlet, wet with sweat and stained yellow in large half-moons under the armpits. He was balding, and what hair he had was plastered to his scalp by a combination of sweat and hair oil. His nose was large and bulbous and mapped with small veins that provided a history of his excessive drinking. His lower jaw jutted out beyond the upper, and his two front teeth were long gone. A rolled cigarette hung precariously from his lower lip, and ash had fallen down the front of his singlet and settled in amongst pieces of his breakfast, deposited there at dawn.

Cookie had the underrated talent of being able to talk without removing the cigarette from his mouth. Sometimes Maysa had observed that he could even open his mouth entirely during an animated conversation with the cigarette remaining adhered to his lower lip.

Maysa turned and walked toward the dam. Under the shade of a tree, Cookie had driven a small wooden stake into the bank. From it, a rope led into the water. Maysa pulled on the rope and drew a wooden crate from the water and across the muddy bank. It contained 6 large bottles of beer, cooled by the water. She took one bottle, covered with mud, from the crate. She washed it clean in the dam water and carried it back to the kitchen.

As she returned, Cookie was carrying half a sheep carcass over his shoulder from the meat safe into the kitchen. He threw it down on the cutting block, which was a solid piece of waist-high red gum. It was worn into waves by knives and meat hatchets, over years of shearing seasons.

He turned to face Maysa as she walked through the door. His appearance was part evil and part comical. His hairy, sweaty shoulder and the front of his singlet were stained with sheep blood and greasy with sheep fat.

'Good on yer Luv, that'll find the spot I reckon.'

He took a carving knife and flicked the bottle top off the brown bottle, and upended it into his mouth. Beer cascaded down his chin. When he finally finished gulping the fluid down, he wiped his mouth with the back of his blood-stained hand, leaving streaks of red across his face. He burped long and loud and then broke into a broad smile announcing, 'Shit, that was good!' It always appeared to take him completely by surprise.

Maysa stood in the doorway, watching Cookie's drinking theatrics. At first, they had horrified her. Now she was no longer threatened by this gentle giant. He amused her in an odd sort of affectionate way. She took a seat by the table and began peeling potatoes for lunch.

'What was you up to with that fella by the tree over there, Maysa? What'd he want with you? Not that I haven't worked that out for meself.'

'That is just Tom. He is one of the stockmen here on the station.' Maysa replied, keeping her gaze fixed firmly on the potato she was peeling and hoping that was that.

'Yeah, I know who he is. What'd he want then?'

Maysa noticed that Cookie had assumed a fatherly role soon after her arrival. A few days of needing to provide protection from the uncouth behaviour of the shearers had only further encouraged him. He provided sage advice on every possible occasion, most of which Maysa ultimately failed to comprehend while smiling and nodding earnestly.

'He just came to introduce himself Cookie, nothing more than being polite. Quite a gentleman, actually.'

'You's were standing mighty bloody close for an introduction.'

'That was not Tom's fault, it was his horse that made us.' Maysa was laughing.

'Whatever, just watch him. You're the only sheila within thirty miles except for Mrs Patterson, the owner's wife. You can't tell me these young fellas are only thinkin' about a polite conversation with you.'

'You are very sweet Cookie, but I am sure I am quite safe. Besides, I have you to protect my virtue.' Cookie felt quite chuffed with the compliment, although he wasn't quite sure he understood what virtue was.

'Well, ok then. Anyway, I gotta get on and butcher up these bloody chops before the flies carry 'em away on me.' Mumbling awkwardly, he waved a couple of blowflies off the sheep carcass.

That evening, Maysa retired to her bedroom at

the side of the kitchen and lay awake for several hours, alone with thoughts of meeting Tom. Moths and insects flew endlessly around the hot light globe hanging from her ceiling. When she finally felt sleepy, and the shouting and raucous behaviour from the campfire had died to a dull murmur, she pulled the light cord, rolled on her side and fell into a deep sleep. She dreamt of her father and her brother and faded images of her mother smiling.

A loud metallic bang from the kitchen woke her as the first light streamed in between the two potato sacks that Cookie had nailed into position over her window.

'*You can take my bunk Luv,*' Cookie had volunteered, showing Maysa the small room off the kitchen. It was nearly a week earlier when Bob Jackson had arrived with Maysa on a Saturday before shearing had commenced.

CHAPTER THREE

Maysa delivered the morning tea to the shearing shed. She stalled on the landing talking to Dean for as long as she could, hoping to see a pall of dust in the distance signalling the arrival of the morning's mob of unshorn sheep. On her way back to the kitchen, she hesitated as much as she could, meandering along, kicking sticks and stirring up dust with her work boots as she walked. She frequently glanced over her shoulder, hoping for any sign of the mob and the handsome stockman. There was nothing. She even walked to the dam after seeing Cookie appear in the doorway, anticipating his routine call for a dam cooled beer.

One day he'd announced, very pleased with himself, 'I need a damn cold beer, someone get me a dam cooled beer.' He'd laughed himself into a coughing fit that had made Maysa worried he would collapse in the kitchen.

'Here's your beer, Cookie.' Maysa placed the beer bottle on the table next to a sheep liver that Cookie was about to slice up for lambs fry.

'Good on yer Luv. What's eatin' you? Yer gone quiet all of a sudden.'

'Nothing.' Maysa feigned a smile. 'Just thinking about things.'

'Things ey? Things who ride horses, I'm guessing. Am I right?'

'Not at all.' Maysa paused for a moment as if considering Cookies comment. 'But it is interesting there wasn't a mob brought in from the paddock today, was there?'

'No, well there wouldn't be, would there? It's Friday. Be Sunday before they bring the next lot in. We'll get a bit of peace and quiet for the next couple of days, 'cep't for those monkeys if they get on the turps around the fire at night.' Cookie inclined his head toward the shearer's quarters.

Maysa's face betrayed her disappointment. She could see Cookie felt sorry for her. He would know it was a dull life for her out here in the bush with only him as a companion. But she knew she needed to keep to herself and to spend most of her evenings quietly in her room. To spend too much time with any shearer might have encouraged unwelcome advances, particularly after a night of beer drinking. Bob had said as much in his not-infrequent warnings.

The day drew on slowly through lunch. The shearers all came to a large room on the opposite side of the kitchen to Maysa's bedroom, where they ate their meals. They sat at two tables and quietly ate lamb chops, lambs fry, mash potatoes, green beans and carrots. Tin mugs of hot tea sweetened by several spoonfuls of sugar washed down their meals. Some of the older men in the team would crack open a beer after the meal and sit on the steps to their rooms until ten minutes before the after-lunch run began. Others would return to the shed to sharpen combs and cutters on the grinding wheels. The roustabouts would eat lunch quickly and return to the shed to fill the catching pens with sheep. They had to skirt and roll any fleeces not attended to when the final sheep were shorn before lunch.

At afternoon tea, 3:30pm, Maysa walked the baskets of scones and cake to the shed again. As she walked, she glanced toward the toilet shed. A stack of empty brown beer bottles was growing like a neatly constructed fence. She wondered at the endurance of these men. They ate three cooked meals a day as well as morning and after-noon tea, then washed it all down with copious amounts of beer. She thought about their jokes and arguments around the campfire until late each evening. Then they were up at the crack of dawn and doing it all again the next day. Yet none of them was overweight, and some of them were as thin as a sheep in a drought.

Tired and slumping in her chair, Maysa finished peeling yet another pile of potatoes to be roasted in the old wood stove for dinner.

'One more meal Luv and then it's the weekend.

You can sleep in tomorrow, and these buggers will look after 'emselves for lunch and dinner. I expect some of them will go to town and won't get back until Sunday.'

The evening meal was served and eaten. The shearers had left and were showering, then drinking around the campfire as they had every other night that week. Maysa and Cookie washed up the pots, pans, enamel plates, mugs, knives and forks. Cookie was on his fourth bottle of beer, well ahead of every other night that week, but was showing no sign of slowing down. Maysa sat at one end of the table with her back to the door, drying the washing with a tea towel. Cookie stood in the middle of the table, sloshing everything through a large galvanised trough of hot water. At regular intervals, the cigarette in Cookies mouth dropped ash, shaken loose by a throaty cough, into the washing tub. It was dark outside, and the moths and other flying insects were circling around the light globe hanging over the table. The light globe swung gently in the breeze generated by the fan, creating moving shadows about the room.

'What'cher gunna do on the weekend, girlie? You've got some free time. Not much you can do I s'pose, unless you get a ride into town. Wouldn't get in a ute with any of this lot though. You'll never get back. Most of 'em drink 'emselves stupid and drive until they run off the road asleep. Two years ago, we pulled one of 'em off a tree halfway back from town. Fortunately, he was going so slow he only buggered his ute, not himself.'

'I don't know, Cookie. I have no plans. I have my books to read. I understand there is a river not too far away. I thought I might go for a walk along the river and take a sandwich.'

'How yer going?' Looking over Maysa's head, Cookie was addressing someone in the doorway behind her. 'Don't suppose it's me yer after then, is it?' Cookie addressed the guest disparagingly.

Maysa turned to see Tom. Her face flushed bright red, and her heart pounded. She was caught by surprise at her reaction. She'd only met and spoken to Tom for a few minutes the day before, yet he'd had quite an impact on her.

She stood up quickly, and the chair she was sitting on caught on the rough concrete floor and toppled over backward. Cookie let out a peal of laughter. Tom leapt forward and picked up the chair as Maysa apologised, embarrassed.

I must look dreadful, she thought as she felt the beads of sweat on her forehead and was aware of her wet and dirty apron. Her old cotton dress had still looked presentable at morning tea time when she'd hoped to see him, and her large dusty work boots were a comical addition to her feet. Her shoulder-length black hair was coarsely fashioned into a bun on the back of her head. Strands of hair escaped in every direction, many of them plastered to her face with sweat.

Tom smiled broadly. He seemed to be enjoying having her at an obvious disadvantage.

'Evening Maysa.'

'Hello, Tom.'

'Would you like me to leave?' Cookie asked, smiling. Maysa answered with a mock angry, but very embarrassed expression.

'Well, bad bloody luck mate. We gotta finish this lot before she can go anywhere. If yer wanna speed things up, then get a tea towel.'

'No . . . no, Tom, please don't,' cried Maysa, as Tom reached for a towel off a neatly folded pile on the table. 'Cookie, please, we have no idea why Tom is here. Don't ask him to do my work.' Maysa paused. 'Ah, I'm sorry, Tom, this is Cookie.'

'Gidday Cookie, I'm Tom.' Tom leant toward Cookie, offering a hand for a greeting. Cookie seemed to take enormous pleasure in pulling a sopping wet hand from the washing tub, grabbing Tom's hand and shaking it furiously.

'How are yer, Boy. I'm Cookie. You can call me . . . Cookie. I'm the Chef.' Cookie smiled. He chuckled and coughed together, obviously pleased with his joke. His cigarette bounced up and down on his lower lip, still firmly adhered to it. Tom smiled and relaxed.

Turning to Tom, who had already started to dry a plate, Maysa smiled. She was unsure of what to do or say next, but so excited she was drying dishes with renewed enthusiasm.

'We've been moving some of the shorn ewes back out into the paddocks down by the river. I was riding back to the quarters when I saw your light on and thought I'd drop in and say hello. I'm filthy dirty sorry.'

Toms clothes were dirty, and his face was stained by rivulets of sweat and dust. The inner leg of his trousers was stained dark by saddle grease. Maysa made little attempt to hide the fact she noticed he was still wearing the shirt that was torn at the stomach.

'Yes, I haven't fixed that yet, washing day's tomorrow. I'll get to it then.'

Maysa was a little disappointed that he hadn't accepted her offer to mend his shirt but didn't like to offer again in front of Cookie.

'You should be worried about what you look like, mate. Look at her. At least she dressed for your visit,' Cookie announced as he pointed at Maysa with a dripping ladle. Again, Maysa was embarrassed by Cookie's comments but more embarrassed when she looked to see Tom smiling.

'So Maysa, how would you like to go for a walk with me tomorrow about lunchtime. I could show you our beautiful river, and we might just see a roo or two on our way.'

'Well, fancy that. A roo or two! Great idea, Romeo. Hey, here's a good idea, how about I come along as a chaperone on this little walk?' Cookie laughed at himself again and lifted a beer bottle to his mouth and took a long swig.

Maysa ignored Cookie. For a brief moment, she tried to imagine Cookie walking any distance other than to an ice chest full of beer.

'That sounds lovely Tom, thank you' Maysa replied, turning her back to Cookie. 'I was just telling Cookie I would like to see the river, so that would be perfect.'

'God struth girlie, he was standing behind you when you said it. Now get on and finish these bloody dishes, and then you can go, 'cause I'm getting bloody thirsty.'

CHAPTER FOUR

Moments later, the dishes were finished and packed away on the shelves, and Maysa was free to leave. She stepped out into the warm evening air with Tom. It was dark, but a three-quarter moon provided enough light to see each other well. Not far away, the shearers circled the campfire, sitting on logs and telling yarns that bore little resemblance to the actual experiences and events. With each year and shearing season, the same old stories took on all new lives with more colour and drama than the previous year. In the dark, all that was visible of the shearers was a circle of brightly lit and animated faces and cigarette tips glowing orange.

Maysa and Tom leant on a timber railing, looking toward the dam and watching the shimmering reflection of the moon darting and weaving on its surface. They stood in silence for some time before Maysa spoke.

'I am so pleased you came to see me tonight. It's quite lonely here.'

'I was a bit nervous, to be honest. I wasn't sure if I should or whether I might just be being a nuisance,' Tom kicked uncomfortably at the dusty earth.

'Nervous! That surprises me. You seem very confident, Tom. Me, well, that's different. I look like a wreck. I feel like a wreck, and I don't know what to say.' Maysa paused for a moment, reflecting and then began again in a confident tone. 'But that doesn't matter. Cookie has taken to speaking for me at every chance he can.' They laughed.

'He seems alright, is he? A bit rough around the edges?' he paused. 'Actually, very rough. He's looking out for you in his own way though, which is good.'

'Yes, it's like having a father with me.'

'Well, fortunately, you don't look much like your father . . . More teeth to start with.' They both laughed again.

'So I will come by to pick you up at about 11:00 am. Is that ok?' Again Maysa could see the admiration in Tom's eyes. She was glad he seemed to be able to see beyond the messy clothes, boots and hair all over the place.

'That will be fine thanks,' Although she kept a calm expression on her face, inside, she was nervous and happy.

'I will make some sandwiches. I hope you like lamb?'

'Gotta love lamb if you work on a sheep station or you'd starve to death. I'll bring something for us to drink then.' Tom replied.

'Will you be wearing a clean shirt?' Maysa asked with a cheeky smile.

'I hoped you wouldn't notice,' he said, looking down at the tear in his shirt. I was wearing a singlet all day and just put the shirt on to ride over here . . . to tidy up a bit . . . funny enough. To be really honest, I do my washing once a week, and I try to keep it to a minimum by going a few days in one shirt. But I do change my underwear.' Tom added. Maysa thought that was an odd comment, but she appreciated he was nervous as well, so she controlled her urge to laugh at him.

'I don't often see a lady out here, and the boys don't care what you look like, of course.'

Maysa thought Tom spoke very well in comparison with the rest of the team and wondered if he was educated. Her father and brother had been educated men, although they both took on menial labouring jobs in Australia. Work was hard to find for a foreigner with any sort of accent. Maysa had taken every opportunity to learn and practise the Australian accent and colloquial terms. Still, she remained obviously a foreigner. She found there was lots of this colloquial language to learn and took great delight in quoting Australian sayings from time to time. Coupled with her accent, it usually resulted in a good laugh. Up here, in the outback, she found the accents were even thicker, and the men all spoke slowly, clipping letters off the start and finish of words. It was very different to Melbourne, and she had to learn some words and terms all over again, which she enjoyed.

'Won't you let me mend your shirt for you, Tom, please?'

'No, don't be silly. I've been darning my own clothes for years. You have to out here. Besides, it needs to be washed and what would your mates over there think if they saw you with my shirt.'

'Another hour and they won't be able to see their way the short distance back to their beds. I insist. Please let me, it's the least I can do. I think it's my fault your horse nudged you yesterday. She is a very jealous girl. Besides, I always sewed my father's and brother's clothes for them. I will need something to do on Sunday. I can wash the shirt for you. I will hang it in my room. No one goes into my room. Cookie would punch anyone who even knocked on my door.'

Over to the side of one of the sheds, two of the shearers, Dingo and his slightly daft mate Darkie were standing pissing into the darkness.

'What do yer make o' that ey Darkie?'

'They're having a chat Dingo.'

'I can see that, you bloody half-wit. But it's a pretty cozy one, isn't it? If you ask me, the bitch wants it. She wants it bad.' Dingo whispered with a drunken slur. 'You see 'em under the tree yesterday, during smoko? She's only known him five minutes, and now she's ripe for the pickin'.'

'Yeah, right Dingo, she's ripe for the bloody pickin' isn't she.' Darkie looked perplexed. 'But they's just talking, aren't they?'

'Shut up, stupid. The bitch wants it. But what she needs is a real man, not a bloody pup like that uppity bastard. I'm gonna have me a piece of that Darkie. What do you say to that then? You in?'

'Shit Dingo, mate, she seems like a real beaut sheila. I don't think you should go near her mate, and you know what Cookie said. I want to keep me balls for a few more years yet.'

'Yer as weak as piss Darkie, aren't yer, Boy. You didn't seem to mind last time, did yer, ey? Shit, look, what'd I tell you, Boy? He's taken 'is bloody shirt off.'

'Ok, I will take off my shirt, and you can wash and sew it for me. But I must say it seems a little crazy. We only just met.' Tom was blushing as he undid the first few buttons of his shirt then slid it slowly over his head. Maysa watched in the moonlight. She found herself just staring at him. He was lean and muscular. Under his shirt, he wore a tight blue singlet, wet with sweat. She wasn't even conscious he was handing her his shirt as she stared at his arms and chest. In the past, she'd seen her brother and father stripped to the waist. She'd even seen men swimming in Melbourne in brief swimming costumes, but it had never had an effect like this on her. Somewhere deep down, she felt a longing that she didn't recognise. And then she was aware he was watching her staring at him, and she looked away quickly and cleared her throat. She took his shirt from him.

'I will have this ready for you by Sunday if that's ok.'

'Yes, that will be perfectly fine, of course, thank you. I better head off ey?' Tom backed away all of a sudden. As Maysa watched him, she couldn't help but notice he'd become suddenly uncomfortable. She wondered what had caused the discomfort. What had he thought of, or perhaps who had he thought of. 'I gotta get Bess back into her paddock and give her a feed and some water. And then I guess I better have some dinner.'

'Yes, of course. Please don't tell Bess you were with me. We don't want another incident.' Maysa smiled. 'Where do you live, Tom?'

'I am in the stockman's quarters about a mile over that way just the other side of the Station homestead. Well, see you tomorrow then.' He smiled, turned away and walked into the darkness.

Maysa returned to her room off the kitchen. She quickly shut the door and placed Tom's shirt on her bed. She was strangely excited to have his clothing in her possession. She lay it out carefully on the bed, smoothing out the creases.

It was Maysa's time to shower, and everyone knew the routine. At about 7:30 she would go to the shower block, and Cookie would broadcast to the group that anyone leaving the campfire would face castration with a butcher's knife. By then, most of the crew were settled into the drink, exhausted from the day's work and lacking real interest.

Maysa gathered her belongings in a small bag for the shower. Each night she would wash her underwear and socks to be hung in her room to dry overnight. Tonight she would wash her hair, anticipating meeting Tom the next day. As she walked to the shower block, she listened to the shearers who were getting louder and more animated as the evening progressed. Tomorrow was Saturday, sleep in day. All of the team were settled in for a long and damaging session.

In the shower block, Maysa locked the door bolt carefully behind her. It was a new addition, especially for the female member of the team. She had found you could look between the tin wall sheets in places, and as was her routine, she took a quick look to ensure that all the men were still at the campfire before undressing. She had been very uncomfortable the first few nights and had undressed, showered and dressed again as quickly as she could. A quick count confirmed they were all at the campfire and drinking steadily. She undressed while she ran a tub of hot water to soak her clothes while she showered. Tonight she had Tom's shirt with her.

As she stood naked in front of the old cracked and crackling mirror, she held his shirt to her face and smelt his masculine odour, sweat and dust. The air was still very warm, yet her skin prickled with goosebumps. Warmth flushed through her stomach. It radiated through her thighs and along her spine, tingling at the back of her neck. Visions came to her of Tom taking off his shirt. Her hands fell to her side, and she looked at her naked image in the mirror. She imagined Tom looking at her, right there and then, naked, admiring her. She ran a hand across her breast and then slowly across her stomach, imagining it was Tom's.

Suddenly a noise outside the shower block brought her abruptly back into the moment. She was startled. She stood still for a moment, then thought no more of it. She pressed Tom's shirt to her face once more and took one long breath before sighing and throwing it into the tub with her clothes.

She showered, washing her hair twice to rid herself of the dust, flour and sweat, dried herself, put on fresh underwear and a dressing gown. With her bare feet in her work boots and a towel wrapped around her wet hair, she wrung out the clothing in the tub, unbolted the door and stepped out of the shower block. Looking at the campfire, she noticed that Cookie, sitting with his back to her, was still drinking steadily and loudly dominating the conversation.

'So, you coming?' Dingo whispered quietly to Darkie as one of the other shearers threw a couple of logs onto the fire, and sparks burst into the still air, rising skyward like fireworks.

'Shit Dingo, I don't know mate. Bloody Cookie's

just there, and he knows she just went in the shower. If he catches us, we're done for, mate.'

'Suit yourself. I'm just going to take a look through the wall. That's all. Nothing more. No one needs to know, and no one'll get hurt. I reckon she'll have one sweet body mate, . . . but you just stay there if you don't want to see it. No problems.'

It was too much for Darkie. 'Ok Dingo, but nothing silly, ok? Not like last time.' Dingo and Darkie stood up slowly and went to turn away from the campfire. As they did, Cookie called sharply to them.

'Ey, where do you pair o' dogs think yer going? Sidown now.' Darkie turned back to sit down.

'Settle Cookie, me an' Darkie is just takin a piss, that's all. We'll just be over there mate. You can bloody well come and watch us if you want to.'

The rest of the shearers who'd stopped talking to watch the proceedings began to laugh. Even Cookies face softened, and he smiled at Dingo.

'Come on Darkie mate, Daddy will take you to the toilet.' Dingo spoke with a strong note of theatre in his voice.

The two men moved away from the others. They stood with their backs to fire and began peeing into the darkness. Looking over his shoulder, Dingo watched Cookie watching them. After a short time, he saw Cookie was satisfied they were not up to anything they shouldn't be, and his concentration had returned to the conversation at the campfire. He watched Cookie lift a bottle of beer to his mouth, upending it for a long gulp. He turned to Darkie.

'Ok Darkie, quietly now, let's go. Slowly.' Dingo and Darkie disappeared into the night.

Moments later, they each stood with their faces pressed to the wall of the shower block peering through holes in the corrugated iron. Inside they watched Maysa run the water in the tub and remove her clothing. Dingo elbowed Darkie and turned to him smiling, and winked.

'What'd I say mate?' he whispered.

They watched as Maysa looked at herself in the mirror and then put a piece of clothing up to her face. They pushed their faces hard against the iron as they watched Maysa. Her fingers traced a line from her nipple over her stomach toward the jet black silky hair nestled below her belly.

Dingo became aware of a movement next to him and turned to see Darkie rubbing himself through his trousers.

'You dirty bastard,' he growled at Darkie and pushed at his shoulder. Slightly off-balance, Darkie stepped backward and kicked a discarded beer bottle.

'Shit, you bloody idiot, she would have heard that,' Dingo whispered angrily. Quickly peering back through the hole, Dingo watched Maysa, running his eyes down her spine to her bottom. She looked over her shoulder and around the room as if looking for something. Then she disappeared out of view and under a shower.

'Stuff it. Come on.' Dingo grabbed Darkie by the shirt at his shoulder and started back for the campfire. Then he stopped. 'Bugger it, come on Darkie, I need to touch that bitch, did you see her?' By now, Dingo's arousal and the drink had teamed up. Any sense of reason or morality he was capable of mustering was gone. His thoughts shot back to two years earlier and a trip to town on a Saturday night with Darkie.

Dingo had always looked out for Darkie. Dingo was a shearer, and Darkie was a shed hand and sometimes shearer. Darkie was slightly intellectually impaired. 'Bloody slow,' his father had told his mates in a disappointed fashion over a beer. He required some support and direction. Dingo had a dark and vengeful nature and was happy to have a boy to handle both his dirty and mundane work.

The pair had finished a long drinking session at a hotel in Bourke one evening when the hotel closed. They staggered outside into a vacant lot, Dingo with his arm draped around a local girl, who he'd been drinking with. Darkie followed a few yards behind. Darkie smiled as he watched Dingo reach down to squeeze the girls bottom. She swung her hip away in protest.

'Come on Girl, don't get all bloody shy on me now. You've been all over me all night.' Dingo's agitation was becoming apparent.

Darkie smiled as the girl said she just wanted to

go home and she wanted to go now. Dingo grabbed the girl roughly by the arm, squeezing it hard.

'Fuck that, you bitch, I just paid out all me hard-earned on you, and now I want what's comin'.' Darkie stepped behind a bush to watch nervously. He knew where this was heading. The girl was crying now and pulling herself away. She clawed at the hand that grasped her arm.

'Shit,' Dingo cried as the girl dug her fingernails into his arm. With a full swing of his arm he struck the girl across the face with the back of his hand, sending her toppling onto her back. Following her to the ground, he pushed her dress up to her waist, tearing at her underwear. Darkie watched in horror and excitement as the girl cried and pleaded for Dingo to stop. Dingo put a hand across her mouth and leaned heavily on her, stifling her cries. 'Happy now bitch, you made me do this. You done it to yourself.'

Darkie watched the whole scene in shock. He was horrified, yet aroused by the violent sex. When at last it was over, Dingo stood up.

'There you go, wasn't so bad, was it?' He turned to Darkie, hiding behind the bush. 'Darkie, get over here. Give me that bloody beer and have a go yourself mate.'

Moments later, Darkie stood up, sweating and panting. Revolted by what had happened, he moved only a few feet away before throwing up violently.

'Steady old mate. You drink a bit too much 'ey?'

'What if she tells, Dingo . . . What if she tells?'

'She won't tell mate. Who'd believe her anyway? They've all seen her in there drinking with the boys. They know what she was after.'

'Come on Darkie, we better go, we got a long drive back to camp.' With that, they left.

All these memories, the smell, the sounds, the taste in his mouth all came rushing back to Darkie. He stood in the dark with Dingo waiting for Maysa to come out of the shower block. She crossed the yard, under the trees, past the dining room and toward the kitchen door. Dingo had picked his position well. A tree near the dining room blocked any moonlight as he stood waiting for Maysa to pass. He'd told Darkie he just planned to take his chances and grab her as she passed him and feel her up before disappearing in the night, that's all, nothing more. Darkie waited behind the water tank at the corner of the dining room, terrified. Maysa would pass the tree, and he would get a full view of Dingo's actions, whatever they were. Darkie knew the look in Dingo's eye. He'd seen it two years earlier in that vacant lot as Dingo had violently raped the girl. It was a mixture of lust and anger, and it frightened Darkie until he shook.

Maysa took the track leading through the compound and headed toward the light of the kitchen. Her mind was awash with thoughts of Tom and excitement for the next day's walk and picnic. She had not been this happy in all of her time in this country. In fact, since before her mother had passed away. She clutched Tom's shirt to her chest, wet as it was, and felt how silly it was that she looked forward to hanging it in her room and mending it over the weekend. She pictured herself, folding it neatly and handing it to Tom. She could hear him praising her workmanship, the best he'd ever seen. She saw him taking her hand, leaning forward and gently kissing her cheek.

She was just past the tree near the dining room when her heart stopped as a hand covered her mouth, pulling her head back violently. An arm wrapped around her waist and clawed at her dressing gown. She felt the hand push inside her dressing gown and squeeze her breasts roughly. Tears welled in her eyes, and she struggled to breathe, too terrified to move at first. She felt the hand push down toward her legs, trying to reach between them urgently. The full weight of her attacker was on her now. She tried to scream for help, but she could not make a sound for the attacker's grip on her mouth. In the dark, she saw a second person move out of the shadows, look at her and then run off into the darkness. She recognised Darkie as he leapt from the shadows, and she pleaded with her eyes. For a fleeting moment, she saw both sympathy and apology in his eyes. It was immediately overcome by terror, and he turned and ran off.

She lurched forward in horror as the attacker

tried desperately to reach between her legs again, and she fell on her knees, tearing and bruising skin. The attacker fell with her. She couldn't help but fall further forward and crash face-first into the wall of the dining room, making a large crash and momentarily dazing herself. Dingo tried to recover his balance as Maysa fell, but he too crashed hard into the corrugated wall, swinging at the last moment and taking the blow on his shoulder. The edge of an iron sheet cut cleanly through his shirt and deep into his skin. Blood streamed down his arm. He grabbed at the wound, stood up quickly and ran off into the darkness.

At the campfire, the conversation stopped midstream. 'What the fuck was that?' Cookie directed to the group as they all looked in the direction of the kitchen.

'Probably a bloody pig going for the meat safe,' one of the shearers offered. As quickly as they'd stopped talking, they began again. It wasn't uncommon for an adventurous wild pig or two to come up to the kitchen and root around the scraps from the butchering. The sheep guts from each days killing was dumped only a hundred yards from the kitchen. It was taken each day by wheelbarrow, and at night you could hear the squeals as pigs fought for their share.

Cookie, however, was still watching the kitchen door. He looked back toward the shower block, and the door was open, and the single light blazed inside, casting a faint beam through the door and into the night. The girl was obviously finished in the shower block. He looked back toward the kitchen door and squinted into the darkness. He saw a figure, Maysa, come around the corner from the water tank, hurrying, slumped over clutching at her dressing gown. Through his drunken haze, Cookie could sense something wasn't right. He stood up and addressed the group.

'I'm turning in boys. It's been a bloody long week, and I'm tuckered out.' He turned and walked back toward the kitchen and smiled to himself as one of the shearers called after him in a slurred drunken voice.

'You big fat weak bastard. You're a nancy boy.' There was a chorus of laughter.

Cookie walked on and into the kitchen quietly, although he wasn't sure why.

'You there, Luv,' he called out tentatively in the direction of Maysa's shut door. He fancied he could hear her crying and worked to shake the drunken haze from his head as he leant on the kitchen table.

Maysa stood in the centre of her room. Tom's wet and muddied shirt lay upon her bed with her other washing. Her knees were scraped and bleeding, and a large bruise was forming down the left side of her face. She heard Cookie call out to her quietly from the kitchen.

'You there, Luv,'

'Yes, I am here, Cookie.' She quietly responded after she'd steadied her voice.

'You ok Luv? We heard a real loud bang, and I wondered if you was ok?'

'Yes, I am fine, thanks Cookie, I am going to bed now.'

'Ok Luv, you're sure you ok then?

'Yes, really, I am.'

'Ok, we'll see you in the morning then 'ey?'

'Yes, see you then Cookie.' She listened as Cookie walked out of the kitchen.

Maysa stood for a moment looking in the mirror. She wiped the tears from her eyes and brushed the dust off her dressing gown, retying it around her waist. She picked up Tom's shirt and walked back nervously into the empty kitchen, closing the external door and bolting it from the inside. She ran a tub of water and re-rinsed Tom's shirt, and rung it out. She nervously unlocked the kitchen door for Cookie for the morning and then went quickly back to her bedroom. She hung Tom's shirt to dry and then bolted the door shut and pushed her suitcase in front of the door. She lay face down on the bed with her head buried in her pillow and cried loud and hard into the pillow until she was exhausted and fell into a restless sleep. She dreamt of her mother crying and her father hugging her.

CHAPTER FIVE

At precisely 11 am, Tom arrived on his horse, with dogs trailing and a bottle of wine in a saddlebag. He was wearing fresh clothes, moleskin pants, polished riding boots and a clean Akubra hat, which he took off as he entered the kitchen. He smiled as he walked in and saw Cookie sitting at the table, head in hands, hovering over a hot cup of tea.

'Morning Cookie, how are you this fine day?' Tom strutted confidently into the kitchen and threw his hat onto the table. He seemed to have grown ten inches in stature overnight. 'So, not feeling too well Cookie?' Tom enquired in a mocking tone.

'Enough, Boy, not so bloody loud.' Cookie mumbled into his hands. 'Yes, I am a little under the weather. It was a long session last night.' Cookie rubbed his forehead. 'I fell off a log near the fire, just before midnight, I think. The bastards left me there to sleep it off. Me bloody back's killing me this morning.'

Tom laughed and thought to himself that six of

the shearers couldn't carry Cookie back to his bunk, even if they were sober.

'So, is Maysa here? I'm here to take her out for the picnic down by the river.'

Cookie lifted his head, enough for Tom to see one eye and a cocked eyebrow. 'You mind you look after her Boy, or you'll have me and Bob to answer to, alright?' With that, Cookie put his head back in his hands and laid it carefully down on the table.

Cookie was no help, so Tom decided to knock on Maysa's door and did so quietly.

'You there, Maysa?'

'Yes, Tom. I'm coming,' came the reply from within. Tom stepped back as the door handle turned slowly, and the door opened. Maysa stepped out of the dimly lit room and into the kitchen.

Tom fixed his eyes on her. His smile was short-lived. Her face was bruised along the length of the left side. Her left eye was slightly blackened, and she had a small cut on her lower lip. She had clearly been crying and not just a little. Tom's chest tightened, he felt his muscles tense, and he worked hard to control a torrent of rage growing within. His throat ached, and he felt tears in his eyes. He rubbed them with his thumb and fore-finger. His reaction was strong and immediate. He knew why and where these feelings came from.

'Good morning, Tom.' Maysa spoke with a forced smile as she looked up directly into Tom's face.

She was ready for the look of shock on Tom's face, but his reaction was far more intense than she had expected. He went to speak, and she hushed him with a finger to her mouth and a pleading look. She beckoned him out of the kitchen, and they walked across to where Tom had tethered Bess to a rail.

'Maysa, what the hell happened? Are you ok? Why are you hiding this from Cookie? Did he have something to do with this?'

'No, no, Tom, of course not. I don't know who it was.' As she said this, Maysa could tell by Tom's face that she'd already said too much too quickly.

'Are you telling me someone did this to you?' Tom said with a level of urgency and aggravation that Maysa found unsettling. She felt safe with Tom. It was the first time she'd been able to relax since the evening before when she'd been attacked. Right now, she needed his steadying hand, and his behaviour wasn't helping her.

Looking at the ground, and in a low and shaky voice, he asked again, slowly and deliberately.

'Who did this to you, tell me please?'

'Honestly, I don't know, Tom. Please, can we go? Don't spoil this. I've been so looking forward to this since you came to see me yesterday. We will talk when we get away from here, I promise. Just for now, please smile and try to be happy.'

'I will,' Tom said quietly, as he untied Bess from the rail, and they walked off in the direction of the river. They were silent as they walked, heads down, watching the ground before them. Maysa quickly found an opportunity to change the topic of the conversation.

'Who's this? I haven't met him before.' A new dog was sniffing at Maysa's leg.

'That's Banjo. He's not my dog, but I said I'd take him out for a run. He's kind of . . . semi-retired. Bloody good dog actually.'

Maysa watched as Tom squatted down and gave Banjo an affectionate pat. It was the most affection she had seen him give any of the dogs. She liked seeing his softer side.

'Where are you taking me, Tom?'

'To the river.' Tom paused for a moment and then added 'Darling.'

Maysa looked at him and smiled as they walked. It was such a nice thing to say. Unexpected but nice.

'Oh, I mean the Darling River.' He corrected himself. Maysa was disappointed, and she tried to hide it, but he noticed.

'The Darling's the lifeblood of this whole area. Runs for miles and miles through towns like Bourke and Wilcania. It's only a mile or two easy walk for us. I know a great place where the river winds around a point and slows down. There's a nice sandy beach there. Otherwise, it's pretty much muddy banks and tree roots and the occasional crocodile and snake.'

'Crocodile?' Maysa shrieked, looking up at Tom as they walked side by side along a sheep track.

'No, no, I'm only joking,' Tom laughed. 'There are no crocs in these parts. But there are a lot of snakes, mostly by the river. Snakes like the water. This time of year, there's not much water out in the paddocks, so they'll all be down by the river. You'll be safe if you stay nice and close to me.' Tom grinned. Maysa wondered whether there was more meaning in the comment than just a joke. He'd demonstrated a strong urge to protect and defend her through his reaction earlier. There was clearly lots to understand about him, and she looked forward to learning more.

As they walked along together and Tom spoke, Maysa watched him closely. Apart from getting steadily nervous about the wildlife, she was enjoying his company very much. She examined his face as he spoke and thought how handsome he was and how comfortable he looked out here in this landscape, so foreign to her. Her gaze was drawn away by a sudden screech above them, and they turned to see a small flock of large black birds take flight from a nearby tree. As they flew past, Maysa shielded her eyes from the sun and watched the birds. Each had splashes of red feathers under their tails. 'They're beautiful,' she said as they flew past.

'They're red-tailed Cockatoos. They're bigger and much more handsome than their cheeky sulphur-crested cousins. You know the white cockies you see in huge mobs out in the paddocks?'

They walked on in silence. Maysa thought about

the huge flocks of birds she had seen on the way to the station while travelling with Bob. They were spread across fields, like patchy snow, in their thousands. She had remarked how beautiful they looked and Bob had replied, *'Flaming bloody mongrel things. Oughta shoot the bloody lot of 'em. They pull the seed out o' the ground faster than the poor ol' bloody cockies can sow it.'* By that stage, Maysa had learnt that a Cocky was a farmer and not just the bird that Bob had described with such distaste, confusing as that was.

They wandered on, discussing wildlife and plants as they walked. Tom still seemed very anxious about the state of Maysa's face, and she was a little overwhelmed by the intensity of his reaction. She dared to believe it was because he was feeling the immediate attraction she was. But at the same time, she struggled to imagine it was entirely the result of affection for her.

Although her reins were held by Tom, Bess walked behind Maysa, as if drawn to her. Banjo settled carefully in and right on Maysa's heels. He never touched her with his wet nose, but she was aware he was so close and was amused by the attention. She could see it wasn't lost on Tom either as he looked down and smiled at Banjo. There was more space than you could see in any direction, yet half the party, including Tom, were vying for space almost on top of Maysa. Billy and Barney strolled along at Bess's heels. Occasionally Bess would snort at Maysa's back, giving her a fright. Once she got used to the sound, she thought it sounded like a very fat and exhausted man blowing a raspberry after climbing a flight of stairs.

'Bess seems to like me, Tom. I think she is enjoying the company of another lady. She is getting over her jealousy. It must be hard for her being out here with all you boys and no ladies to talk to.'

'What boys?'

'You, Billy and Barney of course. You boys are all the same. Strong and silent and only interested in your work.'

Tom laughed. 'Yes. Me, Billy and Barney ey? We're like peas in a pod. Here, you take the reins then.' He handed them to Maysa. She stopped walking for a moment to face Bess, who pushed her head into Maysa's chest and snorted affectionately.

Smiling, he remarked, 'You're a natural.'

An hour later, they arrived near the river. The banks were covered in long wispy clumps of grass. Ancient red gums with gnarled, white trunks were dotted along the edge of the water, providing shade for both domestic and wildlife. Muddy banks led to the water, which, moving slowly, provided a perfect mirror image of the vegetation on the far bank.

'It's not far up here, and there's a good spot to sit above the sandy bank in the shade and have a drink and a bite to eat.' Tom led the way. 'You've

51

got to watch out up here in summer. Seems funny, the shade can save you from the heat, but it can also be a death trap for unsuspecting people . . . and animals too. On the hottest and most still day, days without a trace of even the slightest breeze, not a sound to be heard, these big old river gums drop their branches without warning. There's been plenty of times I have been riding along here when I've heard a crack and a thump and turned around to see a branch just fallen.

'That is strange.'

'The trees seem to stress in the hot, dry conditions, and any weakness is exposed, I guess.'

'Are we safe, Tom?' Tom was a storyteller, but Maysa appreciated that. Her Irish father had loved to tell a yarn, as the Australians called it. She was eager to learn about this country.

'Yes, of course. Except for snakes, falling branches and the odd crocodile, we should get out of here alive.' Maysa smiled at him, albeit a little apprehensively.

Amongst a stand of old river gums, Tom found a patch of soft grass in the shade, and he and Maysa set up their makeshift camp. Tom sent the dogs off down to the water, where they quickly walked into the shallows and began swimming and occasionally barking at each other. He walked Bess to the edge of the river to water her and then tethered her with a long rope to a low-slung branch where she could move about picking at the fresh grass.

★   ★   ★

As he patted Bess to make sure she was settled, Tom watched Maysa. She'd brought a basket with sandwiches, some cakes and a bottle of lemon cordial. She'd also brought the grey blanket off her bunk to use as a makeshift picnic rug which she spread out on the grass with the basket on it. Tom fetched the bottle of wine from the saddlebag, taking his time and watching Maysa as she prepared the picnic. She was beautiful, he thought. From where he stood, he could only see her right side and momentarily, he put the bruise on her face out of his mind. His initial anger and concern had subsided, and he was now settling comfortably into enjoying her company. He had allowed himself to believe that what had happened was probably just an accident. After all, she seemed to be in good spirit.

Maysa was wearing a blue and green floral sleeveless dress that blended, as if by design, with the green of the gum leaves. The dress was gathered at the waist, a rounded neckline and cut just below her knees and showed off her figure to its best advantage. Her olive skin complimented the colours of the dress, and her hair was tied back in a loose ponytail gathered just above the shoulder with a white ribbon. Tom found her natural and relaxed style very attractive. He continued to admire her as she moved about, setting things up. He had to shake his mind clear of thoughts of taking her in his arms and holding her body tight against his.

Taking a seat next to Maysa on the picnic blanket, he asked again how she'd hurt herself.

'Was it an accident or something? How on earth did you do it? Why is it such a secret?' He did his best to appear relaxed.

'I will tell you Tom, but you must promise to stay calm. Your face scared me earlier. You seemed to be incredibly angry.' She paused and took his agreement from the look in his eyes. 'First, have a lamb sandwich before the flies carry them away.' She smiled, and Tom laughed.

'I admit I stole that line from Cookie. Just let me pour you a lemon drink first, and then we will talk. And I will hear all about you also.' She handed Tom a drink. 'I haven't really heard anything about you. Is a lady safe out here in the bush with you?' Her comment was both funny, and not, given the previous night's incident. They both seemed to realise that at the same time.

'You know you are safe with me,' he said seriously. He was reading her expressions, and he knew she was still putting on a façade to protect against something. But then, so was he. She began.

'So, Tom . . . I need this job. My father died a couple of months ago in Melbourne. My brother and I lived off the little money that my father had saved and the small amount of money my brother was earning. My brother, Rick, as he likes to be called here in Australia, works as a cleaner at night at the wharf. It is the best job he could get. His

English is ok, not good. He works with Bob's son Dave. Dave seems to look out for him. He's not much older than Rick.' Maysa refilled their drinks and offered Tom more food which he took enthusiastically.

'When my father died, the money quickly ran out. Our landlord came to collect the rent, and of course, we couldn't pay. We asked him to give us a little time to find good jobs. He said our problems were not his, and he was sorry for our loss, but he was not a 'bloody charity shop'. He said he had a wife and children to feed, and we would have to move out within a week if we couldn't pay. And of course, we couldn't.' Tom lay back on the blanket and propped himself up on his elbow, watching Maysa.

'Well, Rick told Bob's son the very next day. Rick's pay was not enough to pay the rent, let alone feed us. Bob's son came to work the following day with a proposition for Rick and then for me. Rick could take a bed on Bob's back verandah once we left our home, and Bob offered me a job as an assistant cook on the team. He said the usual man was in hospital with '*a lung complaint and his liver's shot*'. According to Bob, he was '*done for*'. Very sad. He said he would pay me good money. Of course, I couldn't expect to get what a man got, he said, but nonetheless, I'd '*make a good living for a sheila, and get to see the country*'.' Maysa smiled and took a break to eat. Although the story was serious, Tom was amused by Maysa's quoting of

Australian colloquialisms and her attempt at an accent when she did.

'Here, Tom, eat up.' Tom had stopped eating and was just staring at Maysa as she spoke. She liked that. She smiled at him.

'How'd you come to meet Bob.'

CHAPTER SIX

Maysa stood at the front gate of their Carlton terrace house. It was 6:05pm, and she expected Rick to come walking along the footpath at any moment. He had been very firm with his instructions in the morning as he left for work.

'You need to be ready to leave as soon as I get home. Bob is an important man. He told me so. Meet me at the pub, he said. You can shout me a couple of pots and then pick up your sister and bring her home for dinner with the missus and me.' Rick had barked the instruction at her as she placed his breakfast in front of him.

Rick was highly agitated. He had changed since their father had passed away just a month before. Although he was two years younger than Maysa, he had assumed the role of head of the family, whether he was ready or not. This was expected and was his rightful place in his home country, as well as this foreign place where they'd found themselves stranded.

The weather was unusually hot for mid-October, and as Maysa stood by the gate, she felt beads of perspiration gathering at her brow. She was awash with mixed emotions; grief, excitement, and trepidation. She was dressed in her best summer cotton dress, with white sneakers. At nineteen, she was very mature for her age. She'd experienced so many challenges so young. She was strong and determined, and whatever this next challenge presented, she had made her mind up to meet it head-on.

She was not quite seventeen when she arrived in Melbourne with her father and brother. They had left India for Australia to escape the grief of her mother's passing from a long illness. They had decided to start afresh in a land of opportunity as her father had promised.

Her brother had changed his name from Vikrant to Rick after his first couple of days in school. Ironically his Indian name had meant brave, which was a quality he would require in spades.

'Some kind of Wog is yer, a dark skin wog, what's yer name then wog boy. Geez, what kinda name's that then, bloody beaut, that's for sure.' The other boys taunted him from the moment he arrived.

Rick was more sensitive than Maysa and far less determined. He changed his name to blend in, but his face, his hair and his dark olive skin betrayed his origin, and the taunts came relentlessly. He had been excruciatingly nervous and lonely at this school in this new place. Eventually, a couple of the Aussie boys had befriended him. No doubt, his running to the canteen, giving up his lunch and fetching the football from over the schoolyard fence on command had helped. The ruffling of his hair, and the occasional slap over the back of the head, accompanied by an affectionate 'stupid', had smoothed his path into a friendship group.

Maysa hadn't entered school when she arrived in Melbourne.

'It is too late for you, my girl. There's no more you need to learn. We need you at home now to keep the house. You need to feed your brother and me. He needs a good education. One day he will be a successful businessman, and our family will grow and prosper in this wonderful place.' She listened to her father with resignation.

She had been a model student in her home country. She had arrived in Australia with poor English and even fewer prospects of anything other than menial labour until she found a husband if she could. In part, she was pleased to keep the house and avoid a life of struggle in employment, sewing, cleaning or ironing. These were careers so many of the other migrant women had fallen into. She kept a spotless house and cooked well. She took on Australian dishes where she could and fended off complaints from her father and Rick that the new country food was dull and tasteless.

She focussed hard on learning her English and quickly diminished the impact of her accent. She borrowed Australian books from the local library. She read Ruth Parks The Harp in the South, then could hardly wait to borrow the sequel A Poor Man's Orange. She was fascinated by the hardships faced by the Darcy's. She read the dialogue from the books aloud, watching herself in the mirror when her father and brother were at work. When she confided with the librarian, she was trying to 'learn how to speak Australian', the librarian laughed and fetched a copy of 'They're a Weird Mob' by Nino Cullotta. She enjoyed and empathised with his struggle with the local language. On shopping trips, Maysa would stand browsing in the greengrocers listening to ladies gossiping over the fruit and vegetables, not interested in the content, just the words, the pronunciation and the inflections. More than once, she received a tut-tut from snooty shoppers, suggesting the strange foreigner was eavesdropping as they turned away from her and moved on. She was undeterred.

Maysa wiped her clammy hands on her apron as Rick rounded the corner.

Rick was somewhat more relaxed when he arrived home. More than a couple of beers had taken the edge off his agitation, and he greeted Maysa with enthusiasm.

'Are you ready to go, sister?'

'Yes, I will just wash my hands and brush my hair, and we can leave for Mr Bob's.'

Bob Jackson lived in a small double fronted brick veneer only 2 streets away from Maysa and Rick's home. The front was bordered by a freshly painted white picket fence. The lawn was mown almost to the dirt. At either side of the front gate, three standard roses were planted at carefully measured intervals. They were about to burst into full bloom.

Rick pushed open the front gate. He and Maysa walked up the front path to the veranda, and Rick knocked tentatively on the fly screen door.

'Ricky, is that you mate?'

'Yes, Bob.'

'Come in, mate. You got young May with yer?'

'Yes, yes, thank you, Bob.'

Bob appeared just as Rick and Maysa stepped into the dark hallway entrance. As her eyes adjusted to the light, Maysa could see that the house was also kept in meticulous order. Like the front fence, the walls were painted white from floor to ceiling. The ceiling was white, and the floor was covered by a beige carpet.

'You must be May are yer Luv? Come in, come on.' Bob was wearing a faded blue singlet, khaki shorts, slippers and no socks. His rotund stomach spilled over the worn leather belt that struggled to keep his shorts above ground level. He was sweating and smelt of beer. He ushered them into a lounge room with a two-seater couch, an armchair on either side, an old piano and shelves lined with an array of china ornaments.

'Edy, come ere Luv, the guests are 'ere.'

A short and obese woman appeared. She was wearing an ankle-length dress that Maysa suspected was a length of material doubled over and sewn down the sides. She was carrying a large carving knife in one hand, wet with blood. Her other hand was covered in flour which she was wiping on her apron.

61

'This is the wife, Edith.'

'Pleased to meet yer both. Bob's been tellin' me about yer. I'm real sorry for yer loss. It's a tough thing for a couple o' youngins, and 'specially in a new country an-all, to find yerselves without yer dad. You're doin' a good job lookin' after yerselves. Me an Bobbie is pleased we can help.'

Edith pointed the carving knife at the kitchen door and addressed Bob.

'You take the boy on through and out the back Bob, and get him a cold one. May, you and me best get some snags in the pan for the boys. You can peel some spuds. Can you peel a potato? Sure you can. If not, yer better learn quick smart. You'll need to know how where you're going.'

Maysa smiled. She was conscious she'd not yet opened her mouth, but it seemed this couple could carry on an entire conversation without a single response from their guests.

Edith turned on the gas at the stove and threw an old steel skillet over the flame. It was scratched clean on the inside and black on the outside. She took a small ceramic jar from the fridge and dug out a lump of hard dripping with a bone-handled knife, and slapped it in the pan. It immediately began to melt and spit droplets of fat.

'Fill that saucepan with water Luv and bring it 'ere.'

Maysa filled the saucepan and then put on an apron that Edith had thrown across the kitchen to her, then sat down at the Laminex kitchen table to begin peeling potatoes.

Maysa could hear Bob and Rick deep in conversation. Bob's voice was grave at times as he delivered his life lessons in rapid-fire. Each was punctuated regularly with a joke or humorous anecdote that Rick laughed over-enthusiastically at. Edith and Maysa sat at the table, preparing the meal, and Maysa felt strangely more comfortable and secure than she had for some time in this strong woman's motherly presence.

'So Dear, how are you coping with all of this?' Edith asked sensitively as she poured a sweet sherry for each of them.

It was the first time in a long time Maysa had sat with another woman. The care and affection in Edith's eyes were more than she could cope with, and she felt tears well in her eyes. She spoke in a broken voice as Edith passed her a cotton handkerchief and rubbed Maysa's forearm gently.

'To tell you the truth, it feels like my world has fallen apart. Two years ago, I was part of a family with a mother, father and brother. My mother died. We moved countries, and then my father died, and then there was just Rick and me. Now even Rick and I are being torn apart.' Maysa paused while she wiped away the tears with the handkerchief.

'I feel like I will be all alone. I know no-one, and I really know nothing about this country.' She wiped her eyes again then folded the handkerchief and sat up straight in her chair and finished peeling the last of the potatoes. 'But I will be alright. I know I will. This country is my home now. I can't go back. Where would we go to? I need this job, and I need to start a new life.'

'Good on yer, Dear. You're a strong one. I can see that. You'll do alright. Where you're going, it'll be hard yakka. It won't be easy up there, and you'll be lonely, probably real lonely at times. But I can tell you'll be ok. You're real pretty, and you're smart too. I'll bet some lucky fella will snatch you up and make you very happy. Just you mind he's a good fella and a decent one too.' Edith paused and smiled at Maysa. 'Now, let's get these veggies on Luv before these boys start complaining.'

A short while later, they sat down to a good Australian meal, sausages, mashed potatoes, carrots and beans. There was much discussion about the trip for Bob and Maysa beginning in two days and then also where Rick would sleep when he moved in. And there was agreement about the board he would pay and the chores that would be his responsibility while Bob was away.

'So Maysa,' Bob began in a severe tone. 'You know I can't have any trouble up there with the team. They're a rough lot o'blokes, but a good bunch. They're hard workers, but they drink and play hard as well. If anything goes wrong up there, it's my reputation at stake. There wouldn't be a second chance Luv, I'd have to pull you out of there quick smart.'

'Nothing will go wrong Bob,' Rick interjected with a note of concern. 'Maysa is a good girl, the best girl, she will be your best worker, you will see.'

'That's right Luv,' Edith added in a stern tone, 'don't go frightening the girl, she's got enough on her plate as it is.'

'It's not her I am worried about Edy, you know that. It's that other rabble. They don't usually work with a woman on the team. Especially not one as pretty as her,' Bob added, pointing a fork with a bean speared on it at Maysa. Maysa looked down at her plate, embarrassed and a little concerned.

'All I am saying is I don't want these galahs playing up. You know what a bunch of fellas up in the bush, a long time by themselves, are like. But don't you worry Girlie, just keep your nose clean. I'll have me ol' mate Cookie look after you. He's a good bloke, and he won't chase you around, I promise. He couldn't run the length of the kitchen table, the big fat bastard.' Bob and Edith burst out laughing, and Maysa and Rick smiled politely.

Two days later, on a Thursday, Maysa and Rick were up early, before sunrise. Standing in the kitchen of their home that they were to vacate that day. They made their last teary goodbyes while they were alone in the kitchen. They were each nervous about what the future held. They would communicate, when they could, through Bob and Edith, with Rick living on Bob's back veranda and with Maysa working up in the North West of New South Wales with one of Bob's shearing teams. But the communications would be few and far between. From Melbourne to the New South Wales outback was more than 700 miles.

'I will miss you, my sister. I wish it didn't have to be like this. It won't be long, I am sure of it, and we will be back together again. Our family. Just you and I. We will settle here in Melbourne very close to each other and grow old together. Our children will be best friends.' Rick held Maysa in his arms. 'Be good and be safe. Here, take this.' He handed Maysa a handkerchief. She kissed his cheeks and held his face in her hands.

'You're a good boy, I mean man, Rick. I won't ever be truly happy until we are back together again.'

A horn sounded on the street out the front of their home. It was Bob, and it was 6:30 am sharp as agreed. Their home was empty now except for Rick's suitcase, a bed and a few dishes. All of their belongings except their very personal effects and keepsakes had been sold to pay for the rent. The account at the grocers, the gas and electricity bills and all of their other debts had been settled. What little cash that was left, paid for food and left a little for each to go on with as their new lives began. Rick would move into Bob's home that evening with Edith and Bob's son, Dave.

Outside Maysa's home, Bob was parked in a sky-blue Holden EK ute of which he was very proud. His dog Rusty, a red Kelpie, stood at Bob's side watching Maysa and Rick as they came through the front gate.

'Here, I'll take that.' Bob took Maysa's brown leather suitcase from Rick and put it in the back of the ute.

'Get up Rusty.' Rusty leapt into the back of the ute. Bob hooked up the Tarpaulin, pulling it tight and leaving just a small corner open for Rusty. He sat behind the driver's side and panted enthusiastically, watching forward over the edge of the ute. Moments later they left, and Maysa watched through the rear window as they rounded the first corner and Rick disappeared from her life for the first time in seventeen years.

Over the next few days, Maysa saw much of the Australian countryside as she travelled north through farmland, only occasionally interrupted by country towns. The main streets were dotted with pubs and small stores and seemed to have a typical pattern. Locals talked on the sidewalks. Dogs ran along the road's edge and barked at the cars. Life moved at a slower and more relaxed pace than Maysa had ever seen. It was almost a relief. Her life was changing so quickly. Yet here she began to see a life that changed so slowly, almost suspicious of change. On their second day, they travelled North on to Dubbo where they stayed at the Commercial Hotel. Then, on Saturday, they left and travelled North through Narromine, Nyngan and into Bourke along the Mitchell Highway.

CHAPTER SEVEN

Tom looked at Maysa as she finished talking about her trip and the adventures on the road with Bob. By now, he was settled on his side, head in hand, feeling very relaxed. Maysa seemed to come back from another place as the story finished. She looked at Tom and smiled.

'Now your turn, Tom. How did you get here, what is your life story?'

'It's dull, I can assure you. I don't want you to fall asleep while I am talking.'

'Oh, come on. I have told you about me. Please, Tom.' Maysa pleaded.

'Ok, but first I am going to light a small fire for a cup of Billy tea for my new Australian friend, and I am going to take a dip in the river. You coming?'

'Where, in the River? Of course not, I don't have a swimming costume, and I am ashamed to say, I can't even swim.'

'I don't have a swimming costume, either. Swimming togs we call 'em out here. But it's not going to stop me.' Tom watched for Maysa's reaction. She looked shocked and very uncomfortable.

'Tom please, I can't go in there. My father would kill me if he knew I was out here with a man and with no, how do you say, chaperone . . . He is not here, I know.' She looked sad as she replied in a quiet and serious tone. 'But I do honour and respect his memory and his wishes.'

'I'm sorry, Maysa. I am just a stirrer. I like teasing you and watching your pretty face. But I took that too far. Especially since we hardly know each other.' In a whisper and looking into his lemon drink, he added, 'I hope that's going to change.' He looked up at Maysa, who was grinning again.

'Now, I am going into the water. Do you mind if I just take off my shirt? It's pretty hot out here, and we'll dry off quick smart.' A smile from Maysa was all Tom needed. She watched as he kicked off his boots and pulled off his socks. He stood up, and she looked away shyly as he took his shirt off, then rolled up the legs of his moleskin trousers to the knee. He held out a hand to her.

'Maysa.' She turned to face him. Her face had reddened, and she looked embarrassed as he stood before her naked to the waist. He could see she was trying not to look, but couldn't help herself. He had a strong and athletic build. His arms were tanned from the elbow to hands, and his torso was white in stark contrast. His arms were well-muscled from physical labour. Placing her hand gingerly in his, he helped her to her feet.

'You best kick off those shoes, or they'll get wrecked.' Reluctantly, she removed her shoes and placed them carefully on the rug. 'Let's go,' he said, and he led her by the hand toward the river. His heart was beating fast from both the thought of the water and the touch of her hand.

'It'll be beautiful in, you'll love it. The current's nice and gentle here. It slows right down to get around that corner and all those old trees,' Tom remarked, pointing down the river. 'That's why there's so much sand here. It comes roaring down the river, floating along until the water slows down, then it all sinks to the bottom. It's created this beautiful beach here in the middle of the outback.' The river meandered out at right angles from just downstream of where they stood, then weaved back on itself almost creating an island where Tom and Maysa had been sitting. 'Let's go. This way.'

Tom led Maysa down a narrow, steep path between tufts of long wiry grass and thorny bushes. Maysa walked along closely behind Tom, craning over his shoulder on tiptoes trying to see the beach area. Her eyes gave away her excitement and anticipation.

All of a sudden Tom stood still, and Maysa crashed into his back. Tom felt her soft body against his. It was a moment before she pulled away from him.

'What is it?'

'Sshh. . . . Snake, just stay still.'

Lying on the path directly in front of them, no more than five feet away and looking at them, was a King Brown snake. It was looped around in the dust with its head a few inches off the ground. It was staring directly at the pair through beady evil eyes. In truth, it was as scared as Tom and Maysa were. It was a flight or fight scenario for them and the snake. In the outback, a bite from a brown snake would nearly always be lethal. With more than an hours walk back to the camp, it was a dangerous situation.

Maysa stood deathly still, with one hand on Tom's shoulder and one on his back. She watched the snake over his shoulder. Ever so slowly, Tom lifted his hand toward his hat.

'What are you doing?' Maysa whispered. 'Let's run.'

'No, don't move . . . And be quiet. If we move, it might strike, and five feet is not enough space between us.' Their entire conversation took place in a barely audible whisper and with almost no movement, even in their faces, to give away the exchange.

After what seemed like an eternity, Tom's hand reached his hat, and in one swift movement, he tore it off his head and flung it at the snake. The snake reared and struck the hat violently and as quick as lightning. Tom and Maysa reared backward. Maysa all but fell over Banjo. He'd had been standing still and leaning against her leg throughout the whole ordeal. Tom steadied her as they turned and ran back several paces. Maysa was shaking, and they both began laughing madly.

'Shit. Excuse me, but that was close,' Tom

panted. A bark startled them, and they turned and saw Barney leaping through the grass bouncing on his back legs, furiously barking and heading away from the track.

'Come here, you bloody idiot,' Tom yelled at him. 'I'm not going home until after my swim, so if you get bitten, you can die out here.'

'Tom, that's awful.' Maysa chided him and slapped him gently on his arm.

Tom walked forward and retrieved his hat from the dusty track and examined it closely. He dusted it off with his hand and placed it back on his head and turned around and smiled smugly at Maysa. 'Come on then.' He beckoned her to come forward.

'You're joking, surely.'

'No, it's alright, it's long gone now.'

'But you can't see anything in this grass.'

'Barney sent it scurrying, the poor bloody thing won't be back 'til next week I reckon.'

'Tom, that was terrifying. I can't walk to the water now. What if there is another one?'

'Not likely, with all that barking. Come here.'

Maysa edged forward slowly watching the grass on each side of the track carefully. Tom was laughing. He extended his arm and Maysa took it as she drew closer. She stepped slowly and carefully as though on a balancing beam. At the last moment, she leapt forward, and he caught her in his arms. 'Here,' he said, as he whipped her off her feet and into his arms. She shrieked with a start.

'What are you doing? You're mad.' Tom turned and trotted off toward the river carrying her like a feather. She bounced in his arms as he ran, with her arms about his neck. He ran onto the soft sand and out into the river with water splashing about them and Maysa shrieking. She had never felt so happy. The water was up to Tom's knees when he put Maysa down into the water. She grabbed at her dress, trying to keep it from getting wet. She pulled it up above her knees. Tom couldn't help himself, and he looked down at her bared flesh. He caught his breath again.

'My god what happened to your knees,' Tom asked in astonishment. Both of Maysa's knees were badly bruised and scraped. One was bleeding slightly after all of the swinging about.

'It's nothing, please, Tom. We are having so much fun, don't spoil it now.'

Tom felt the anger desperately trying to surface again. Anger at an unknown assailant. He held his tongue as she dropped the hem of her dress, covering her knees and let the dress float in the water. She had gone from the happy, beautiful young woman he was admiring to a sad, scared-looking child in a moment, and he felt guilty. He forced a smile and took both of her hands.

'Here, sit down in the water.' He sat down with a splash. Maysa looked tentative but eventually smiled and sat down in the water with her dress billowing about her. The cool water rushed by them. They sat quietly for a moment allowing the tension to subside before resuming where they had left off just moments earlier.

They talked for some time about the countryside, the birds and animals. A kookaburra burst into a long laugh, and Tom told Maysa it was laughing at her, and she splashed him. Tom looked longingly at Maysa and wished he could kiss her right then and there, but he'd only known her for a couple of days. What's more, something odd had happened the day before which filled him with a mixture of anxiousness and anger. Anyway, he couldn't be sure what her reaction would be if he did try to kiss her, so he sat and listened to her talking. He answered her myriad of questions about Australia and the bush while they soaked in the cool water.

'Come on, it's time for a cup of tea. That billy'll be boiled dry.' Standing up, Tom offered Maysa a hand. He helped her to her feet, and they trudged through the water. The dogs were running along barking furiously and excitedly as the couple came to the edge and Maysa smiled as Tom yelled at them to sit down.

'That better not be another snake,' Maysa said nervously. With that, Tom swept her off her feet again and into his arms. They walked back to the picnic site, both pleased and thinking themselves a little smart to have found themselves so innocently back in this pseudo embrace.

At the campfire, the billy was sizzling away on the dying coals. Tom took a handful of tea from his saddlebag and threw it in the blackened and battered tin-pot along with a gum leaf. He threw a couple of sticks onto the fire to push the billy to the boil. Then he pulled out two chipped enamel mugs, stained brown inside from tea, and placed them on the ground next to the fire.

'Stand back!' he directed after a few minutes, and he took the billy off the fire and stepped away. Maysa watched in astonishment as he swung the billy at arm's length right up high over his head and around in a circle 3 times before pouring the tea. 'That really gives the tea its final mix. It draws out the tea, and adds the real flavour,' Tom added as an afterthought when he saw Maysa's surprised look. 'Just gotta keep that billy moving otherwise you get a hot shower.' Maysa laughed. Tom was pleased with himself.

They sat together and drank Tom's tea and ate cakes. 'Thank you so much for showing me your country, Tom. I've had a wonderful day. I wish it wouldn't end. Now you were going to tell me about yourself and how you came to be working here. On this station.'

'Well, I don't live too far away from here, actually. About twenty-five miles that way as the crow flies.' Tom pointed off beyond the river to the east.

'Is your home on a farm too?' Maysa prompted Tom as he slowed.

'Yep. It's a little patch of very beautiful land. My Mum and Dad live there. I have a brother who is in school in Sydney in his last year. He's got no interest in the land. Wants to be a lawyer. Good luck to him. And I have a little sister who is fifteen years old. She's also in Sydney at school and cheeky as a galah.'

Maysa was fascinated as Tom began to sketch out his family and his personal life for her.

'So why aren't you working on your farm, Tom. Is it too small for you all?'

'Well, it's a very long story. I was going to work there. But Dad and I were always banging our heads together. I wanted to do things differently. Do some of the things I learned at College in Hawkesbury. He's old school, changing how we do things, but slowly. Geez, we would fight. You could hear us a mile away. Poor Mum was always worried we would give each other a hiding.'

Maysa smiled and listened intently. Tom had stopped again and was rubbing his face in his hands in an agitated fashion.

'Go on, Tom. Please,' Maysa encouraged gently.

Tom looked at Maysa as his mind drifted far from the place they were. Refocussing on Maysa, he felt like talking. Like telling her everything. Like really talking for the first time in two years. He sensed he could trust her and that she would care about him, and about what he had to say.

'Two years ago, I was nearly finished college. I was living in an old boarding house at college with a mob of other fellas. Good mates.' Tom shuffled his feet uneasily and spoke with hesitation. Maysa could see his discomfort. 'There was a call. A telephone call . . . on the phone in the hallway . . . just down from my room . . . for me . . . a call for me.'

Maysa sat still, transfixed as Tom spoke. He drifted deep into dark places as he recounted his story.

CHAPTER EIGHT

Tom was sitting on his bed in his dormitory room, reading some study notes when he heard his name yelled out.

'Tommy, phone.' A good mate was holding the phone with a hand covering the mouthpiece. Tom stepped out of his room and into the hallway. 'Hurry up, mate, it's the ball and chain. It's Milly.' His mate spoke in a mocking tone. Tom told him to get lost while taking the receiver from him and trying to slap him across the back of the head.

He was surprised and pleased to be hearing from Milly, although it was unusual for her to ring on a Wednesday night. They had a routine. They were like an old couple. She would ring one Thursday, and he would ring the next. But it was Wednesday and the night before it was his turn.

Tom and his girlfriend, Milly Patterson, had been childhood sweethearts from the time they were barely ten years old. They had attended primary school, church, Sunday school and regular family picnics and tennis days together for as long as each could remember. Left to make their own entertainment as their parents socialised, they would play together.

They walked and rode horses through the countryside and even played tennis when the adults turned to tea and drinks. From an early age, they had shared an affinity with the countryside in which they lived. They shared their first kiss at 15 on a Sunday afternoon horse ride during school holidays and fell comfortably in love with each other. It was meant to be. Even their parents, who were neighbours and already close friends, loved each of them as their own. They planned in a joking fashion for the inevitable and happy union. They were separated only by school and college.

Milly returned home after boarding school to work on the family station. She couldn't be separated from her horses, dogs and the livestock. She took an active supervisory role on the farm. She was well respected by the stockmen. She would ride alongside them in the musters, work alongside them fencing, and also take an active interest in accounting for the property's financials. Tom had also loved her ability to transform into the perfect lady in both behaviour and dress, supporting her mother on social occasions with ease and grace. She was equally at home in both environments. By the time they were in their late teens, they were deeply in love and committed to each other. Milly had grown into a beautiful young woman. She had the pale skin of an English rose, long auburn hair and the figure of a model. Tom was the envy of all of the young men in the district.

Tom waved his friends away who were still mocking him as he answered the phone. He turned his face to the wall and whispered, 'Hey Milly baby, how are you?'

There was silence for a moment, and then an unsteady voice replied.

'Tom, it's mum.'

'Geez, sorry, mum. That idiot Alex said it was Milly. I'll give him a good floggin' for his trouble. So how are you? How's Dad?' He asked, finding it a little hard to disguise his disappointed that it wasn't Milly.

'Tom,' his mother said quietly again and then stopped. Tom began to feel uneasy.

'Mum, what's up? Are you ok, is dad ok?' he asked with a growing sense of urgency.

'Yes, your father's fine and so am I. Actually . . . your father is on his way to see you now, he'll be there in a couple of hours.' She paused and then added, 'to get you Tom, and bring you home.' Tom's agitation was growing now, and he was getting confused.

'Why, why is Dad coming here? Something's obviously wrong!'

As he said this, Tom was suddenly aware that Mr Brookes was standing close by and watching him. He was an old bachelor who lived in a self-contained living area within the dormitories. His job was to see to the students and their welfare and knew all the boys well. He lectured in Pastures by day and then strolled the halls of the dormitory by afternoon and evening, supporting students in their study.

Tom, perplexed and uncomfortable with this

attention, turned back toward the wall again and whispered into the phone.

'Mum, please, what's wrong?'

'Tom, sweetheart, I have some awful news.' She hesitated again. Her voice was breaking, and Tom was aware she was crying and battling to speak. 'I am afraid it's Milly.'

'What? For Christ sake, Mum. What?' Agitation gave way to shock and defensiveness at the mention of Milly's name.

'Tom, I am afraid there has been an accident . . . We've lost Milly. I am so . . . so sorry . . . She's died.'

The words hit Tom like a sledgehammer. His head throbbed with every beat of his heart. He thought he was going to pass out, and as he wavered on his feet, he felt two arms catch him. Brookes helped him toward a chair.

'Alex, come here now. Here look after Tom.' and Brookes took the phone and spoke with Tom's mum. 'He'll be ok, we've got him. I'll sit with him until his father arrives. How long do you think that will be?'

Tom's vision swam. He listened distantly to Mr Brookes speaking with his mother and was aware Alex sat beside him with an arm around his shoulders. He slumped, head in hands and felt nothing, no pain, no tears, no understanding and no acceptance. Just blank. Tom's mother had been forced to ring him with the news before the country grapevine reached him first through one of his many friends from their area.

Two hours later, Tom was sitting on his bed. Alex

had packed Tom's bag and was sitting on Tom's desk just watching his mate when he heard Mr Brookes approaching talking in hushed tones. Tom's father appeared in the doorway, looking grave. 'G'day, Alex. How are yer Boy?'

'Yeah fine thanks, Mr Sutherland. I am really sorry for . . . Well, you know.'

'Tommy, how are you, Boy? You ok?' Tom's father stood over him, and awkwardly ruffled his hair gently. 'Come on then Boy, we better get going I guess. Get some miles done before it gets dark.' His father took his bag from the bed and walked with Tom out into the hall. Tom walked, slumped over, with his father's arm around his shoulders. His father nodded at Mr Brookes as they left. Most of Tom's friends were standing in doorways awkwardly watching and mumbling sorry and good luck and chin up mate as Tom, and his father passed.

The first hour in the ute was spent in silence. Tom stared out the window but saw nothing. His father looked at him periodically and then returned to concentrating on the drive.

'How did it happen?' Tom finally spoke, his voice breaking.

'Truth is, we're not really sure yet mate. She was missing for a while. They put a few blokes out to track her down. They found her up a hill in amongst some rocks. We don't know if she'd fallen, or . . .' Tom's dad hesitated and then continued. 'Well, anyway, she was in a bad way.' He hesitated a moment before going on.

'She was dead when they found her, Tom. Her horse was found first, not too far away, fully saddled, reins broken, but still saddled. The first thing they all thought was she'd come off the horse, but when they found her, it was obvious it couldn't have been the case. There's no way the horse could have gotten in there amongst the rocks. She'd have had to walk at least 40 or 50 yards to where she ended up. But what for, that's the question. Well, I guess the police will work it out. They've been all over the place.'

Tom was feeling sick, and he asked his father to stop the utility. It was getting dark outside. He staggered from the car and supported himself against a tree rubbing his eyes aggressively as the reality of what his father had told him set in.

'So, are you saying that someone did this to her?' Tom spat the words out at his father.

'Mate, we really don't know yet. It'll do no good jumping to conclusions until we hear something from Len.' He spoke of Milly's father.

'But they must think that, if the police are involved,' Tom pushed.

'It's routine mate. If you don't know how someone died, you have to investigate. Probably just a terrible accident. Let's wait and see, ey?' His father spoke in a calm and consoling tone.

'But what do you think, Dad? You knew her. She was as good and as smart in the bush as any bloke we know. And she knew that country as well. Why would she be out there with the horse running loose and in the middle of all that bloody rock?'

'Yeah well, I don't know, mate. Doesn't seem to make much sense to me either.'

The initial reports from the police said Milly had been found partially clothed and badly bruised. Their comments indicated she had appeared to have been whipped with a stock whip, punched and possibly hit on the forehead with a rock. A rock with dried blood had been recovered from nearby to where she had been found.

The police had told Tom's father quietly on the verandah of Patterson's homestead, that in all likelihood she had been sexually assaulted. They had spoken as Milly's parents sat distraught in their living room with the local doctor and Tom's mum, comforting them as best they could. They'd said that she had been found naked from the waist down and that her hands and fingernails showed signs of a fight – they were covered in dirt and blood. They suggested the killer would most likely be bearing the scars of the attack, but they couldn't be sure. Some of her clothing was never recovered. All this, his father kept from Tom.

'If someone did this to her, Dad,' Tom started in a low unsteady voice. 'I will fucking kill them. I promise, Milly.' Tom punched the tree hard, and blood burst through the broken skin on his knuckles. His father rushed forward and held his son's shaking wrist as his son collapsed to his knees.

'I promise you, Milly.' Tom let out a mournful wail and began weeping. His father knelt beside him with his arm around Tom's shoulders and cried quietly with him.

At the campfire, Tom sat with his head in his hands, talking quietly. Maysa sat in silence, watching him with tears streaming down her face. She reached out and took his hands in hers. He looked at her with tear-filled eyes.

'The police never worked it out. They know this much; she was murdered, and she was . . . raped.' Tom struggled to say the word. 'She almost certainly died from a blow to the head from a rock they found. We sat through a coroner's case and heard all the bloody horrible detail. It nearly killed her Mum and Dad. It killed part of me. It actually nearly finished me. I went to town every opportunity I could. I got drunk. In fact, I think I was drunk for six months. Every man I looked at looked like a bloody killer to me. I got in fights. I spent a few nights in the lock-up in town. Everybody was sick and tired of me. I was sick and tired of me.' Tom stopped and looked at Maysa. He took a sip from his tea which was long cold, then stared wistfully into the bottom of the mug, swirling the tea leaves.

He stopped for a moment and stared deep into Maysa's eyes. She squeezed his hands, and he knew she understood now why he had reacted so powerfully to her bruised face.

'Go on,' Maysa prompted in a careful and caring tone.

'Well, it all came to a head about six months after Milly died. Mum and Dad had the Pattersons over for afternoon tea. Everyone was working hard to move on, to pull it all together. I turned up, and I'd already had a couple of beers. The afternoon wore on, and I got drunker and drunker, and aggressive and embarrassing. It was too much for my father. He tried to rein me in politely. But he'd had it. Looking back, I don't blame him. He had a go at me, and I got as mad as hell, and it erupted into an enormous argument, right there in front of Milly's parents.' Tom rubbed his face again as was his habit when he was stressed and agitated.

'Finally, Milly's dad leapt out of his chair and stood up between Dad and me.

'*Enough,' he said, 'enough, Tom. You come with me now.'* Well Old man Patterson, as the shearers call him, is a big bloke and I respected him, drunk as I was, I still had enough sense to shut up. He walked me out into the garden.'

'*Tom' he said, 'Tom, that's enough Boy. We've all suffered through this. Don't you think Mrs Patterson and me have suffered? Poor Irene, it nearly bloody killed her. We know how much you loved Milly, but she's gone Boy . . . she is gone. We all need to start to live again, somehow, even you. Your parents need a break, lad. You can't keep doing this to them.'*

'Well, we talked on for a half-hour. He told me

he would never feel easy until he knew what had happened to Milly, and he knew how I felt. He talked about how he felt he had let her down, that he hadn't protected her and that his heart had been ripped out of his chest. He said he felt his life had become worthless. But then he said he needed to be there for Milly's mum and for her brother, Jeff and that there was still a purpose in his life.'

'After some time, he said to me, *'Tom, I want you to come home with us. You can work for me. We need another hand on the property. You can bunk down in the stockman's quarters. Give you and your Dad a rest for a while. God knows you both need it. Go and pack a bag, Boy and we'll head off shortly.'*

'And with that, I packed my kit. A half-hour later I was sitting on my bag in the back of the ute watching my mum on the verandah of our house, waving, as she disappeared in a cloud of dust. I didn't go home for a long time. By the time I did, I'd pulled myself together. I spent a lot of time out on a horse with Len Patterson and the boys in those first few months, fencing, and just working hard. I worked a lot of heartache out of my system. By the time I went home for short visits, I was able to behave like a pleasant human again. But I decided to stay on here for a while anyway.' Tom sighed and took a moment.

'It was 18 months ago Dad and I had that big fight and Mr Patterson, Len, rescued my backside. And here I am today . . . with you.'

Maysa and Tom sat in silence for some time. Finally, Tom broke the silence.

'I guess we better get going then. It's late, and I don't want ol' Cookie chasing me down and giving me a beating.' Tom stood up and took Maysa by the hand and helped her to her feet. As quickly as he'd begun talking, he had finished. Maysa was clearly extremely saddened and moved by this story about Milly. As he stood up and began packing up their picnic, he tried to smile a smile of resignation at the story.

Tom tipped the remains of the billy tea on the dying embers of the campfire which hissed furiously, then he kicked dust all over it as well. He packed up the picnic basket and put various items back in the saddlebags.

Maysa stood watching Tom, with her picnic basket at her feet. He was securing the saddlebags and tying on the picnic rug. He turned to face her and could see a flicker of disappointment in her eyes as she watched him. He realised he'd become distant.

'You know, I've had a wonderful time. I'm sorry it's over so soon. I am, really. I want to spend more time with you.' He paused to watch Maysa's face. He reached forward and took her hand in his. 'Would that be alright? Maybe I could teach you to swim. There's an idea.'

Maysa smiled as Tom stepped toward her. He placed his hands gently on her waist, and she put her hands on his upper arms. Electricity rocketed through his body, and his heart raced. He leant toward her, so close that their noses touched, and he could feel her breath on his lips.

'I would like that very much,' Maysa whispered, barely moving her lips as he felt them touch his. He could smell her perfumed skin and feel the curve of her waist just above her hips under her cotton dress. They held this gentle kiss for seconds before breaking. Maysa remaining for just a moment with her eyes closed as Tom reluctantly pulled back slowly, admiring her.

An hour later they were walking into the shearers camp quietly talking. Most of the shearers were sitting about the campfire already having a beer. It would no doubt be another night of hard-drinking. Cookie was in the kitchen when they walked in.

'Ah, good lad. You've returned the valuables,' he said with a smile while chopping through a rib bone with a meat cleaver. 'Did you have a good time, lass? Did he look after . . .?' Cookie stopped mid-sentence. It was the first time he'd seen Maysa's face, bruised and with her eye blackening. He was preparing to ask a question when Tom, standing behind Maysa, pulled a firm face at Cookie and shook his head from side to side to indicate he should keep quiet, so he did. He seemed relieved that Tom had stopped him, and although this was what Tom had wanted, he couldn't help but lose some respect for Cookie.

Maysa excitedly told Cookie the story of the snake and the lunch and the river and hastened to add they walked into the river fully clothed when Cookie raised a cheeky eyebrow. Cookie winked at Tom who smiled behind Maysa's back.

'Well, I best be off then. Thanks, Maysa for a great day.' Tom went to move toward her awkwardly, then thought better of it. 'And thanks Cookie for letting her come out with me.' Tom nodded and tipped his hat at Maysa and backed out of the kitchen.

With an afterthought, he leant back through the doorway and spoke directly to Cookie.

'I'll be doing the killers this week. I'll be in after morning tea after we've mustered and I'll do one then if that's ok?' And then, directed to Maysa, 'We'll catch up for a chat then.'

'No worries mate,' Cookie replied without looking up from his butchering. He took another swig from his beer bottle and then mumbled to himself, 'Now bugger off. You're hanging round here like a mangy dog.' Maysa laughed and playfully slapped Cookie across his sweaty, hairy shoulder, and Cookie let out a feigned moan of pain and pulled a sorry face.

CHAPTER NINE

At morning tea, Maysa walked nervously to the shed. She'd been carefully avoiding Darkie since the attack. She felt sure Darkie wasn't part of the attack, but she was suspicious and scared of him, particularly the fact he hadn't tried to help her. She was watching for the new mob of sheep to arrive, to see Tom and to feel secure. She'd avoided all of the shearers for the rest of Saturday. She washed in the kitchen, well after Cookie had gone to bed, avoiding the shower block. She kept busy, avoiding the dining hut during the shearers' meals on Sunday and Monday morning.

Maysa stood uncomfortably on the landing at 9:20am, as was the routine. When Dean emerged from the shed and said good morning, she kept her head bowed and the bruised side of her face away from him. She handed the basket to him and mumbled good morning quickly then darted down the stairs as soon as possible. She moved away from the shed and stood behind the trunk of a large gum where she couldn't be observed from the shed. At morning tea, the shearers would often

91

lean out the windows smoking and drinking their tea while watching the activity in the sheep yards. Windows along the edge of the shed were simple wooden swinging frames, clad with corrugated iron, hinged at the top and held open by a swinging piece of timber at the bottom. They were typically closed at night, and so it looked like there were no windows at all. They were opened each morning to provide fresh air and flush out the ammonia-like stench of several hundred sheep defecating and urinating all night. In this particular shed, they had the added bonus of providing a view of the pretty young woman walking back to the kitchen hut.

On this morning, however, Maysa disappeared well before the 9:30am bell rang to signal the end of the morning run. The shearing plant powered down soon after. The last of the sheep reluctantly appeared head first out of the shoots, freshly shorn. Maysa had always been vaguely aware of the shearers watching her as she walked from the shed. Although she was aware that she was the only woman for miles around, she had found it slightly flattering. But this morning, everything had changed. The feeling had gone and had been replaced by one of fear. It was fear of another attack and fear of losing her job with this team.

She had thought long and hard about telling Cookie, but she couldn't help but remember Bob's words, *'Can't have any trouble up there with the team.'* So, she stayed silent. Where would she go, where would she live, how would she make money to simply survive? She thought about telling Tom the detail, she'd managed to avoid it at the river. She knew he wanted to know desperately, but had reluctantly respected her wish not to talk about it and to focus on having a lovely day together. She had been worried enough by his initial reaction. Still, she was further terrified by what he might do having heard about Milly and his behaviour after her death. She had also wondered about the attack and what might have happened if she hadn't fallen. What if the attacker hadn't crashed into the wall? And was the attacker a shearer? Suddenly she began to think, maybe, just maybe it wasn't a shearer. The attacker may have been frightened off by the failed attempt, whoever he was. Or perhaps it was a silly drunken attack based on a misjudgement of her willingness to comply. Before too long, she had diminished the violence of the attack, pushed her fear down below the surface, and justified her silence. At least to herself.

At last, in the distance, she saw the dust of the next mob. Faintly, she heard the barking of the sheepdogs, and the whistling and yelling of instructions by the stockmen. Slowly, she recognised the individuals. There amongst them was Tom, tall and handsome on his horse. His face shadowed by his hat, his stockwhip in hand. His dogs were running and barking at the heels of the sheep. All her fears dissolved in an instant.

★   ★   ★

Tom squinted as the dust clouded over his face, getting in his eyes and leaving a gritty film on his teeth. The dogs barked and ran hard, even after two hours of mustering. Tom cantered forward to a gate to the yards and opened it from the saddle and then cantered away again. He was looking around for Maysa. He finally spotted her standing in the shade of an old tree, and he waved.

The sheep were herded into the yards. Tom and Paddy dismounted and tied the reins of their horses to one of their stirrups. This kept the reins out of the dust and prevented the horses from standing on them and breaking them. The horses were then set free into a small yard with a water trough and some hay.

Tom was free of the mustering now. There was time to say a quick hello to Maysa before killing a sheep for the shearers' rations. Paddy and the other stockman would take a break and have billy tea and biscuits before organising the sheep from the mornings run. They were marked with an ink brand that identified them as belonging to the Pattersons. After that, they would draft the lambs off the ewes that were to be shorn the next day. As Tom and Paddy walked past the shed windows, Stan the wool classer called out to Paddy from a window.

'Hey, Paddy. You can back off yer numbers by a pen for tomorrow. We'll be down one today as well. One of these boys won't be shearing until Wednesday at the earliest. He's buggered his shoulder.'

'What happened?' Paddy called back in an irritated voice. This meant that at least 150 sheep yarded the day before would need to be let out to feed and then penned up again overnight for a second night.

'Dunno really. I think he hit the turps pretty hard on Saturday night and fell over drunk somewhere. Shoulders all bruised up and pretty stiff apparently.'

'No worries. Thanks, Stan, we'll sort it out after smoko. Give him a good kick in the arse for me, will yer.'

'Yep, good on yer Paddy. I got the silly bugger tramping wool for the next couple of days. Nothing wrong with his legs. He'll wish he stayed sober by the time he picks up a handpiece again.'

Every shearing team had a wool presser. His job was to take the wool, which had been sorted by the wool classer, and roustabouts into various classes including fleece wool, pieces, bellies, locks and more. They pressed it into large hessian sacks called wool bales, for transportation to the wool sales. Thirty fleeces or more could be pressed into one bale. Loose, this was a large mass of wool. It took hard work to stand in the wool press, tramping the wool down around the edges of the bale until finally a lid was placed over the wool. A large handle 6 feet long was used to pull down the lid, drawn with steel cables, compressing the wool. The wool pressers often swung full weight on the handle trying to apply enough tension to cap off the wool bale with steel hooks. In this shed, more than five hundred bales were pressed a season. Dingo was definitely paying penance for his sins. He kept his head low, his mouth shut and sweated hard, up in the wool bale.

Tom listened to the exchange between Paddy and Stan with little interest other than the additional mustering work it would cause them. He was eager to get away from Paddy and get on with his next task, which would allow him to catch up with Maysa.

'I better go and get on with the killer. I'll see you after.'

'Ok lover boy, get on yer way then. Don't forget to fit a bit of work in with yer bloody play though will yer. Yer not paid just to chase skirt 'round the bush.'

Tom looked at Paddy and made no reply. There was no love lost between the two stockmen. If Paddy hadn't been Len Patterson's nephew, he might have given him a piece of his mind. But out of respect for the Pattersons, he received, and he ignored, many more insults than would be reasonably expected by anyone. It wasn't just the insults that grated on Tom, it was the way Paddy showed little respect for machinery and equipment. More importantly, his treatment of the stock and the working animals, horses and dogs disgusted Tom. One day, Tom had seen Paddy take a dog in a rage, two hands on either side of its neck and ram it tail down into the ground while it yelped in pain and terror. It had limped off with Paddy screaming obscenities after it. His fit of rage had been spurred on when a mob of sheep broke away at a gate. They backtracked on the stockman heading all directions into the bush. On another occasion, Tom had seen him swing a steel branding iron onto the backs of freshly shorn sheep. He was desperately trying to push one more sheep than could possibly fit into the race for branding. Tom sensed there was something almost evil and desperate about Paddy, but he couldn't put his finger on it. He knew a little of his background and his upbringing. He knew it was far less fortunate than his own. The wealth and social status that the Pattersons' had enjoyed had not been shared by Paddy's family.

Len's sister Mary had married Patrick O'Brien senior, against the wishes of her family. It was an unhappy marriage from the outset. Patrick was a hard worker and a heavy drinker, labouring for the local shire. He always finished his working day at the pub, staying through until six o'clock closing and always came home with a skin full of beer. Any disagreement, and in fact most discussions, ended in at least a slap for Mary. On many occasions, Paddy junior saw his mother thrown across the kitchen before receiving a beating from his drunken father. More often than not, the arguments related to money. Patrick spent the housekeeping on grog, and the lack of food Mary could buy, as a result, ignited regular arguments. With an empty stomach, Paddy often went to bed to the sound of fighting, slapping, crashes and muffled crying. In time, Paddy's mother took to drinking the cooking sherry to calm her nerves before her husband came home. On occasions, she put up a solid fight before being punched and sometimes kicked into submission. Mary died relatively young, an unfortunate alcoholic by the time Paddy was fifteen. Out of respect for his estranged sister, Len took Paddy on at the station soon after. This took Paddy away from the violent father from whom Paddy had become the new target of rage.

By fifteen, Paddy had a healthy disrespect for his position in life. He resented the Pattersons. He resented the fact he'd shared none of his grandfather's (Len's father) love or wealth even though he was as close a blood relative as either Milly or Jeffrey. He resented the treatment of his mother by her family. He blamed them for her early death at the hands of a drunkard from whom she should have been rescued. He resented the fact that his cousins and others like them in the district, from the big properties, had everything when he struggled to be fed. He watched them in the town when they returned from their private city schools on their school holidays, and how they socialised in their groups and looked down their noses at the town kids like him. And then, amongst them stood his relatives, his cousins who also looked through him as easily as looking through the glass in a shop front window.

To add the final insult to injury, when he was finally

98

rescued from his living hell by his uncle, he was relegated to the stockmen's quarters with the other paid hands. So outwardly Paddy put on a brave and contented face when inwardly he desired some compensation for his lot in life.

The Pattersons' son Jeffrey had stayed in Sydney after a miserable and failed attempt at university. Likewise, his efforts to work on the home station as a stockman had been a miserable experience for him. He didn't like the work, and the staff didn't like or respect him. After some perseverance, his father had relented and agreed with his mother that the boy should be cut loose to pursue whatever would make him happy. Len quietly feared what that might be. Once it was settled and the boy moved permanently to Sydney, Len found it easier to say the boy was working and doing well in retail and leave it at that. Other local gentlemen, who had known Jeffrey, were also happy to leave it at that, for Len's sake. So, Jeffrey rarely featured in Len's conversations. Both Irene and Milly genuinely loved Jeffrey and had appreciated his softer personality. They'd also met and enjoyed the company of Jeffrey's partner, John, with whom he lived in Paddington. In the protective way of women, particularly mothers and sisters, they had shielded Len from the details of Jeffrey's private life. At the same time, they added spark to descriptions of Len's interest in Jeffrey when passing on his father's salutations.

★　　★　　★

With Milly having passed away some two years earlier and Jeffrey hidden in Sydney out of sight and mind, and being the next of kin to the Pattersons, Paddy could see himself firmly in control and eventually inheriting the property. He was rapidly gaining confidence in his status. However, except for the title of supervisor, reluctantly bestowed upon him by Len Patterson, he had had no indication from the Pattersons, formal or otherwise, that he stood to inherit the property or any other belongings for that matter.

Tom left Paddy where he was and quickly made his way over to Maysa where she waited. Paddy stood for a moment and watched Tom. He couldn't put his finger on it. He knew he didn't like this Silver Spooner. He wasn't really sure why he was still here on the Patterson's station. Surely after his girlfriend died, there was nothing left here but sad memories. He really disliked how friendly he and Len Patterson were. He resented the occasional dinner invitations that Tom would get when he himself received none. He often watched him walking up to the homestead at dusk through the window of the stockman's hut and cursed him under his beer-laced breath through a puff of cigarette smoke. He'll be the first to go he'd think. When I own this show, things will change around here.

He felt the anger bubbling in his stomach and leaving a bitter taste in his mouth as he watched

Tom talking to the girl. He turned and walked to the yards yelling at the dogs.

'Get 'ere'.

'Hello, Miss Maysa,' Tom smiled broadly.

And with a smile disproportionate to the occasion, Maysa replied. 'Hello, Mr Tom.' They laughed.

'I am here to slaughter the lamb, Mam.'

'How disgusting! I don't know how you do it.'

'Well it's either I do it, or this lot of hungry ragamuffins will starve to death, which would you have?'

'Have them starve.' They both laughed again and set off in the direction of the kitchen, happy and excited to be in each other's company.

'Paddy's as cranky as a snake. One of the shearers has hurt himself, and now we have too many sheep in the yards. We've got a fair bit of messin' around to do to get things reorganised.'

'Oh, what happened? Who got hurt?'

'Dingo, apparently he fell over on Saturday night, drunk, and cut open his shoulder, so he can't shear for a couple of days until he comes good.'

Maysa was shocked. Her memory flashed back to Saturday night, the moment she fell to her knees, and her face hit the iron wall. She was aware that the attacker had fallen, unbalanced, over her shoulder and driving their own shoulder into the wall.

She was frozen on the spot for a moment before she composed herself. She could see Tom watching

101

her and no doubt wondering why the sudden change of demeanour. Her stomach was in knots, and her arms were covered in goosebumps as she was suddenly aware of who her attacker was. Tom was watching her closely now. He stopped talking and observed her. Maysa turned away quickly, and the moment passed.

'Come on, Tom. Come to the kitchen. Do you have time for a cup of tea?'

'Yeah, sure, as long as Paddy doesn't see me.'

'Come on then.' They walked into the kitchen where Cookie was having a cup of tea and feeding his face with a cake. Maysa made Tom a tea and put a cake on a plate for him after ushering him to a chair at the table. Cookie looked at Tom resentfully and a little suspiciously. He kept his cake hovering inches from his mouth between mouthfuls as if it might be stolen. Tom looked straight back into the eyes of this fat and sweaty man stuffing his mouth with cake. They each held the stare for a moment until Tom smiled. Cookie sat, half hunched over like a giant old bullfrog on a riverbank watching an insect. He didn't smile back.

'What?' Cookie questioned aggressively spitting cake on the table. Maysa watched them both, bemused by their behaviour, then excused herself, and said she would return in just a moment. She left Tom and Cookie to their odd standoff, flattered by her understanding that she was the source of the psychological duel.

Leaving the kitchen, she walked outside and turned left walking along the front of the kitchen and then the dining shed. At the end of that wall, she reached the water tank. She was nervous. It was broad daylight, the shearers were all up at the shed, but she was still worried. She walked past the tank slowly. Her fingertips were gliding lightly along the edge of the corrugated tank. Walking carefully and quietly, at the corner of the square timber tank stand, she turned in left again almost on tiptoes, moving very slowly. She reached the next corner of the tank stand. She was looking at the ground now, where she had fallen Saturday night. She recognised what were obviously both hers and her attackers scuff marks in the dry grass and red dust. There was no one else there, of course, so she relaxed a little. She stepped forward to the wall, and there was a dent where she guessed her head had struck the wall and to its left, where two sheets met, an edge protruded out from the wall with a dark red bloodstain. On the ground, there were a few preserved drips of blood, only noticeable by someone looking specifically for them. She walked slowly along that wall, and there, on the corner was another bloodstain. This one, obviously where the attacker's shoulder had brushed against the wall as he staggered around to the back of the shed, misjudging the corner in his desperation to escape the scene.

So that was it. Maysa knew who her attacker was now. He was here in the camp with her.

'What are you doing?' Maysa visibly jumped and turned around to face Tom, panting from her fright.

Sitting in the kitchen, staring at Cookie staring back at him, seemed like a huge waste of Tom's morning tea break. The kitchen was hot, and the smell of greasy food was not enticing Tom. He decided to take his tea and step out into the fresh air. He had caught a glimpse of Maysa mysteriously creeping around the edge of the water tank beyond the dining hut, almost as though she were sneaking up on someone. He wandered, not deliberately quietly, up behind her. He watched her from just behind the water tank as she seemed to be inspecting the wall, running her fingertips over a dent in it, low down on the wall. Then he watched her walk slowly to the corner and then stop to inspect something on the wall at about her eye level. He walked up behind her, still undetected. He had been quiet as the moment seemed to have a mysterious air about it. He didn't mean to frighten her when he asked her what she was doing.

'What are you looking at?' Tom frowned with a quizzical look, 'You're behaving strangely.'

'It's blood.' Maysa said quickly recovering.

'Blood from what? . . . Or blood from who? Come on, what's going on?' As he was saying this, Tom suspicions became clear. 'Does this have something to do with your face, and your knees?'

Maysa stood still looking up at Tom who put his

hands on her arms and held her firmly, perhaps a little too firmly, but with an overwhelming sense of a need to protect and defend her.

'Tell me, please.'

'I will,' she started slowly, 'but you must promise me to stay calm. You won't help me one bit if you lose your temper. Promise me.'

'I promise.' Tom was already fighting to arrest his temper. He knew it frightened Maysa. 'I promise I will be sensible.'

'Ok then,' and Maysa paused for a moment. 'The blood is from my attacker, at least that is what I suspect.'

Tom looked at Maysa, and her words took a moment to make sense.

'Attacker?'

'Yes. I was attacked on Saturday night. I didn't just fall over. It was here on my way back from the shower hut. I was attacked from behind. He . . . whoever it was, grabbed me from behind so hard that as I tried to break free, I fell forward onto my knees and then hit my face on the wall. He fell over the top of me and crashed into the wall. I am sure he was very drunk.'

'But why haven't you said anything to anyone about this. It was probably one of those bloody shearers or someone else in the team. They might try and do it again. Why haven't you said anything?'

'Tom, I need this job. I have nothing in the world now. All I have is this. No home, almost no family, no money yet and no useful education. What would

I do without this? Bob said I was '*out*' if there was any trouble, any trouble at all. What would I do? And we, we've only just . . .' Maysa stopped mid-sentence, but Tom knew what she was saying. 'They'll send me away, Tom, they will.'

'Surely bloody Bob's rules don't stretch to letting women get attacked and keeping their bloody mouths shut about it.' Tom's anger was building rapidly now.

'Tom, you promised. Please stay calm.'

'But who did this?'

'Have a look at the corner of the shed, Tom. See that big bloodstain like someone dragging a wound across the tin? Go and stand next to it please.' He did.

The bloodstain was roughly level with his shoulder, just slightly below.

'It's a cut shoulder, Tom. I think it's a good chance we now know who did it.'

The reality hit Tom in the stomach like a blow from a clenched fist.

'When I hit the wall, I was stunned for a moment, and by the time I could think, the attacker was running off around the corner, so I didn't see him. But as I was attacked, I did see the one they call Darkie in front of me, near the water tank, but he ran off just as I was attacked. Tom, we know who it was, but we have to be so careful. I need this job, and I don't want any trouble.'

Tom was overwhelmed with anger. Old feelings he'd pushed deep into submission threatened to overwhelm him. His desire to protect Maysa was powerful. He had only known her a few days, but already he had fallen in love with her.

'I won't do anything stupid, I promise you. I need time to think. You need to be protected just the same. I just need to think about this.'

A voice shouting broke their concentration.

'Maysa, where the bloody hell are yer? You gotta fit a bit of bloody work in between yer socialising, Girlie.'

CHAPTER TEN

Maysa returned to the kitchen to placate Cookie. Appealing to his ego, a few compliments on his cooking and some giggling at his jokes, did the trick. He was putty in her hands.

'You best get out there and wash them tea towels and the like, Luv. We're nearly out. And while you're there, you can tell yer butcher mate, that when he butchers yesterday's sheep, he can run the forequarters out into chops the whole way through please.'

Maysa took a basket of washing through to the wash hut, ran a tub of hot soapy water and emptied the contents in to soak. Here was an opportunity to see Tom again. She knew she could finish this job later after she'd spoken to Tom, and Cookie would be none the wiser.

Maysa rushed across to a small yard set away from the shearing shed in the shade of a couple of large gum trees. There was a dozen sheep in the yard. Tom was standing off to one side, sharpening a knife on an oil stone. His dogs lay at his feet, watching him attentively. They leapt to their feet and ran over to greet Maysa as she arrived.

'What are you doing here?'

'I have come to see what you are doing.'

'Well you can't stay here, I am about to kill a bloody sheep.'

'Why not?'

'Well, you're a woman. It's just not really done, and there will be blood and guts. It's not a nice job.'

'Huh, don't be silly.'

'It just seems pretty bloody odd to me. Don't know why you'd even want to be here.'

'Tom, I used to help my mother kill the chickens, pluck out their feathers, and take their guts out and the same with the fish.'

'Fish with feathers?' Tom mocked, and they both laughed. 'Ok, but don't say I didn't warn you. I hope you've got a strong stomach.'

'Yes, of course. Tell me what you're doing.'

Tom explained as he went. They kept a small mob of sheep, that was known as the killers, in a paddock near the yards. These sheep were either for the homestead or for seasonal workers like the shearers. They were bred just for meat, not wool. Most of the sheep on the station were medium wool merinos with a wool staple mostly used in clothing and other cloth. The killers were bred from Merino Dorset-cross ewes and Dorset rams. Their wool was of little value, but they were well-muscled and far superior meat sheep than pure merinos. Tom had kept the sheep in a small yard overnight, and it was from them that he would select one to be butchered. He explained to Maysa that keeping others with the sheep to be killed, kept them all much calmer. A sheep that had been frantic and upset at the time of killing had a very unpleasant, gamey taste. He put that down to adrenalin running through their system. The sheep were kept in overnight to 'empty out' with no food or water. Therefore, when he was gutting a sheep, if he accidentally pierced the bladder or bowel, there would be no mess on the meat.

Tom pushed the sheep into a corner of the pen where he selected the sheep he wanted. Grabbing the sheep by the snout and twisting its head back on itself whilst pulling its hip toward his leg, he put the sheep off balance. He effortlessly sat the sheep on its backside in the same way the shearers did all day long in the shed.

'Open the gate and let the others out please.' Maysa did as he directed. Tom smiled to himself. She seemed to move about in a very relaxed and natural manner with the animals. He allowed himself a fleeting moment to imagine her as a farmer's wife, hands-on in the field, as Milly had been. As Milly would have been. Could there really be two women, so right in every way? Each so different in so many ways, but both very beautiful, very capable and very strong.

Maysa locked the gate and turned back to watch Tom as he took a long straight-bladed knife and he drew the blade back and forth across the sheep's neck in a few quick motions. Blood from its main arteries spurted out onto the soil, and Tom held the sheep still as all four legs lashed at the air. In seconds, the life had drained from its body. He lay the sheep on its side whilst its nerves drove the last few eerie kicks from its legs. At last, it was motionless.

'That was quick.' Tom looked up as Maysa spoke. He was still uncomfortable that she had watched the whole process. She, however, seemed quite comfortable, and he wondered how different her life must have been before she had moved to Australia. To him, she appeared pretty and fragile, yet, at the same time, strong and determined.

It took only minutes for Tom to peel back the skin on all four legs and to open the skin from the sheep's groin to its neck, branching this main cut out to each of the legs. Two butcher's hooks were inserted, one in each of the sheep's back legs between the muscle and tendon just above the hock. Tom then hooked these to a steel frame which resembled a coat hanger and then hoisted the sheep by rope into a tree. He took a large knife with a curved blade which he used to peel back the skin from the legs and around the brisket. Once he had enough skin to grip, he used his free hand to punch between the skin and muscle, tearing the membrane that held the skin to the tissue. In about ten minutes, he had skinned the sheep. A tidy carcass hung from the tree. He made a careful incision through the stomach muscles of the sheep. He ran his knife down to the brisket, being very careful not to pierce any of its gut as he did. With a couple of quick cuts, he disconnected the sheep's gut from its groin, and its innards fell out onto the ground. Tom reached into the chest cavity and pulled the heart and lungs free, and the job was all but complete.

'Pass me that enamel dish will you please, Maysa.' He removed the liver and kidneys, placing them in the enamel bowl. 'You can take these to Cookie when I carry the sheep over to the meat safe.'

Standing outside the yard, the two dogs were staring intensely at Tom and the carcass and were drooling. Tom took the carcass in his arms and hoisting it upward, it came free of the hanger. He draped it across his shoulder and led Maysa and the dogs back to the meat safe where he hung the carcass overnight for butchering the next day. It was now time to butcher yesterday's kill.

Cookie was leaning out of the window, smoking a rolled cigarette and watching this young couple walk across from the yards. The pretty young girl with the enamel basin filled with sheep offal, and the good-looking young fella with the carcass strewn across his shoulder. They made a fine-looking couple. He felt strangely comfortable and happy with this developing relationship.

He'd asked Maysa gingerly what had happened

to her face the day after the attack and had been pleased and relieved to hear she had just fallen over. Somewhere deep down inside, he didn't believe that for a moment. He didn't want to have to deal with this. He was getting on in years, and he just wanted to cook and drink a few beers with the boys. As much as he was becoming very fond of Maysa, he couldn't for the life of him understand how Bob could have sent her up here, way to buggery in the bush. How did he not expect there to be some sort of trouble? Especially with her being so bloody good looking and all. He fancied, if he'd been a younger bloke with some decent prospects, he might have taken a shot at her himself, but he was well passed it now. Anyway, something was niggling at him though and the fact she was with that young fella Tom, who seemed like a bloody good young fella, made him much more comfortable.

Tom spoke quietly to Maysa.

'Listen, I better get going. I will be back tomorrow morning, and I'll come and see you. Paddy's getting a bit jack of me at the moment, so I have to keep my head down. Tonight, I want you to be careful ok? Just keep clear of that bloody Dingo. I promise you I won't do anything . . . yet anyway. But if I get a sniff of him even looking in your direction, I'll make him wish he cut his head off on that tin, not just his stinking shoulder.'

'Tom, please be careful. It is not worth making trouble for yourself. He is nasty and dangerous. But his time will come.'

'Too bloody right, his time will come.'

CHAPTER ELEVEN

It was just on dusk when Paddy watched Tom heading off up the track to the Homestead. During the day, Tom had spoken with Len Patterson and asked if he could come and see him and Irene that evening and Len had responded with a dinner invitation. Tom had washed up, put on clean clothes and polished boots, and set off, determined to sort a few things out that would put his mind at rest.

Paddy leaned on the sill of an open window in his room, drawing cigarette smoke deep into his lungs. He spat a small piece of tobacco, from the rolled cigarette, off the tip of his tongue. He squinted as the smoke climbed gracefully upward from his nostrils in hypnotic tendrils. He took a swig of his beer and felt the warm flush to his head from the alcohol, heightened by his day of hard work in the sun. Tom was nearing the garden gate, and Paddy didn't take his eyes off him, he barely moved a muscle. He was deep in contemplation. He wondered and wished he knew what was being discussed up in the big house. Somewhere deep in his stomach, the faintest nervous flutter served to dampen his agitation just a little. Somewhere deep down, there was a solution for this agitation, and it comforted him and excited him as well. Tom disappeared into the homestead garden, and Paddy turned his attention absent-mindedly to two rabbits running cautiously across the paddock just 50 yards away. He butted his cigarette on the window sill amongst the flaking paint. He'd been following this routine for some time, and the sill was stained black and slightly burnt. He flicked the butt out of the window, and it lay with a pile of others in the dirt. He turned away from the window and stood on the leg of one of his dogs that had been lying on the floor behind him loyally. The dog yelped. Paddy got a fright and kicked the dog violently in the stomach and yelled at it.

'Get out of the way you stupid fuckin bastard.' The dog yelped again and ran off quickly. Paddy punched the door jam as he passed through the doorway, muttering, 'stupid bloody bastard.' He paused for a moment in the hall outside of his room, then turned, went back into the room, opened the closet where a couple of pairs of pants and shirts were hanging and pushed them aside. From the back of the closet, he took a .22 calibre rifle. He opened a drawer in the closet and took out a small box of bullets and thrust them in his trouser pocket. He left the building with the rifle and his dog skulking along carefully at his heel.

★ ★ ★

Tom strode up the garden path to the homestead, up four concrete steps and onto the timber floored veranda. The old Victorian style red brick homestead stood grandly in this harsh landscape. The lawns were green, and the gardens were well kept. Standard roses were in flower in well-defined garden beds. There were the typical palms, that seemed out of place so far from the coast, but were favoured by the country folk. Tom knocked on the door. It was answered just a few moments later by Len.

'G'day Tom, come in, Boy.' Len greeted Tom with a broad smile. 'There's no need to come through the front, Boy, next time come straight to the laundry door and throw your boots off there and come in. You're not a stranger here. Irene, Tommy's here. Here mate, go into the kitchen and say hello and I'll get you a beer.'

Tom walked into the kitchen, where Milly's mother, Irene, was drying her hands on a hand towel. She turned and smiled at Tom, greeted him and strode across the room, grasping his arms and kissing his cheek.

'Sit down, Tom. Sit down, please. Here give me that hat.' She took Tom's hat and placed it on an old pine dresser. She pulled a chair out at the table and sat down next to him. 'How are you, dear?'

Irene Patterson was a strong, capable and attractive woman. Milly had been her mother's daughter. Until Milly's death, Irene had been active in the

117

community, particularly in the Country Women's Association. She played tennis, supported many charitable functions and frequently hosted social occasions at the Patterson's homestead. After Milly's death, Irene had shrunken physically and socially. But she was still a strong woman, just more withdrawn. Tom was still a favourite with Irene. Time was not diminishing the affection she felt for him at all.

'So, Tom, what's up with you? Len said you asked to come up and see us. I am always pleased to have you for dinner any time at all, you know that. Please feel free to come up anytime at all.' She rested her hand on his forearm and watched him closely.

'Well, it's . . . um.' Tom wasn't sure how he would put this to the Pattersons. He was feeling terribly guilty, but at the same time, felt he shouldn't be. 'Well, it's . . . well it's up the shearing shed, in the team, the cook's hand . . . she's, well she's a woman . . . a lady.'

'Ah, I see, and is she pretty?' Irene was smiling and speaking in a teasing tone. 'Len, come here. Apparently, there is a pretty young lady working in the shearing team. I take it she is young. Is she, Tom?' Irene called through the open door of the kitchen to Len. He appeared mid-sentence with his large hands carrying 2 glasses of beer and balancing a glass of wine between his fingers.

'Ok, Irene. Take it easy. You'll frighten the boy off for good. Here, Tom. Get this into yer. She's a good-looking young Lassie, isn't she mate. I've seen her once or twice when I've been up there, but I haven't met her yet. She'd be keeping Cookie on his toes I'm guessing.'

'You've never mentioned any attractive young ladies up with the shearing team before, Len!' Irene rebuked her husband.

'So, Tom, what's up then?' Len asked. 'Mate, if you're looking for our blessing to ask this young lady out for dinner or a dance, then you don't need to. Whatever you do, we'll always be proud of you and happy for you.' Len spoke on with sensitivity. 'It'll never take away from Milly. We know how you felt about her. But she's gone now, and we've all got to keep going. Irene and I would both be real happy for you if you found someone nice. Wouldn't we Luv?'

'Of course we would.' Irene replied quietly, staring at Tom and knowing this was another moment that put distance between the world now and her daughter's life. One more connection that was somehow being severed. 'Yes Tom, tell us about this girl.'

'Well it's not that simple,' Tom began. 'Yes, she is attractive. In fact, I think she's very beautiful. I have to confess, I have already taken her out on a picnic. Pretty sure she's keen on me as well. She's all alone, you see. Her dad passed away recently, and her mum several years ago. Now she and her brother have been split up because they were desperate just to make ends meet. She's not an Australian girl. She's a foreigner. She's from India, her mum was Indian, but her dad was Irish.' Tom paused for a moment. Rubbed his face in his hands and then took a swig of his beer.

'You see, there's been some trouble up at the shed. With Maysa, that is. That's her name, Maysa.' And over the next half hour and a drink refill, Tom relayed all he knew of the attack including who they suspected. He also had the Pattersons pledge not to make a huge issue of the attack in the same way as he had to Maysa, although he and the Pattersons knew this could only be for so long.

Tom and the Pattersons ate dinner and talked on into the evening. When the meal was complete, Irene washed, and the men dried the dishes. When the last dish was washed, and in the rack, Irene took off her apron and hung it on the back of the kitchen chair.

'Right then, that's settled, Tom. You and Len can make the necessary arrangements tomorrow, and I'll not hear any arguments from anyone. I am quite looking forward to this now. I think we've made the right decision.'

Tom left shortly after and walked back to the stockman's quarters. The stockman's quarters was simply an old weatherboard cottage that was shared by Tom and Paddy. Old Neville, or Nev for short, lived in a second smaller cottage close by. Each had their own bedroom. They shared the kitchen and bathroom and an outdoor long-drop toilet. The house had a full-length verandah, eight feet wide, with a timber floor right around it.

As Tom approached the building, he had a sense that someone was watching him, and he turned to see a figure disappear into the moonlit shadows near the tank stand where the dogs were sometimes tied up.

Two and a half hours after Paddy had seen Tom disappear through the garden gate into the homestead, he saw him reappear sauntering along looking happy with himself. In his left hand, he balanced .22 rifle. His finger brushed the trigger absentmindedly. Blood dripped down his right leg from two dead rabbits whose carcasses he held by the back legs. He stood deathly still as Tom passed by, like a predator, partly camouflaged and watching its prey.

It was no more than a tiny movement that caught Tom's attention, and he turned to see Paddy standing by the tank stand. He was not deliberately hidden, but there was something odd about how he stood, half in the shadows and so still. It was the dog lying at his feet, wagging a tail in recognition of Tom, that caught his eye.

'Christ, Paddy. You frightened the shit out of me. What are you doin' over there?'

'Not much. Just shot a couple of rabbits for the dogs. Stopped here by the stand to skin and gut 'em. Then I can wash up and come in. How about you? What er you been up to then?'

'Yeah, not much mate. Just catching up with the Pattersons about a couple of things. See you inside.' Tom walked on, feeling a little uneasy. When he reached the door to the house, he turned back. Paddy was still standing there, he hadn't moved at all, just watching him. He moved quickly inside and then stepped into the living area where he left the lights off and moved over toward the window. In the moonlight, he could see Paddy, who was still standing by the tank stand, watching the door now. After a moment Paddy moved, like a shop mannequin coming to life. He put the gun down and began to skin the rabbits.

CHAPTER TWELVE

At morning tea, Maysa dropped off a basket of cakes and sandwiches to the shearing shed and made her way back toward the kitchen. Tom arrived early with Paddy, Nev and the next day's mob. He waved to her as he passed nearby on his horse, shouting good morning, and calling out he'd see her shortly. She smiled and waved from the shearing shed landing. As she walked past the big old sliding iron door, she glanced into the shed where the shearing had stopped for morning tea. Leaning on the wool press, Dingo was taking a long drag on a smoke. He was watching her walk past. She looked away quickly and felt a shiver down her spine, leaving the hair on the back of her neck and arms standing on end. She quickly walked down the stairs and headed back to the kitchen.

There was a ute parked near the kitchen. Maysa had heard it pull up behind her as she was walking to the shed earlier and had turned to see Len Patterson getting out of the driver's seat. As she drew closer to the kitchen, she could see Tom's horse, Bess, tied up to a rail just beyond the kitchen, and she could hear voices coming from within. She paused for a moment to listen. Cookie was talking loudly but politely. He sounded a little irritated, perhaps defensive, but Maysa couldn't make out what was being discussed. She thought she heard a woman's voice. She stepped slowly into the kitchen.

There at the table, sat Cookie, Len Patterson and a well-dressed lady of about Mr Patterson's age, who Maysa assumed must have been his wife. In an instant, Maysa thought of Milly, of Milly and Tom, the search for Milly's body, and the grief this mother must have felt. She almost felt the weight of that emotion in this lady's energy, although she seemed to be strong and amiable. Behind them all, standing in the corner, was Tom. He was obviously part of, or at the least, a close observer of the conversation.

The conversation stopped dead, and everyone looked at Maysa. She blushed. Tom stepped forward quickly.

'Maysa, I'd like you to meet Mr and Mrs Patterson. Of course, you know they own the station, and it's their sheep you've been shearing for the past couple of weeks.'

'And eating too,' Cookie added with a smile.

Immediately regaining her composure and confidence, Maysa replied.

'Don't be silly, I haven't shorn a sheep yet, Tom. Even after two weeks here.' The group all laughed, and everyone was immediately at ease.

124

Len Patterson got to his feet.

'Good to meet you, Maysa, Tommy Boy has told us all about yer. Haven't yer, Tom.' Len looked to Tom for confirmation.

'Well, ah yes, a bit I guess,' Tom replied a little self-consciously.

'Only good things I hope.' Maysa paused and then gave Tom a cheeky smile. 'Tommy.' She added.

'Tom'll do thanks, Maysa.' Tom replied.

'Oh, Tommy,' Irene pinched his cheek as she stood up.

'Hello, Maysa. I'm Irene.' She shook hands with Maysa. Maysa felt an immediate affection for her. She was taken by Irene's motherly connection with Tom and her cheeky teasing style. She also felt connection and empathy for the shared life's tragedies, yet to be spoken of and yet shared between them.

'Tom, you were not pulling our legs when you said how pretty Maysa was.' Irene smiled as she looked Maysa over like a prize cow. Both Maysa and Tom were scarlet with embarrassment and couldn't look at each other. Although they had shared some intimate conversation and very personal time together, their affection for each other was just days old. They were still very shy with each other.

'Anyway, enough of this.' Irene's tone turned serious and business-like quickly. 'Maysa, Tom has told us about the incident here.' As she said this, she shot a sharp look in Cookie's direction. He kept his eyes averted, instead, choosing to stare at a dusting of flour on the table in which he was drawing nervous swirls with a wooden spoon. Irene continued to look at Cookie, and Maysa could see she thought Cookie should take some responsibility for the incident. She felt sorry for Cookie but remained quiet along with the others in the room.

'I must say, when I heard about this, I told Len to take a shotgun and run this dog of a shearer into town to the police. At the very least, off the property. But Tom spent some time persuading us not to take any action, against our better judgement, at least for the time being. But this matter is far from finished.' Irene held court, and everyone listened attentively.

'Tom explained your situation as best he could, and we appreciate the importance of this job for you with the team. There is still two and a half weeks of shearing here before the team moves on. Whilst you are on this station, your welfare is Len's and my concern and quite obviously, Tom's.' Again, she darted a piercing glare at Cookie who had let his guard down and dared to look at her as she spoke. Like a chastised child, he quickly turned his attention away again.

'For the rest of this contract, you will move to the homestead with Len and I.' Maysa was dumbstruck, uncharacteristically unable to form a comment.

'There is a perfectly good spare room which is much more suitable than this setup for a young lady. Once you have completed your chores with Cookie each day, you can come straight over to the homestead. I can't see why you can't be in by dark. This afternoon, you'll need to pack up your belongings, and we will send Tom over in the ute to pick you up. Can you ride a horse?'

Still taken aback by what was happening, Maysa took a moment to answer.

'Ah . . . no . . . Mrs Patterson. Walking Tom's Bess along the other day is as close as I have ever really been to a horse.'

'She's a natural.' Tom chipped in, and everyone turned to look at him, including Maysa. 'Well, I just mean that she looked comfortable with Bess and Bess clearly likes her.'

'You'll have no problems on a quiet horse, Maysa. You're a strong and fit young girl, and you should be able to ride. Tom, you bring in Angel and ride her around a bit and settle her, then get Maysa on her. She can carry Maysa back and forward each day. She can take Banjo with her as well. He'll follow Angel anywhere, and he'll be good company. Banjo will look after you Maysa.'

There was silence in the room now. Maysa was shocked at how quickly everything had been turned upside down, even if only temporarily, and was overwhelmed and excited all at the same time.

Unbeknown to Maysa, this was a huge gesture from Irene. Angel was Milly's horse, a mare who had remained out to pasture since Milly's death and Banjo was Milly's old Blue Heeler, Kelpie cross. Banjo was now old and wise at 9 years old. He followed Len around, but lived a semi-retired life since Milly's death and had never regained his spirit and desire to work. He was part of the family.

'Well Maysa, I can't tell you how much I am looking forward to some feminine company in the old house, it has been too long. So, if no one's got anything to add, then we will see you later this afternoon.' Irene looked about the room, but everyone knew better than to interrupt or compete.

'Early enough for Maysa to wash and be ready for dinner at seven-thirty please Tom.' Again, Irene looked around the room at the three men in turn, as if inviting or perhaps daring comment. On receiving nothing, she turned and left the room looking very satisfied with herself and her new project. Maysa watched Irene march out of the room, then looked to both Len and Tom who stood in silence. The faintest smile showed Tom was very happy with the outcome.

Maysa quickly followed after Irene, who was making her way to the ute. She made a small and very shy attempt at thanking Irene for her generosity.

Still inside the hut, Tom went to leave, and Len stopped him.

'Just a second, Tom. Now, Cookie . . .' Cookie dared to look up from the table, now this powerful and intimidating woman had left the room. 'Listen, mate, this is far from over. This bloke can be thankful to Maysa for the fact neither Tom nor me, or for that matter, Irene, has laid a finger on him. Don't let him give us an excuse. You tell Bob when you see him. That bloody mongrel bastard Dingo is finished on this station forever, or this team is. He can decide. And you can tell him that Dingo is finished in this district as well. I'll see to that. And if he ever steps foot in this district again, Tom and I will dump what's left of him at the police station when we're done with him. It's Bob's reputation, he puts a mongrel like that back in a shed belonging to anyone I know, and he'll regret it. You got all that?'

'Yeah, bloody oath, Len. He's gone as soon as we can mate. You can rely on me.' Cookie replied. Both Tom and Len looked at Cookie, and he read the disapproval on their faces. Cookie thought of Dingo with bitterness and anger. This was a good contract, with good people he had known for more than ten years. Bob would be wild with anger.

What's more, Cookie had become really fond of Maysa. Now he felt he had done nothing and had let her down. He hadn't known what had happened until this morning, but he suspected something bad, and he'd done nothing which had left him as guilty as Dingo in the eyes of a decent bloke.

★   ★   ★

129

Later in the evening, Maysa was packing the last of her belongings into her suitcase, when she heard the sound of a vehicle arriving outside. The shearers were fed and sitting around the campfire, quietly drinking. Cookie remained in the kitchen, partly to see Maysa on her way and partly because he didn't want to be seen associating with the boys, who included Dingo. Tom strode through the door into the kitchen, looking pleased with himself.

'G'Day Cookie. You there, Maysa?'

'Coming Tom.' Maysa appeared in her doorway wearing a clean dress and carrying her suitcase, which Tom quickly took from her.

'Come on then, let's get going.'

'I will see you in the morning then Cookie.' Maysa patted Cookie's shoulder as she passed, giving him a sympathetic look.

'Yeah good on yer, Luv. 'Ave a good night, ey.'

Outside the shearers were all watching the kitchen when Tom emerged with Maysa carrying her suitcase. A couple of them yelled out comments to her, 'where you off to Luv?' and 'yer not leavin' are yer?' Maysa smiled back at them nervously and waved, shaking her head to indicate no. Tom put her suitcase in the ute and then opened the door for her as the shearers watched on. The gentlemanlike gesture was not lost on Maysa, the shearers, or Cookie for that matter. Maysa got into the ute which was facing away from the shearers. Tom walked around the front of the ute and then opened his door.

'Get up, Billy.' The dog leapt into the back of the ute as Tom tapped the side of the vehicle. He paused for a moment to look back toward the campfire and picked out Dingo sitting next to Darkie. They locked eyes for a moment, and an understanding passed between them. Tom held his gaze until Dingo could no longer. Dingo tried a calm 'What's up?' look, but he lost his nerve and broke the stare. Taking in the scene, Tom made the assumption that the other shearers knew nothing of what had happened, yet. When old Bob turned up next week that would change though. Tom knew that. He might even move that bastard on straight away. Tom thought for a second about Maysa sitting in the ute, flashes of Milly came to him. Something bit deep in the pit of his stomach. He had a couple of days to deal with this, but quietly. He stepped into the ute, turned the engine over and smiled at Maysa. She returned his smile then looked out her window at Cookie who was leaning in the doorway. She gave him a wave. They sat in silence for a few moments as the ute bumped its way down the track. Dust billowed out behind the vehicle. Billy ran backward and forward from side to side, smiling into the cool breeze. After some time, Maysa spoke.

'You'd think I was going forever the way poor Cookie looked.'

'Yes, well he has a bit to answer for.'

'Tom, no. It's not his fault at all. You can't blame him.'

131

'Mmmm.' Tom growled, and he kept his eyes on the track.

Ten minutes later and three gates on, each having given Tom a moment to admire Maysa as she insisted on leaping from the vehicle to open them, they arrived at the homestead. Len waved as they passed by a machine shed where he was tinkering with a small piece of machinery. Irene appeared at the back door immediately as they arrived at the back gate. She strode down the back path toward them.

'Welcome, welcome Maysa. Tom get her bag and bring it in. Come on, hurry up.' Irene locked her arm in Maysa's as they walked.

Irene opened an old timber door with two frosted glass panels, and she ushered Maysa into the laundry and wash-up room.

'Come in, Dear. This is the laundry. You can wash up here and leave your boots there on the newspaper, and hang your coat there when you have one. The boys often wash up outside at the tank. There's soap and an old pan there if you're really dirty and you want to clean up a bit before coming in. Old Len always leaves his soapy water in the pan for the poor dogs to drink.' Irene laughed. 'Poor things. He says it kills the worms in their gut, and it's a waste just to throw it out. A load of hogwash I say, but men. You know what they're like, all sorts of silly ideas. Come in, and I'll show you your bedroom. I've made up your bed and put some things out for you; a towel, and some brushes and perfumes and things. I didn't know what you need so just let me know.' Irene seemed very excited and spoke in rapid-fire.

They walked from the laundry into a hall that led all the way to the front door. The floors were polished hardwood, and the walls were clad with dark dado panelling to waist height. From there to a picture rail just above eye height was a cream wallpaper with a red fleur delis design. The ten foot high ceilings were lined with pressed tin. Along the hall were photographs of the family; adults and children. Some were quite old, hanging from the picture rail in ornate frames. One group of pictures was of family members who were Australian soldiers in the great wars, in uniform with the famous Australian slouch hats. As they walked along the hall, Irene guided Maysa.

'That's Jeff's room, that's Len's and my room, this is Milly's room.' She paused and stroked the door frame tenderly. The door was closed almost completely, but ajar enough for Maysa to see a made bed. She suspected it was just as it was when Milly was alive.

'And this, Maysa, is your room,' and Irene pushed the door open. She stepped in, and Maysa followed her.

'Is this ok?' Irene smiled broadly and gestured to the surroundings. Maysa stood just inside the doorway, saying nothing but looking around the room.

'It's absolutely beautiful.' Maysa replied quietly. The room was larger than the living and dining rooms combined in her Carlton home. A beautifully sewn patchwork quilt, in an array of pinks, adorned an ornate iron-framed four-poster bed with polished brass knobs atop each post. There were piles of pillows in floral patterns. She walked to the bed and gently stroked the soft cotton of the hand-sewn quilt. On one side of the room, a large window looked out over the garden. It was dark now, but Maysa imagined the view of the garden would be lush green and beautiful, and resplendent with blooming roses. Such a contrast in this harsh dusty environment. On another wall stood a large Mahogany wardrobe, with doors to hanging space on either side of drawers. To the other side, beyond the end of her bed, was a mahogany chest of drawers with a mirror. On it lay hairbrushes, perfumes, and other beautiful silver objects, including a jewellery box, all laid out carefully on a delicately embroidered doily. The tour stopped when Tom appeared in the doorway.

'Ah, excuse me. Here's your suitcase, Maysa,' Tom announced overly formerly. Both the women greeted Tom with big smiles.

'How's your room, Maysa. You like it?'

'Like it? It is beautiful, Tom. I have never slept in a room like this or stayed in a home like this. I don't know what I have done to deserve such kindness.' She turned and smiled appreciatively at Irene.

'Nonsense.' Irene replied in a business-like manner, although clearly moved. 'Now, off you go, Tom. Let Maysa settle in and get ready for dinner. Would you like to come up for dinner? Of course, you would. I have cooked a little extra for you. I anticipated you saying yes to an invite.'

'I wouldn't say no, to be honest. Don't feel like cooking now. It's getting on. I'd have to try and put something together.'

'Yes, yes.' Irene cut Tom off mid-sentence. 'Nothing to do with a certain, very pretty girl then.' Irene winked at Maysa who blushed. Tom smiled, embarrassed, turned and walked away.

'Seven fifteen,' Irene called after him. 'Maysa, I expect you'd like a shower or a bath in a real bathroom. Back down the hall toward the laundry. Last door on the left. There's a fresh towel there on the bed. We'll see you in the kitchen just before dinner if you like. But we'll eat in the dining room tonight since it's your first night.'

'Can I help?'

'Not at all. Well, not tonight. Settle in Dear, and then we'll get going as a team 'ey?' Irene paused and looked at Maysa affectionately. She took Maysa's hand gently. 'I can't tell you how pleased I am you're staying with us.' She smiled and gently squeezed Maysa's hand, then left.

Tom parked the ute in the machinery shed and headed for the stockmen's quarters to clean up before dinner. He walked through the front gate of the garden, which was no more than patchy grass and dust. Paddy was sitting on a chair on the veranda in a blue singlet and khaki shorts with bare feet. He was leaning forward, arms on legs, a rolled cigarette smouldering in his fingers and two butts crushed on the floor at his feet next to a half-finished bottle of beer. As Tom walked up the steps and onto the veranda, Paddy picked up his beer and took a swig.

'Watcha been up to, lover boy?' Paddy asked. Tom knew Paddy knew the answer. He'd seen him bagging grain at the silo next to the machinery shed as he'd arrived earlier with Maysa. He'd seen Paddy straighten up from where he'd been bent over at the grain hatch and noticed he'd stayed watching them. Always watching, Tom had thought, irritated.

'Beer?' Paddy asked Tom. Tom was a little surprised. He and Paddy tolerated each other, but typically in silence. They lived in this old house together, but they organised themselves quite separately. Although Paddy was the supervisor, Tom took most of his direction from Len and often worked entirely independent of Paddy. This only served to heighten the tension between the pair.

'No, I'm right thanks mate, got stuff to do. Thanks anyway.' Tom went to move off, but Paddy went on speaking to him.

'So what are you up to that you ain't got time for a drink?'

'I'm heading out for a while, so I want to go and freshen up first.'

'Where you off to then?'

'Just up to the homestead to see the Pattersons.' Tom responded reluctantly and was getting impatient with the barrage of questions. He knew where this was heading and was having trouble heading Paddy off.

'What for? You just got back from there didn't yer?'

'Yeah I did, and why are you so bloody interested in what I'm doing all of a sudden?'

'Steady, steady.' Paddy held up his hands in a gesture of surrender. Tom was getting agitated. Paddy looked pleased with himself. 'Take it easy, Boy, just being friendly. No need to get your nuts in a knot. Off you go then, go put yer face on. Better get some perfume on too. Don't want to stink like an old sheep when you're up there getting the silver service.'

Tom was getting really annoyed. He knew damn well he was being baited. And he knew he should have walked off, but he stood and listened to these jibes. He had been in a good mood heading back from the homestead and seeing Maysa settled safely with the Pattersons. But now he was agitated, and his temper was rearing its too often ugly head. He knew this was what Paddy wanted, but he was having difficulty controlling it.

'Listen, Paddy, I don't know what's up your

scrawny arse, but firstly, what I do in my spare time is my business and not yours. And secondly, I'm not your bloody boy either. You're about two or three years older than me at best mate, so drop the 'boy' bullshit. We don't have to like each other, but for now, we gotta live together and work together.' Paddy broke in over the top of Tom.

'Live together for now? What's that supposed to mean? You moving up to the big house and into bed with your girlie from the city, eh?'

Tom stepped toward Paddy, his fists clenching. Paddy gave him a sly smile, taunting him. It was as though Paddy wanted Tom to punch him. He didn't seem in the least bit afraid. But Tom wasn't giving him the pleasure. He knew if he hit him, Paddy would be up to see Len a minute later. It wasn't worth the heartache.

'You can piss off Paddy, you sad bastard. I'm not wasting my time on you. I've got better things to do.' And then he added as an afterthought back through the doorway, 'as you well know.' He forced a smile at Paddy.

The Spooney was getting angry. Paddy had him just where he wanted him.

'You moving up to the big house and into bed with your girlie from the city, eh?' Paddy baited Tom.

Paddy pushed his chin forward toward Tom. Offering it for sacrifice. He'd be happy to take a fall. To sustain a few bruises. It would be a compelling argument for old man Patterson. He could tell him, this boy you got here Len, he's lost it. Not quite right. Look at me face, bruised, cut. Never laid a finger on him. He just went off. Everyone knows he does. You remember. In town last year. In and out of the lock-up, drunk, punching the shit out of poor innocent bastards. Yeah, he thought, I've got this prick where I want him.

Paddy was disappointed as Tom strode off, mumbling and swearing under his breath.

CHAPTER THIRTEEN

'Tom, come in. I believe Maysa will be here in a moment. I found her some dresses that fit her like a glove, and she's changing for dinner.' Tom smiled at Irene as Len walked into the kitchen.

'How are you, mate? You seem to be eating up here as often as I am. What's going on. You keep this up, and you'll have to take a pay cut or pay board.'

'Don't be so rude, Len! Don't listen to him, Tom. It's nice to have a handsome young man about the house. I remember when Len was young and handsome. Well, I can just remember, it was a long time ago.' Irene laughed at her own joke, and so did Tom, carefully watching for Len's reaction.

'Enjoy it while you can, Tommy. That's what I say. They turn on yer pretty damn quick.' Len spoke in a dejected tone and pulled a face to match.

There were footsteps in the doorway, and everyone stopped the joking and turned to see Maysa. She wore a light pink cotton dress gathered tight in the waist which showed off her figure. Her hair was gathered in a ponytail, and her eyes sparkled as Tom had never seen before. She broke into a huge smile as she became conscious of the three admirers, who stood a moment in silence, taking in the vision.

'Well,' Irene broke the silence finally, 'going to be a bit hard to concentrate on dinner tonight is it boys?' She winked at Maysa as she spoke and then looked at the two men who were still having difficulty hiding their admiration. Maysa was blushing and looking down at her feet, clasping her hands in front of her. The pose only served to make her more attractive to the two men.

'Well, you know what?' Len announced, having composed himself finally. 'It's not too often we get such a pretty young lady around here is it, Irene? You know what, Maysa, I remember . . . well, just remember, when Irene was young and attractive.' Tom burst out laughing, and Irene slapped Len across the arm. Maysa was shocked.

'Don't you worry about him, Maysa. He's very rude to me. No consideration for my aging feelings at all. But I am still more than this old bull can handle.' Irene swung an arm affectionately around Len's waist and kissed his cheek. Tom and Maysa darted a glance at each other and smiled.

The rest of the evening went very well. Irene served roast beef and vegetables, followed by ice cream and rice pudding. She supposed Maysa couldn't possibly stand the sight of another 'lamb anything' on her plate. It was the most enjoyable meal Maysa had had in months, perhaps even years. At times during the evening, she thought of her father and her brother. And when watching and listening to Irene, she thought of her mother. But mostly she watched Tom, as discreetly as she could. She was embarrassed to see that nearly every time she dared to look at him, he was watching her. She noticed Irene, watching them both closely and noticed Irene smiling at Tom, but when she looked toward Tom, he was staring at her and not looking at Irene at all. Irene was clearly pleased with how this was all working out. Lots of stories were exchanged, and many questions were asked of Maysa, who struggled to eat her dinner whilst politely answering questions. Two bottles of wine were shared, and Maysa felt the warm and fuzzy feeling of being tipsy. Try as she might, the excitement, the alcohol and the day's work were finally catching up with her. Finally, Irene announced they should leave the table and sit in the lounge.

'Come on you boys, a quick cup of tea and then Tom, you'll have to go home. This young lady's exhausted, and she has to get up and work tomorrow. There is plenty of time for socialising. So Maysa, can you drive since you can't ride a horse yet? We need to know how you will get to the shed each day. It will take fifteen or twenty minutes to drive or half an hour if you ride a horse straight across the paddocks.'

'Oh.' For the first time, Maysa began to think about getting to work and the logistics of her new-found accommodation. 'Well I can't drive, and I have never ridden a horse.'

Irene smiled. 'Well, it seems there is work to do. Len. You can give Maysa driving lessons in the ute on the weekend, alright?' Len nodded and sipped his whisky. 'And Tom, as I've already said, I want you to bring Angel in.'

Tom and Len both stopped and looked at Irene, still surprised and a little shocked. Irene looked back at both of them defiantly.

'Yes Tom. You know how I feel. Maysa should be able to ride a horse if she is going to be out in the bush for a while. There is only so much you can do in a vehicle out here. You'll need to ride Angel a few times and get her under control. She knows you, and she'll settle quickly with a bit of exercise. Take Maysa with you, and she can feed Angel a little grain and some apples. They'll be best friends in no time at all.'

Len and Tom remained silent. Angel had been Milly's beloved horse, perhaps her most precious possession.

That night, Tom lay in his bed for quite some time staring through the darkness at the ceiling. He was thinking about Maysa and dinner, and he was still buzzing from the evening. He was sure now he was falling in love with her. It had been so fast, he'd been caught by surprise. Rarely an hour went by during the day when he didn't spend some time thinking about her. He'd begun to picture her working alongside him on the land, riding horses, mustering sheep, and even allowed himself to think about what their children might be like. Beautiful young girls with long black hair and lean and muscled young boys, bronzed by the Aussie sun, all tearing around the countryside on ponies and making mischief.

But different thoughts nagged at him from below the fuzzy happy surface. Faint pictures of Milly came to him from time to time as he lay there, often her face was bruised and bleeding, although he'd never seen her after she'd died. His mind had created memories made up of grizzly pictures from what he'd heard of her death at the Court case. And Paddy, sitting on the verandah, swimming in booze and watching Tom from under his hat with dark eyes buried in a dirty, unshaven face. Standing by the tank stand watching, always watching. And then in sharp piercing clarity, a vision of Dingo sitting at the campfire, his sharp features and evil squinting eyes. Darkie, sitting nearby like some dopey, eager sheepdog.

Although he knew he shouldn't, he couldn't help but imagine ways to take revenge on Dingo. The thought of Dingo leaving and never facing the music tore at Tom's guts until they ached. He suspected that Bob would appear this weekend and that Dingo may even be asked to leave the station immediately. It would be an unhappy and nasty couple of final weeks of shearing. He worried about how Maysa would cope during this period.

Then he began to think, not for the first time about what happens next for Maysa. She would have expected to do her best in this job and then be offered another shed straight after this one was complete. What were the chances now? Slim at best. She would very likely be sent straight back to Melbourne, however much the Pattersons argued. But he hated the thought of her leaving. So much to think about. How to find a legitimate reason for her to stay on the property. To remain where he could be with her.

But then back to Dingo. The shearers wouldn't be happy with the fuss, although there wasn't much love lost between any of them and Dingo. The fuss this bloody sheila brought to the shed. 'What'd yer expect,' would be the comment, he could hear them now. 'Shed's no bloody place for a sheila. There was always going to be trouble.' And to his undeserved defence, 'He's a bit of a mongrel, Dingo, but underneath he's alright. He's just a bloke, that's all. What'd yer expect?' He couldn't stand the thought of them defending Dingo. It made him bitter and angry.

Tom rolled onto his side to try and get comfortable and shake off all the thoughts. He needed sleep. He stared at the wall and pictured Maysa walking to the river with him. Soon his thoughts seemed to wash together. He drifted off into a deep but dream-filled sleep.

CHAPTER FOURTEEN

At 5:00am, Tom's alarm rang out through the darkness and pierced his sleep like a sharp knife. He needed to get up, eat something, make himself respectable and be up at the homestead by 5:45 to pick up Maysa and get her across to Cookie. He put on his trousers, socks and boots quickly and threw his shirt over his shoulder, grabbed a towel from where it hung on the doorknob, and headed out to the tank stand. He relieved himself behind the tank stand then filled an enamel basin with cold water from the tank. He splashed his face, arms and chest and wet his hair, then towelled himself off before heading into the kitchen. There, he made himself 3 fried eggs on thick slices of toast and washed it all down with a hot black tea. At a quarter to six, he was leaning on the back fence at the homestead. He watched the light in the kitchen and waited for Maysa to appear. Moments later she walked out the back door accompanied by Irene in a dressing gown. Irene squeezed Maysa's arm and sent her off in Tom's direction while waving to Tom.

'Good Morning,' Tom smiled as he spoke and felt his face redden. He was still nervous and not used to this new relationship and all of its feelings.

'Good Morning to you, Tommy,' Maysa said with a huge smile and was visibly much more relaxed.

'Enough of the Tommy,' he replied, laughing. 'Like I said, Tom'll do just fine, thanks. Let's go. Come and jump in the ute.'

Tom led the way to the old machine shed, which had four bays filled with all sorts of machinery. It had no front wall and was opened toward the back of the homestead. All that lay between the back garden fence and the 50 yards to the machine shed was red bulldust as they called it. Soft as talcum powder. It covered your boots to the ankle in a puff as soon as you began walking in it. It would be like that until the rains came when it turned sticky before trying to send grass shoots up to compete with the endless tyres travelling overhead.

At the ute, which had been reversed into the shed, Tom opened the door for Maysa.

'You're such a gentleman, Tom. Thank you.' She paused, placing her hand on his wrist where it held the door. Her hands were cool and soft, and her fingers were long and lean. A searing heat flew up Tom's arm, and his stomach erupted in butterflies. He longed to kiss her. She looked at him, almost expectantly. He was embarrassed. He couldn't believe how nervous she made him. He had never felt like this with Milly. They'd always been friends. Everything had been easy. He just knew he had always loved her. Their first kiss was almost experimental. Almost clinical, as he remembered. But this was different, this girl drove needles into his nerves.

'It's my pleasure.' He smiled awkwardly. Maysa released her hold on his wrist and sat down in the ute. Tom shut the door and was disappointed with himself. He glanced around him instinctively and noticed Paddy leaning, both elbows on the fence to their cottage, taking a long draw on a rollie and watching Tom and Maysa. Tom stopped for a moment staring back. Just as it looked as though they were in a standoff, Paddy dropped his cigarette in the dirt, stubbed it out. He spat some loose tobacco off his bottom lip, as was his habit, before standing up and walking away.

Maysa looked at Tom, staring into his eyes. She believed he loved her. The way he looked at her, the shy and nervous way he behaved around her, the streams of exaggerated compliments. He made her more comfortable than any man had ever done before. He awoke feelings in her she had only ever briefly experienced in dreams and occasionally in daydreams. She realised they hardly knew each other, yet they were rocketing toward each other and the future at such a rate. But it felt right. Len and Irene's behaviour the evening before told her this was right. She longed for him to kiss her. But it wouldn't be on this occasion. Tom stuttered nervously.

'It's my pleasure.'

Tom closed the door for Maysa then got in himself and took Maysa across to the shearing shed. They spent the trip speaking politely about the Pattersons and how kind they were.

CHAPTER FIFTEEN

At the shearer's kitchen, Maysa was greeted like a long-lost friend by Cookie who was already flustered and sweating as he smoked and cooked the breakfast. Maysa slipped quickly into the morning routine, cracking eggs and frying bacon, chops, lambs fry and boiling water for tea.

At morning tea time, Tom, Paddy and old Nev arrived with a mob of sheep, yarded them and agreed to have smoko before they began drafting off the lambs. Tom walked by the shorn ewes as he did most mornings and looked at the quality of the shearing and checked there were no shoddy jobs or badly cut sheep. The sheep were routinely knicked and cut during shearing, especially the very wrinkly merinos. The wrinklier they were, the more skin, and of course, the more wool. But the wrinkles were also a cause of headaches for the farmers, with the shearing cuts getting fly struck. Flies would lay maggots deep in the damp protection of the wool and skin folds. This was a common cause of death in sheep. Occasionally, a shearer would take a long piece of skin off a wrinkle before he realised he was cutting the sheep. This was named after the bootlace it resembled. The shearer would call, 'tar here' and often a young boy, employed in the shed, would run with a pot of sticky black tar. He'd dab the tar on the wound, and this would keep the flies away until the wound healed.

On this morning, as Tom strolled through the yards, he noticed Darkie, his back to Tom, relieving himself on a fence post in the yards. Tom walked quietly up behind him. He slapped Darkie quite hard on the shoulder blade. Darkie jumped and hurried to zip himself back up inside his pants.

'Shit mate, you frightened the crap out of me,' Darkie spat out at Tom as he watched him nervously over his shoulder and fumbled with his fly.

'You're a bit nervous are yer mate? Just saying good morning, that's all. You can relax for Christ's sake. You got something to be nervous about have yer?'

'No nuffin. But always nervous when some Toff comes up behind me when I got me dick out.' Darkie, gaining a little confidence, laughed nervously at his own joke. Still standing and facing the puddle he'd made, Darkie shyed away nervously as Tom put his arms around his shoulder. Looking back toward the shed, Tom noticed a couple of the shearers leaning out the windows of the shed, tin mugs of tea in hand and smoking rollies. They were watching Tom and Darkie with expressionless faces.

One of the two shearers mumbled through his cigarette to his mate.

'These bastards got it comin' you know. You can't do that shit and think you can just walk away. All I can say is, I wouldn't like to run into that Tom on a dark night with that on me conscience.'

'Yep, reckon so.' His mate replied and then spat on the dust below the window.

'Maybe we might just take a little walk for a minute,' Tom almost whispered in Darkie's ear who was visibly panicking. Everyone knew of Tom's reputation; nights in the lockup after drunken brawls. He was known to be a strong and controlled fighter, even with a gut full of grog. Tom wanted Darkie out of sight of the shed and the shearers. He knew they'd say nothing, but he wanted no one interfering. He'd promised Len there'd be no trouble and as far as he was concerned, there wouldn't be. But there would be some payback, however small. Every time he pictured Maysa's bruised face and thought of those two bastards, his anger boiled. Invariably he would think of Milly at this time as well, and the fires of fury were fuelled to explosion point.

Tom grabbed a fistful of Darkie's shirt and pushed him in the direction of a gate behind the shed that led to a holding yard. Tall trees provided shade for the yards and a little privacy for a confidential conversation.

'Come on, I want ter talk to yer.' Tom kept his arm around Darkie's back while he guided him.

'Here, get the gate will yer.' Darkie complied reluctantly. He unlatched the chain slowly, and it dropped, swinging from the post. They were huddled uncomfortably close as Darkie pulled the gate back toward them. In a flash, catching Darkie entirely by surprise, Tom drove the gate and Darkies hand fiercely back into the post, jamming Darkie's fingers between the steel gate and the wooden post. He let out a shriek of pain.

'Fuck, what did you do that for yer bastard.' With that, Tom shoved the gate again. The blood was draining from Darkie's face.

'I want some information, and I want it now,' Tom spat the words into Darkie's face from just a few inches away. 'What did you and that mate of yours do to the girl. Come clean right now, and I'll take it easy on you at least.'

'Nuffin, I swear . . . nuffin,' Darkie cried back in a pleading tone.

'Mate, I am not a bloody idiot. You can make this easy on yerself, or do it the hard way, and that's gonna hurt, I'm tellin' you.'

'I swear I didn't do nuffin, I didn't. It wasn't me. It was Dingo. I didn't want to be in it. No shit. It was Dingo. He made me, but I did nuffin.' The words spilt out of Darkie as fast as he could talk.

'Tell me what your mate did then, and hurry up.' Tom lent harder on the gate, and Darkie drew a sharp breath. His middle finger was caught and being bent backward like a banana. It felt like it would break any second.

'I can't tell you nuffin. Honest, mate. Dingo'd kill me . . . honest. He said he'd cut me balls off if I blabbed anything . . . he did . . . and I believe him. He will.'

Tom's anger was rising to the surface like a volcano ready to break a fragile crust. 'Bugger this shit. You're wasting my time.' With one enormous shove, Tom pushed the gate in harder again and with that Darkie's finger dislocated at the middle joint. Darkie went white. The pain was excruciating. Tom eased off the gate and pulled Darkie backward by the shirt.

'What the fuck have you done,' Darkie coughed out the words as he held up his finger which was bent at a right angle at the middle joint and rapidly swelling and going purple.

'You better talk now you piece of dirt and fast, or the next one will be your neck.'

'Ok, ok. For Christ sake, take it easy. I didn't do nuffin, I said. It was bloody Dingo. He wanted a piece of the sheila. He said she was easy going. We'd had a couple of beers, and he was stirred up. He said she wanted it bad. Parading around here in her dressing gown and towel. I told him no. I swear. I told him to go root a sheep or som'fin, Just get it out of yer system. He smacked me across the head and told me I was weak as piss, and if I didn't go with him and help, he'd tell everyone about . . .' The cascade of words stopped for a moment.

'Get on with it before I break another finger.'

Tom glared at Darkie daring him to see if he'd follow through. The confession flowed on. A waterfall of words.

'Well anyway, he's got some shit over me, and I went along. But I swear I didn't do nuffin. I couldn't. She's a good sheila, I know that. She didn't deserve that. He grabbed her from behind, and she fell forward, and I ran for me life, honest I did. That's all'

'You didn't think to stop and help her, even though you reckoned it was wrong. Ey?'

'Mate, it was all too bloody quick, and I was a bit sloshed, and Dingo was real wound up. Real mad.'

'Yeah, well too bad for you. You're too bloody weak, Darkie. Weak as piss, and yeah you're not too bloody quick either.'

Darkie never saw it coming. Tom threw his head back and forward like a whip being cracked. The top of his forehead hit Darkie's eyebrow at a blistering pace, splitting the skin open. An inch and a half long and gaping wide, the bone was almost exposed. Time stood still for a moment. Darkie looked dazed, staring into Tom's face, which was still only inches away. Then the blood began to pour from the wound and gush down Darkie's face and onto his shirt. His knees gave way. Tom let go of him and stepped back to let Darkie fall to his knees then forward onto his face in the dust. Tom looked at him, lying there in the dust. He pulled his foot back and prepared to crush a couple of Darkie's ribs for good measure with a savage kick from a riding boot.

'Enough! Enough now, Tom!'

Tom stopped mid-kick and spun around to see old George, one of the shearers standing near the shed. He'd known George for many years, and they shared a mutual respect. George had been around the sheds out this way for years, long before Tom was born. Over the years he'd seen Tom grow into a man. Sadly, a troubled man. He'd seen the fallout from Milly's death. He knew Tom still carried a lot of pain and that he needed release. He feared how that might finally come. He knew a man instinctively needs to protect those he loves, even a young man, like Tom. He knew Tom suffered from his helplessness when it came to Mille and what had happened.

'That's enough, Tom. Off you go and get out of here. He's copped his lot. You know he's not the real problem here.' George walked over to where Darkie still lay in a stupor on the ground. Tom nodded at George, said nothing and quickly disappeared. He had what he wanted.

George looked down at Darkie. He took a closer look at his bent finger and wobbled it about a bit.

'Shit!' he exclaimed, and Darkie groaned with the pain. 'One thing for this, and better now while you're still half out of it,' George mumbled to himself. He put his foot down on Darkie's wrist with all of his weight, leant down and quickly pulled Darkie's finger out straight letting it pop back into the joint. Darkie yelped and sat up holding his finger and looking forlorn with blood across half his face and tears streaming from his one clean eye. George turned and walked away, saying nothing. He returned a moment later with a bucket of soapy water from where the shearers washed their hands. He threw its contents full force into Darkie's face and dropped the bucket beside Darkie.

'You'd best clean yerself up, stop your howlin' and get ready to go back to work. Come up the shed, and I'll stitch yer eye. We'll tell them you fell over. And don't go whining, yer got off bloody light, Boy.'

CHAPTER SIXTEEN

Thursday and Friday passed in quiet routine. Bob Jackson was expected on Sunday morning to see how things were progressing and to stay through until Monday morning smoko, before moving on to another shed. It wasn't widely discussed, but it was expected that Bob would clean up the unspoken mess on this visit. He might even arrive with a replacement shearer for Dingo.

Saturday morning started like most. Everyone slept in, and through the fog of a hangover, Cookie organised breakfast for the shearers.

Maysa had the weekend off and had nothing planned. She woke to the sun streaming through a break in the curtains and rolled sleepily over to check the time. She got quite a shock to see it was 7:30 already. She was not sure how Saturday mornings would work at the homestead. Every other morning had been an early business-like start, where she ate her breakfast cooked by Irene and left for the shed shortly after with Tom in the ute.

She rolled out of bed, feeling refreshed, put on

158

her dressing gown and opened the curtains to look out at the morning. In the distance, she saw Tom, Len and Paddy standing next to the ute in conversation, with dogs milling about their feet. Outside appeared fresh and crisp with the slightest dew quickly drying away. She surveyed the garden and planned a walk through it later in the morning. She watched as Len and Paddy call the dogs onto the ute, then got in and drove off across the paddock. Tom disappeared into the shed then reappeared momentarily with a wheelbarrow and then disappeared again around the other side of the house yard. Maysa observed all this activity and felt wonderfully contented, excited and inspired. She wandered off to the kitchen.

'Good morning, sleepy,' Irene greeted Maysa with a welcoming smile. 'I expect you're ready for breakfast? It's 2 hours passed your normal brekkie time.'

'Yes, I must say I am very ready to eat. It looks to be a beautiful day out there.'

'Yes, it is. Lovely now, but it is going to be a scorcher. You mark my words, Dear. Len and Paddy are off to make sure all the stock have good water.' Irene spoke as she set a place at the table for Maysa and told her to sit down. Maysa protested, she could surely get her own breakfast. But Irene insisted and was clearly enjoying this new sense of purpose and diversion. Maysa was inwardly enjoying being nurtured in such a fashion after the long absence of her own mother.

'So, you haven't asked what Tom is up to today,' Irene asked with a cheeky grin as she placed a bowl of porridge on the table in front of Maysa. Maysa spooned raw sugar on to her porridge and accepted a glass of orange juice. She did her best to look only politely interested as she took Irene up on her prompt.

'Yes, what is Tom doing, if he's not with Len?'

'To be honest, I don't know what his work entails today, except I know he's starting with splitting stove wood. We're a mile behind with the wood because of the shearing. He'll be at that for a few hours the poor tyke, and that'll probably nearly see him through. He works until early afternoon then he is free to do as he pleases.' Watching Maysa closely, she added. 'And with whomever, he pleases of course. Anyway, eat up. It's not a free ride here you know. We have lunch to prepare. Before that, we'll get a batch of scones on for morning tea, and you can take some out for Tom with a cup of tea.' Irene smiled as she watched Maysa begin eating quickly.

After breakfast, Maysa dressed in a casual dress and sandals and joined Irene in the kitchen.

'Here, put this on.' Irene threw an apron to Maysa. Maysa put it on and loosely tied back her hair out of her face. Irene started putting containers on the table, flour, salt and milk.

'I think we'll put some raisins in this lot, Maysa. Tom likes raisins in his scones. Always has.' Irene smiled at Maysa, who smiled back. 'Run and fetch some eggs from the chooks please, Dear. We'll make cakes as well, for lunch and afternoon tea.'

'Yes of course.' Maysa ducked out the back door and headed for the chook pen. As she walked around the house, she could hear the axe striking the rock-hard red gum logs. As she got closer to the chooks, she could see Tom at work, swinging the axe. She stopped in the shade of a lemon tree and watched Tom, who was unaware of her presence. He was wearing moleskins, riding boots and a khaki cotton shirt with the sleeves rolled up. His back was wet with sweat. His broad-brimmed hat shadowed his face. Maysa watched as he picked up the grey logs with the red centres and with precision blows, he split each piece to a size suitable for the woodstove. After a while, he stopped and threw the pieces into the wheelbarrow. Maysa felt a growing excitement as she watched Tom work. He was sweaty and dirty, but she found it very attractive. Shaking herself out of the daydream, she realised she had stood and watched him for a quite a while. She brushed down her apron, let down her hair and shook it loose and strode on toward the chook pen. As she got level with Tom, twenty or thirty feet away, he looked up, catching the movement from the corner of his eye. She waved at him and smiled.

'Oh, hello Tom.' She pretended she'd just noticed him. He stood up from the wheelbarrow, tipped his hat and bid her good morning. She walked on as he watched her, and she could feel his eyes like warm sun on her back. He stood watching her, and when she reached the door to the pen, she turned and looked back at him, catching him. She smiled at him as he flushed with embarrassment and stumbled over a log on his way to the wheelbarrow. He headed off to stack the load without looking back, and Maysa laughed to herself.

At 9:30, the scones were cooked, and cakes were in the oven. The kettle was boiled, and the tea was brewing.

'You can take these scones, and a cup of tea to Tom now please Maysa. Take some for yourself if you'd like to sit with him a while.'

'Is that ok?' Maysa asked.

'Of course, you're not officially working today Dear, but we all need to tuck in and help where we can over the weekend, especially during shearing time. Not much time during the week to keep on top of things.'

Maysa picked up the tray of scones and the teacups and walked toward the back door.

'Just a minute, Dear.' Irene came around the table and met Maysa at the door. 'Let me look at you.' She took Maysa by the shoulders and looked at her. Irene gently brushed some flour from Maysa's cheek and then put her hands behind her head.

'Let's let your hair down again 'ey? You are so very pretty. Mmmm. Look at you.' She smiled a tender smile at Maysa and opened the door for her. 'See you in a while.'

162

'See you soon, Irene,' Maysa smiled over her shoulder at Irene as she walked out into the blinding sunlight. The day was warming up quickly.

At the woodpile, Tom had just started another wheelbarrow load. He placed a log on the chopping block and took a full swing to split the piece in half. It split easily, and both halves fell from the chopping block. He picked one up and put it on the block. He was tiring when he swung again and misjudged the smaller target skimming the edge of the wood, sending the axe darting in one direction and the log in another. A small piece of wood rocketed through the air and struck him in the chest, grazing skin and drawing a drop or two of blood. He looked at the scratch, wiped away the blood with a dirty hand and thanked the Lord that it missed his face, particularly his eyes. He took a deep breath and began swinging the axe again with a trickle of blood running down his chest.

Maysa appeared quietly behind Tom with her tray of morning tea. She stopped with a start when she saw Tom again, swinging the axe, but this time bare to the waist. His muscular arms were pumped hard from the exercise. He had not an ounce of fat obscuring muscle, and his torso was glistening with sweat and streaked with dust. Maysa drew breath at the sight of his half-naked body, of him, hard at work in the sun. She was amazed by how this made her feel, and in such a primitive way. Tom finished chopping the barrow before Maysa declared herself.

'Tom, I have your morning tea.' Tom turned around and faced Maysa, smiled and threw the axe aside.

'Thanks. I could do with a break.' He picked up his shirt from the woodpile and wiped the sweat from his face. He went to put it on, but seemed to think better of it. He threw his shirt aside on the grass instead. Maysa was staring at his chest and flushed red with embarrassment as she realised she'd been caught by Tom.

Snapping back into a conscious state, Maysa stepped forward to place the tray on the chopping block.

'Two cups. I'm not that thirsty. And enough scones for 2 blokes ey? Who else is coming?' Tom laughed cheekily. Caught a little off guard, Maysa realised he had the upper hand. She smiled and confidently replied.

'Perhaps another show-off like you.' She poured tea and broke open scones and smothered them with jam and cream.

'I put some raisins in the scones, Tom, because that's the way I like them. I hope that's ok, is it?'

'Bloody beauty, I love 'em like that too. Fancy that.'

Who's the clever one now, Maysa thought to herself. She handed him a cup of tea, and as she did, she noticed the blood on his chest that had started afresh when he wiped it with the shirt. She was genuinely and disproportionately concerned.

'What have you done?' And before she thought,

she put her fingers to his chest near the small wound and leant forward to inspect it more closely. She stood motionless, her fingertips on his chest. He stopped still and looked down at her face.

'I am fine. It's nothing. Just a scratch . . . really. It's just a scratch.' The attention was clearly a surprise but seemed far from unwelcome.

Maysa stood, still not moving. Her fingertips still on his chest. Tom placed his free hand on Maysa's forearm. Still looking at the wound, her mind was swimming. She didn't really see the injury at all. Very slowly, she lay her palm flat on Tom's bare chest across his breast. He gripped her forearm more tightly. She was breathing as deeply, as his breath was shallow. All of a sudden, they both became aware of the clanking of china, and together they looked down. Tom's hand was shaking, and the teacup was rattling. They both smiled.

'Let me get a cloth and clean this for you.' Maysa wet her handkerchief under a tap and returned to Tom. He hadn't moved except for a nervous swig of his tea.

'Here, give me that,' Maysa directed and she placed the empty teacup on a log. She stood in front of Tom and gently cleaned the wound with the damp handkerchief. Tom laughed a little.

'It's really just a scratch, I would have just cleaned it up in the shower later on.' Maysa looked up and into his eyes for a moment, and the smile disappeared from his face. He continued in a

165

whisper, seemingly as much for himself as her. 'I guess it's not a bad idea cleaning it up a bit.'

Maysa was feeling the warm flush of excitement again that she felt so often around Tom. The world beyond their immediate space seemed to vanish. Beyond Tom, the rest of the world was a blur.

'Maysa.' Tom whispered. She looked up to meet his eyes. He cupped her chin gently in his hand, tilting her head back to face him. Her eyes half-closed as though in a sleepy trance. He looked at her adoringly, then kissed her gently. They stood motionless, lips touching, but not moving. She placed her arms around his neck. It was the first passionate embrace of her life. Tom wrapped his arms around her and pulled her towards him. She felt the warmth of his chest through the cool cotton of her dress as her breasts pressed against him. His body was hard and muscular, and the smell of his sweat and sun-baked skin was intoxicating. Her lips parted slightly, as Tom began to kiss her more passionately. The tips of their tongues gently touched and Maysa tasted the salty sweat on his lips. She pulled him to her with a deep hunger. They kissed for a few minutes, which seemed to last only a few seconds. Finally, they parted still holding each other and looking into each other's eyes. It was a half happy smile and a half relieved smile. She could see in his expression, they had complete and open acknowledgment of their feelings for each other. Finally, Maysa released her hold on Tom and he on her.

'Here let me get you something to eat. You must be starving after all that work. Maysa immediately assumed a loving proprietorship over Tom. They ate morning tea, sitting on logs in the shade of a tree. They talked about work, the shearing shed and living at the homestead. When they knew they could no longer avoid getting back to work, Maysa stood. Tom walked to her and holding her hands, he kissed her cheek. Maysa took Tom's chin in her hand this time and kissed him on the lips and smiled at him again and left for the kitchen.

CHAPTER SEVENTEEN

'Tom, I think you should bring Angel in this afternoon and give Maysa a riding lesson. Let's see how much she really likes being in the country. Out here Maysa, everyone does their fair share. You can help with mustering, checking the stock and all sorts of things if you can ride.' Irene gave out directions for the afternoon's activity.

Maysa looked nervous but was determined to try everything. She was conscious that her future and her happiness depended on her being able to take on everything that was thrown at her. Sometimes that could mean the unthinkable, like the Dingo incident, and sometimes stretching your boundaries like horse riding. She watched Irene and was impressed with her strength in this harsh environment and in the face of such personal tragedy. She knew that the way to survive was to be strong. And she knew the power of her personal strength and determination.

'I will look forward to it, thanks Tom,' she replied with feigned confidence. Either way, she had decided it would be good to be with Tom all afternoon.

'Good, it's settled then. I will find some riding breeches and a decent shirt and boots for Maysa, and she will be ready in a half-hour Tom.' Irene looked very pleased with herself.

A half-hour later, Maysa walked beyond the sheds to some cattle yards which were principally for the house cows, which provided the homestead and workers with milk, cream and cheese. There were yards and small holding paddocks there for the horses, with sheds, feed and water troughs. Tom was standing in the paddock with Angel. She was a buckskin, fifteen hands high with kind eyes and a sleepy disposition. She was an excellent instinctive stock horse. Seven years old and had been broken for Milly.

Tom had saddled Angel in Milly's stock saddle which he had personally kept dusted and oiled. He stood with Angel's forehead against his chest, loosely holding her reins.

'Tom,' Maysa called, and both Tom and Angel looked up to see Maysa strolling across the paddock.

Maysa wore fitted moleskins that showed off her figure, leather riding boots and a work shirt. Tom was taken aback. She was beautiful in a dress, and she was stunning in breeches, her long hair waving about her shoulders.

'Come, Angel,' he whispered to the horse, and he led her to Maysa. 'Come meet your new best friend.'

Angel snorted and eagerly walked to Maysa. She carried an apple in halves and sugar cubes that Irene had given her to start the friendship. As carefully instructed by Irene, Maysa held her hand out flat with a piece of apple on it and offered it to Angel. She sniffed it and then scooped it up with her hot breathy horse lips and crunched it in her teeth, swinging her head about happily before nudging Maysa for more. Maysa laughed, relieved and excited.

'Ok, we will start in a small yard over there. In case you come off on your backside, it's got a nice sandy and soft floor. I'll lead you around for a while then I will let you guide her about and see how you go.'

All went well with Maysa and Angel striking up an immediate friendship. Tom hoisted Maysa on to Angel and led them about for a while before letting Maysa guide the horse about the small yard and then the larger holding paddock. Maysa loved the riding and took to it comfortably. Irene and Len came to the yards in the mid-afternoon and marvelled at Maysa's progress. Maysa even urged Angel into a slow trot. They all laughed as Maysa bounced up and down on the saddle, trying to match the rhythm of the trot. Maysa shrieked with joy for a brief moment as she managed just a few smooth strides.

The afternoon progressed happily, with Tom explaining in detail how to look after a horse. He impressed Maysa with a few tricks on Bess, including cracking the stockwhip. The sound of the whip excited the dogs into a frenzy and made Bess a little jittery. It terrified Maysa, who thought poor Bess was bound to get hit. But Tom was an expert with the whip. He deliberately made it all look much more dangerous than it was and she could see he delighted in terrifying her even after she pleaded with him to be careful.

When the afternoon was finally over, and Maysa declared herself too sore to go on, the horses were unsaddled, brushed and fed, then put out in their paddocks. They stood for a moment at the yards, talking about the afternoon and recounting all the funny and terrifying moments from the afternoon's intense instruction. As they chatted, Maysa became aware of a dog sniffing at her leg. She looked down. It was Banjo again. Milly's faithful friend. She squatted down to pat him, and he wagged his tail enthusiastically, licking her hands. She smiled at Tom, who was equally as amazed and pleased.

Finally, they had to call an end to a wonderful afternoon. Tom walked Maysa back to the homestead. As they walked, Banjo fell into step right behind Maysa as he had done on their first date. It wasn't lost on either Tom or Maysa.

CHAPTER EIGHTEEN

The next morning was Sunday, and Tom was out riding around the stock when he saw a pall of dust billowing out behind a ute heading along the track to the shearing shed. He knew who it was immediately and quickly decided to find something to do over at the yards so he could watch the goings-on at the camp. He was a little disappointed he hadn't been able to get to Dingo before Bob arrived.

Bob Jackson arrived at the shearers camp at 11:00am after camping the night in town at the Royal Hotel. He sat across the table from Cookie in the kitchen, having a cup of tea and a sandwich.

'Shit, Cookie. That bastard's gunna go and quick smart. I don't wanna see him out this way ever again. I should have known the bastard would be trouble. You've heard the stories. He's not called Dingo for nothing. He might be a bloody good shearer, but he's dangerous. He's usually cunning as a dunny rat, but not so smart this time. I don't know what I was thinking of . . . sending a young sheila like her up here by herself, and such a bloody good lookin' sheila as well.'

'You weren't to know, Bob. Mate, she's a top sort. Good worker and a quick learner. Her only problem is she's a looker. She'd been better off being dog ugly and the bastard would'na given her a second look. I agree, get rid of him mate. It's cast a bloody shadow over what's usually a damn good shed. You got someone to replace him?'

'Yeah, young fellah off a property at Nyngan's comin' in this afternoon. Can't shear a pen like Dingo, but as long as he keeps his pants on and his hands to himself, I don't care.' Bob paused, drew deeply on a cigarette and then coughed into his shirt sleeve. 'Well, I better go and get this bloody well over with I suppose.' He rolled his eyes, rubbed his face, then got up from the table and left.

Cookie got up a moment later and walked to the door. He flung the last of his tea from his enamel cup onto the dusty ground, put down the mug and lit a cigarette. Leaning in the doorway, he watched Bob knock on the door to Dingo and Darkie's hut.

Tom found a task to do at the shearing shed where he could watch the goings-on. There were several shearers and roustabouts, already sitting around a smouldering campfire, smoking and drinking tea. They were planning a roo hunting trip for the afternoon. They all called G'day to Bob as he passed and then turned slowly to watch him. They all knew what was coming, the word had finally got around.

Darkie answered the door.

'G'day Bob,' he said with a smile and seemed genuinely happy to see him.

'G'day Darkie. How are yer mate?' Bob peered past Darkie to see Dingo lying on his stretcher, one arm behind his head and pulling on a cigarette. He looked relaxed but wasn't. He chose to ignore Bob. Darkie stood in the door in front of Bob like an eager sheepdog.

'Righto Darkie, fuck off and make yourself scarce. I gotta talk to Dingo. Go on off you go.' Looking forlorn, Darkie wandered off to join the other shearers at the campfire.

'Out here Dingo, we need to talk.' Dingo got up reluctantly from his stretcher and wandered out into the sunlight squinting. Bob looked at him and thought what a sorry sight he was, no doubt, hungover from the previous night. He secretly hoped Dingo's head was hurting like hell.

Tom had carried some branding equipment and a couple of buckets across from the shed and was now standing next to Cookie and within earshot of Dingo and Bob.

'Dingo, yer gone. You've done it this time mate. I can't have this shit on my run. We both know what I am talking about. I don't want to get into the details. Let's do this nice and easy. You get your kit together and put it in the ute, and I'll take you down the road a bit, and you can hitch into town.' Bob was staring at Dingo with a stony face. Dingo was standing, feet apart, hands on his hips. He said nothing for a moment and didn't move. After a tense standoff, Dingo spat on the ground and kicked dust over it.

'Well, I don't know what the fuck you're talking about, Bob. I don't sees why yer trying to turf me off the run. I done years of good hard work for you. I helped pay f'yer shiny new ute over there. I think I deserve a bit more respect than this, don't I.'

'Respect! I'll give you the bloody respect you deserve you mongrel dog.' Bob exploded and shouted at Dingo. 'Don't bullshit me, Boy, we both know what happened. Everyone here knows. None of 'em want yer here no more.' Bob spat the words at Dingo while pointing a thumb at the other shearers over his shoulder. 'Pack yer bloody bags now, before I kick your arse out on the road and yer can walk to town. Yer got no mates 'ere, Boy. Even bloody Darkie's had enough of yer. You got twenty minutes, and I'm leaving. If you're not ready by then, the local cop'll be out, and I'll leave it to him to do what he sees fit with yer.' Bob turned away in disgust and walked back in the direction of the kitchen.

Darkie leapt up from the campfire and walked over to where Dingo stood. He watched perplexed as Bob walked away.

'Hey Dingo, what was that all about buddy? What'd Bobby want with yer?'

Dingo ignored Darkie for a moment before finally turning to him and barking his response.

'What? What d'you say you bloody half-wit? Buddy, I am not your friggin buddy. You're just a bloody idiot.'

'Geezus Dingo, what 'n' bloody hell'd I do?'

'You been mouthin' off Darkie?' Darkie stared at Dingo perplexed. 'Well have you, stupid? Have you? You bin mouthin' off haven't you and I'm gonna give you a bloody good flogging for yer trouble.'

'I didn't say nuffin.' Darkie pleaded. 'He tried to beat it out of me, but I didn't say nuffin.' Dingo smelt a rat. He was suspicious and angry as hell. Dingo was sure Darkie had spilt the beans about the incident with the girl. He knew how to fool Darkie. It wasn't hard.

'You sure, Boy? You sure you said nuffin? It's alright mate. You can tell me. We bin mates for a long time. You'll be right. Tell me what you told what's his name.' Dingo cajoled Darkie now. The other shearers were all watching the goings-on but couldn't hear the muffled conversation. Dingo was working Darkie like a misbehaving sheepdog. He could see Darkie was confused, but he knew he was just smart enough to suspect he was going to cop it, so he spoke softly to him until he seemed to relax and get his confidence.

'Bloody Tom, he fair flogged me Dingo. Over

176

the bloody sheila. He was gunna ring me bloody neck if I didn't spit it out. I didn't fall over mate . . . he smashed me. I had to tell him it was you. But he already knew anyway. He just wanted me to say it. Fair dinkum mate, I didn't want to.' Darkie stammered and looked like he was about cry. 'He bloody near broke me finger, then he all but knocked me out cold.' The blood drained from Darkie's face as the expression on Dingo's face changed from friendly to a fierce rage. Dingo had him tricked, and it wasn't hard. As far as Dingo was concerned, now Darkie was really going to cop it sweet.

'You bloody mongrel. You're as weak as you're stupid.' Dingo drove a clenched fist into Darkie's stomach at the base of his rib cage and knocked the wind right out of him. He doubled over in pain, clutching his stomach. Dingo turned as if to walk away, then swung back around with a full kick into Darkie's face, smashing his teeth and breaking his nose. Darkie reeled over backward and landed on his back in the dust. The shearers were on their feet and gathering in a semi-circle around Darkie and Dingo. As much as they preferred a fair fight, they had little time for either of the pair and were pleased to see them belting each other, although this was almost over as quickly as it began.

Watching from the kitchen, Bob began to move as quickly as he could to intervene in the fight. It was rapidly turning into a blood bath. Darkie rolled over slowly onto his stomach and got himself on to his hands and knees. His face was covered with blood, his two front teeth were missing in the dust and others were badly broken and chipped, his lips were split open, and his nose was swelling rapidly. He spat blood out of his mouth and coughed. Dingo had now found a fence paling nearby and was preparing to finish off Darkie. The shearers protested as a group, but no one stepped forward to help. Dingo was swinging the paling about like a mad man, swearing and cursing Darkie and everyone else when Bob burst into the group.

'Put the timber down, Dingo. You've done enough damage. You're only making this worse for yourself'. Bob stood talking calmly to Dingo, attempting to diffuse the situation.

'Fuck you, Bob. I'll do him.' Dingo poked Darkie in the ribs with the paling. 'Then I'll do you next you fat bastard.'

'Come on mate, drop the bloody timber now. You've given the poor bastard a fair floggin'. Give him a chance.'

'Yeah, yer right.' Dingo pointed the paling menacingly in Bob's face. Bob was reeling backward with each swing of the stick. 'It's your turn now.' With that, Dingo made a backswing with the paling like a baseball bat and prepared to take Bob's head off his shoulders. As he began his forward swing, the paling stopped dead like it was caught on something. He turned to see Tom, gripping the paling firmly. Staring into Dingo's eyes with a cold, steely look. Tom spoke in an unnervingly, slow and calm voice.

'This is our fight, Dingo. You could've walked away from this, but you chose to keep it going. So now you're gonna get what's coming.'

The excitement in the circle of shearers was palpable now. This was going to be a good fight, and they were all keen to see Tom in action first hand and find out whether the stories in the pub and round the campfires were even close to fair-dinkum.

'This ain't your fight, Boy. Bugger off before I spread yer nose across your face.'

'That's where your wrong, mate. This is entirely my fight. Someone should've done this to you a long time ago.' With his left hand firmly holding the paling and Dingo still trying to pull the paling loose with both hands, Tom drove his right fist into Dingo's jaw with a sickening thud. Dingo was dazed and stood like a roo dazzled by a spotlight. Searing pain shot through Tom's fist as bone smashed against bone. One end of the paling fell to the ground, and now it looked more like Dingo was holding a golf club which doubled as a crutch, propping him up. Tom seized the moment and swung a left hook toward Dingo who, although dazed, saw the blow coming and dipped his head and caught it on the top of his forehead. This blow stunned Dingo again but inflicted more pain on

179

Tom. He steadied himself and shook his hand. Dingo acted quickly and swung the paling into Tom, collecting him in the rib cage to his left side, tearing open his shirt and splitting skin. It drove the wind out of him.

Seeing Tom hurt, Dingo moved to land a second blow when the sound of a rifle being cocked stopped him in his tracks. Old George had appeared from his room. He had just loaded a 12-gauge shotgun and had it firmly pointed at Dingo.

'Drop the timber Dingo, or I'll drop you where you stand.'

'Bugger off you old bastard and mind yer bloody business.' Dingo turned away, seemingly not concerned about George's threat. He lifted the timber again to hit Tom who had regained his composure, and although sore and bruised, he steadied himself, fists up ready to fight on. There was a loud bang, and dust sprayed up across the fighters. Everyone jumped with fright, then looked at George. He'd fired a cartridge into the dust at Dingo's feet.

'Shit, you're fucking mad.' Dingo threw the paling aside and turned to face Tom. Tom drove his right fist hard and fast collecting Dingo on the shoulder and followed quickly with a left hook that split Dingo's lip open. Blood streamed down Dingo's chin, and blood streamed from the cut on Tom's ribs. Dingo returned a punch which Tom blocked. It left Dingo's face wide open, and Tom drove a straight arm punch hard into Dingo's face, breaking his nose. Dingo staggered backward. As Tom advanced, Dingo kicked a boot full of dust into his face. He was momentarily blinded and didn't see the punch coming that split his forehead open above the left eyebrow.

Tom was barely containing his rage when he felt this blow. He fought in what he considered a fair and gentlemanly manner, even if his opponent was not worthy of the courtesy. But this man, this animal, was lower than a pig dog in Tom's opinion. He put his hand to his face and felt the warm blood dribbling down his cheek. He wiped away the blood to clear his eye. The blood was the trigger that brought images to him in terrifying clarity. In that moment, he saw Maysa's bruised face. He saw and felt Milly's pain and the pain of missing her. A switch turned. He hardened like forged steel. He looked at Dingo who was advancing with a bemused look on his face. Dingo was half stupefied by the blows he'd received but seemed to believe he had Tom's measure. To the onlookers, he was clearly in bad condition. He took a wild swing at Tom who coolly tipped his head and took the blow high. A second wild blow took Tom on the side of the face. He made no attempt at all to block the punch. He had gone to another place deep within himself. With two open palms, he slapped Dingo on either ear, startling him. Dingo's face contorted in pain. Tom drove his forehead into Dingo's face while pulling Dingo's head by the ears toward him. Dingo's broken nose was shattered even more, and blood splashed across Tom's face. Hell had broken loose in the camp. Still holding Dingo's ears, he drove a knee hard into Dingo's balls. Dingo coughed up blood. His legs were going to jelly as he tried to double up, but Tom held him upright like a huge rag doll. In one motion Tom stepped back, pulled Dingo's head downward and drove his knee into Dingo's face. Dingo was unconscious when he fell flat on his face in the dust. Bob and Cookie grabbed Tom by either arm to pull him off Dingo.

'Enough, Tom. You're gonna kill him, and that'll do no one any good, least of all the girl.'

Tom stopped, exhausted and in pain, panting from the adrenalin and the exertion.

'Cookie, George, get Tom in the back of the ute and let's get him to the homestead.' With the fight over, Tom was winding down quickly. He was feeling the pain in his ribs, his fists and over his eye. He felt like he'd been run over by a mob of wild brumbies.

CHAPTER NINETEEN

It was morning tea time. Len, Irene and Maysa were sitting around the kitchen table when they heard the ute pull up. A car door shut, the back gate squeaked as it was opened, and crashed as it sprang shut. Len got up from the table and looked through the back window. He saw the ute disappearing off toward the Jackeroo's cottage and Bob Jackson walking up the back path. Irene got up and followed Len to the back door where Len greeted Bob with a serious face and a handshake.

'How are you, mate?'

'Not bad Len, G'day Irene.'

'So, you've dealt with him have you Bob?'

Maysa heard Len refer to Bob and got up from her chair, smiling. As she got near to the back door, she could hear the conversation more clearly and stopped, quietly listening.

'There was a bit of trouble at the shed, Len. Young Tom. There was a bit of a blue. Dingo gave Darkie a good floggin', then Tom cleaned up Dingo. And I mean, really cleaned him up. He's still lying over there in the shade of a gum tree, out cold.'

'Shit Bob, what happened, and what the hell was Tom doing there anyway?' Len's tone was both annoyed and disappointed.

Maysa stood quietly, listening, worried and concerned for Tom.

'He actually did the right thing, Len. Someone should have done it years ago. We all know that. Someone had to step in today and stop Dingo. He'd a killed Darkie if we'd let him go. Tom fairly gave it to him. He was defending me, and that bloody fool Darkie, who didn't deserve defending anyway. So don't go too hard on Tom. He's done us all a favour, and he's done the right thing by the girl. We all know he's got some stuff to get out of his system. That bloody Dingo will be leaving town with a few scars. He won't forget today for a while.' Irene and Len stood listening, while Maysa hovered, discretely hidden from Bob's view. She was worried about Tom. She was shocked by the fact Dingo might have still been lying unconscious in the paddock. And she felt guilty but thrilled that Tom had defended her honour with such passion and vengeance.

Len stood for a moment, stroking his chin and considering all this news.

'Well, yes, you know Irene and me both reckon you're right, Bob. We don't want that kinda bloke anywhere near this property, or in this town for that matter. We couldn't wait for you to get here and to get rid of that piece of work. But you know what Bob, me and Irene have still got big plans for Tom. He's as good as a son to us. He's gotta shake this behaviour though, and he needs to do it soon. He's gotta grow up a bit. We've all had to come to terms with a lot of loss in the last couple of years.'

Just then, Paddy appeared around the corner of the house. Len looked shocked. Irene put a hand up and touched Len lightly on the forearm in a gesture of concern. Paddy stopped at the group. Maysa stepped back another step. She knew the tension between Paddy and Tom and was as wary of Paddy as she would be a snake.

Paddy had seen the ute come roaring across from the shearing shed. He'd been over at the sheds tending to his horses. Keen to see what was going on, he had taken a short cut through the homestead garden when he heard talking and had stopped, undisclosed. He'd listened to the whole conversation between Bob and Len but rounded the corner as if he had only just arrived.

Paddy was careful to mask his feelings as he smiled broadly at the group. The last thing he wanted was for anyone to suspect he'd heard the conversation.

'G'day, Bob. How are you, mate?'

'Yeah not bad Paddy, yerself?'

'Can't complain. Nobody'd listen even if I did.' Paddy laughed and turned to Len. 'I am off to town Len, to see old Ron Sanders. He's as crook as a dog and up in the hospital. He and dad were good mates. They reckon he's not gonna last the week, so I better see him now. I'll bunk down in town and be back in the morning. We've got enough sheep in the holding paddocks for a couple of days work now and but I'll be back for drafting by morning tea. Can you and Tom handle the sheep work tonight?'

'Yeah, sure, Paddy. Off yer go, mate. Good luck with old Ron. Give him our best would yer?' Paddy could see Len looked almost relieved he was heading into town.

'Ey Paddy, would you do me a huge favour mate?' Bob asked. 'I finished up Dingo this morning. There's been a bit of a blue over at the shed and Dingo's pretty crook, but he'll come good. Would you mind carting him into town for me? Here's a few quid. See he gets a cuppa tea and a sandwich then he can go to buggery after that. Pardon me, Irene.'

'Yeah, no worries Bob.' Paddy left and moments later was heading off toward the shed in his ute.

Maysa listened to all of this fascinated. Plans for Tom. She wondered for just a moment what that was. She tried to imagine the fight.

'Listen, Len,' Bob began again as soon as Paddy was out of earshot. 'Tom's in a bit of a bad way as well. He's gonna be fine, but he's a bit beat up. Gonna be real sore and sorry for himself for a few days. That's the price you pay, I guess. George took him down to his hut in the back of the ute. Your gonna need to tidy him up a bit, Irene.'

'Christ,' Len cursed. 'I just let Paddy go to town, the bloody prize fighter's laid up, and we got a load of work to do at the yards.'

'Be quiet, you cranky old bull,' Irene squeezed Lens forearm hard. 'You've got Maysa and I here. Between us, we can keep the house and sort out your sheep.'

Standing in the background, Maysa was shocked with the reports of Tom's condition. She couldn't wait any longer, and she stepped forward.

'Is Tom ok?'

'G'day girlie, how are yer?' Len and Irene turned as Maysa appeared behind them. Irene extended an arm to Maysa who joined her. Irene put her arm around Maysa's shoulders.

'You best get a needle and cotton Irene, you gotta bit of sewing to do. But he'll fix up right enough, and quick. He's young and strong.' Bob turned to Len. 'Tell you what Len, remind me never to pick a fight with him will yer, geez he went off. Dingo didn't know what hit him.' Len rolled his eyes, and didn't look nearly as impressed as Bob.

'You get a basin and some clean rags from the laundry, Maysa, and I'll get the sewing kit and a bottle of brandy.' Being so far from town, Irene was a dab hand with stitching up anyone who injured themselves. A wound scrubbed and doused with alcohol usually mended well.

★　　★　　★

187

Paddy arrived at the shearing shed twenty minutes later. The shearers were still sitting around the campfire. Darkie was sitting on the step outside his room looking sorry for himself, mopping up blood from his mouth with a rag. Dingo lay in the shade of a tree only semi-conscious. He was no more than twenty yards from the shearers who were taking turns to re-enact the fight and roaring with laughter at their own antics. They were completely oblivious to Dingo and his condition. Paddy nodded at the shearers and smiled as he passed by. He walked over to Dingo, who by now had rolled onto his back and was moaning.

'Up you get Dingo and clean yourself off. Gotta get you off the property quick smart. You can tell me all yer troubles when we get going. I'll take yer to town and get yer a couple of beers.'

When Maysa and Irene got to the Jackaroo's cottage, George was standing on the veranda having a cigarette. He had blood on his shirt.

He tipped his hat to the ladies as they arrived.

'Missus. Girlie. He's inside on the bed. He looks pretty rough, but he's not as bad as he looks.'

Irene charged into the cottage and through to Tom's bedroom with Maysa following tentatively.

'My God, Tom!' What have you done with that handsome face? Prepare yourself Maysa, you might not find him quite so attractive at the moment.'

Tom smiled weakly through his blood-streaked

face as Maysa crept quietly through the door. She wasn't prepared for the shock. Tom lay on his bed. His left eye was already going dark purple and was swollen half-closed. His right eye was bathed in blood from a gaping split through his eyebrow and into his forehead. His shirt was torn and drenched in blood, some was his, and just as much was Dingo's. His fists were half clenched, and his knuckles were swollen and turning purple. Both women stood for a moment, just looking at Tom lying there on the bed.

Irene turned to Maysa, who was looking at Tom with reddened eyes filling with tears. She sprang into action.

'Ok dear, go and fill that basin with some warm water. Use the kettle off the stove and some cold from the tap and come back quickly, please. Oh, and bring back a mug. Tom'll need a couple of brandies.'

Moments later, Maysa returned. Irene directed Maysa around to the other side of the bed. Between them, they tried to sit Tom up, supporting him under the arms. He moaned loudly, and they stopped. Irene poured a brandy and helped Tom gently sip it. The fiery liquid made him cough.

'Get a good sharp carving knife please, Maysa.'

When Maysa returned, she and Irene took turns cutting Tom's torn shirt to shreds with the knife and gently prizing it off him and out from under his back.

'Right Luv, you're going to have to gently clean

him up while I get a bit more brandy into him, then I'll go and sterilize the needle. Concentrate on his face and his stomach first, where we have to stitch him up.' Maysa gulped at the thought.

Irene gave Tom another sip of brandy then left for the kitchen. Maysa began gently wiping Toms face clean with a wet rag. He smiled at her.

'Tom, what have you done?' Maysa stuttered through tears.

Tom lifted a bruised forearm and placed it on Maysa's.

'I'm ok. A spit and polish and a few repairs to the Duco and I'll be good as new.' He was doing his best to look cheerful, but she could see he was in a lot of pain as he winced with every move. Maysa smiled at him through her tears.

'At least you still have your lovely teeth, I guess. That is something. But you sure are ugly now,' and at last, she laughed, relieved. She continued to clean his forehead and face and quickly had him looking presentable. She leaned down, close to his face. 'Thank you,' she whispered as she kissed his forehead gently.

'Ahem.' Maysa turned to see Irene standing in the doorway with one raised eyebrow.

'Ok, let's get started.' One more swig of brandy and Tom was about to be stitched. Irene dabbed the wound generously with more brandy and began to sew Tom's eyebrow back together. Tom grimaced. Maysa continued to clean Tom gently with a rag, dabbing his chest and cleaning the wound on the side of his stomach, avoiding watching Irene work. Irene finished the eyebrow then sewed up the stomach wound. Tom groaned through the process and once or twice squeezed Maysa's forearm until she was in pain, but neither uttered a word until it was done.

'Well Maysa, I think we deserve a cup of tea. You best sit with him for a while, although I suspect, with all that brandy he'll soon be asleep.' And he was. Maysa and Irene relaxed, with a cup of tea on the veranda of the Jackeroo's hut.

'So, you really like him,' Irene asked after they'd sat some time in silence, staring out across the paddock.

'I do,' Maysa replied softly. Looking into the distance, she smiled. 'I like him a lot.' There was silence for some time, and then Maysa spoke again. 'I just hope he doesn't get himself killed or badly beaten. He seems to have a terrible temper. I have never known a man like Tom. My father and brother were much softer than Tom. But it's his strength I find attractive. I can't imagine why he is interested in me.'

'Can't you?' Irene replied, and then she smiled. 'Well, he is a good young man Maysa. He has had too much grief for a boy of his age. He'll grow out of this, and he will get over his demons, and very soon, I suspect. I think you're just the distraction he needs. In fact, I believe you are just what we all need. Now is not really the time to talk about this, but Len and I would like you to consider staying on here at the station. There is plenty of work for a girl who can turn her hand to different things. Of course, there is work in the house, but there is work with the stock as well. You seem to have a natural affinity for animals, we've seen you with the dogs and horses. Some people have it, and some don't.' They both looked down at Banjo who had settled down to sleep at Maysa's feet. He'd hardly left her side since the riding lesson.

'I suspect you have it. You're a hard worker, and you're very pretty. It's just what we need around here to breathe some life into this old establishment. I want you to think about it for a couple of days. If you need to.' Again Irene smiled, looking at Maysa who had been listening intently. Maysa turned back to look into the distance, for a moment seeing her future and remembering her past.

'Of course, you and Tom need some time to get to know each other. I am not entirely silly. Two young kids out here, both of you good looking and intelligent and both of you searching for something, something to replace what was. It's not hard to get carried away under those circumstances. I think you have to be a little careful and patient.' Irene paused, then stood up.

'Well, I am going up the house to get Len's lunch and put a roast on for dinner. You can stay here with Tom and watch him. He won't wake up for a couple of hours, he'll need the rest. Paddy won't be back tonight. It'd be better if you were back up the house shortly after dinner though, please. You've got work tomorrow.' As Irene walked off, she stopped and added. 'And watch out for that Tom. He might be bruised and sore, but he's still a man, and you're still a very pretty girl. You'll find food for your lunch and dinner in the kitchen. I'll see you later.'

Maysa sat and watched Irene disappear up to the homestead and through the back gate and into the house. As soon as Irene was gone, she returned to Tom. He was fast asleep. She found a chair and put it next to Tom's bed where she could watch him sleep.

He lay on the bed, bruised and battered and naked from the waist up. Maysa stared at him, lying there. She felt a guilty pleasure, having this handsome man lying half-naked before her, with no need to be guarded as her eyes explored every inch of him. In fact, she comforted her conscious with a legitimate reason to be there, after all, he needed nursing in his time of need. And moreover, he was here as a result of revenging her honour.

Maysa woke from a nap after falling asleep watching Tom. Quite some time had passed, more than she realised, perhaps two hours. She leant forward quietly and gently touched Tom's bruised fist. She ran two fingertips along his forearm, occasionally checking his eyes for any sign of awareness. Her stomach swarmed with butterflies.

Shivers ran from the nape of her neck down her spine and radiated through her ribs as she traced the muscles of his upper arm. The touched thrilled her. She allowed herself to imagine she was lying next to him, as lovers, just a sheet covering their naked bodies. She imagined tracing the muscles on his chest with her fingertips, his arms around her, her breasts against his skin.

Tom appeared to be still dead to the world. Perhaps he was enjoying a dream of her as he slept, she thought, as she watched the slightest twitch of his eyelids and the almost happy look on his bruised face.

Maysa drew a sharp breath as her arousal began to overpower her senses. Although she dared not, she allowed herself to lay her hand on Tom's shoulder and then gently run it down his chest. It was broad and muscular, and she came to rest with her fingertips lightly on a nipple. Her hand lay there for some time, rising and falling with his breathing. After a while, she became aware she was breathing in time with him.

Eventually, his arm moved, and he put his hand over hers. He opened his eyes slowly and reached out to her face with his other hand. He grimaced as he opened his hand from the clenched injured fist and stroked her cheek. She smiled and leant closer, her hair fell on his bare chest. He stroked her face then pulled her to him. She kissed him gently, conscious of his wounds and rubbed her cheek against his.

He put his arms around her and pulled her down to him.

She lay next to Tom, running her hand from his chest to his stomach, gently and tentatively, wanting him. He kissed her and following her lead, he traced her arm with his fingertips, lightly caressing her neck before tentatively seeking out her breast. They kissed passionately for some time, exploring each other before Maysa stood up from the bed with Tom watching. Not a word was spoken, but an intimate understanding was shared. The afternoon sun was fading into an orange glow through the curtained windows. Tom watched as Maysa slowly unbuttoned her dress and let it fall to the floor. She stood in her underwear. He was breathing quickly, and she was shaking with nervous anticipation. She unclipped her bra and stood for a moment. Her skin was olive, her breasts were full and firm, and her nipples were the colour of melted chocolate. She placed her dress and bra on a chair, then lay back down with Tom. He kissed her again. She watched as he supported himself on an elbow, his eyes devouring her. His fingers traced her bare chest, her breasts and her nipples. He kissed her neck, and as he began to kiss her chest, her breathing became shallow and rapid. His hand was on her stomach, and as he began to explore her lower belly, she grasped his wrist.

'Not now, Tom. I'm sorry, but I want to wait. A bit longer, at least.'

Tom smiled and rolled onto his back, pulling Maysa over him. He smiled, kissed her, and then with a serious face, he whispered.

'I love you, Maysa. I know it's only been a few days, a few weeks, but I really love you. I think I loved you from the moment I laid eyes on your beautiful face.'

'I love you, Tom,' Maysa whispered, so close to Tom's mouth, he could feel her breath. 'I loved you as soon as I saw you. I knew we were meant to be together as soon as you said hello.'

It was dark when Maysa finally tore herself from Tom's arms. He showered while she cooked his tea. After he had eaten, she kissed him and insisted he went and lay down while she tidied up. He surrendered to her directions without a fight. He was stiff and sore, but she could see he was as happy as her. It had been a terrible morning but a wonderful afternoon. When she was done, she blew him a kiss in the doorway to his bedroom, smiled happily and left.

As she opened the door to leave, she was startled as Paddy appeared right in front of her. She tried to squeeze past him, but he deliberately entered the doorway at the same time, making it impossible. His breath was laced with stale beer and cigarettes as he leant in close to her, one arm propped against the door jam preventing her from passing through.

'Hello there.' Paddy breathed the words quietly and slowly into Maysa's face. She squinted as the foul breath assaulted her senses.

'Hello,' she replied, trying to match his stare and not look intimidated.

'What're you doing here so late? As if I don't know.' Paddy grinned, but his face showed no signs of humour, more like a dog stalking its prey. 'How's the pretty boy then? He gave poor old Dingo a fair old flogging. He's in a bad way you know . . . a real bad way. Pretty boy's got a nasty, nasty temper, hasn't he? I mean what did poor old Dingo do to deserve that anyway?' Paddy paused as if waiting for a reaction. Although she maintained an indifferent expression on her face, she hoped her eyes didn't betray her.

'You know, I have a good temper if you're ever looking for a real man. A good man. I could give you everything pretty boy does.'

Maysa was starting to panic, but she could think well, even when she was under pressure. You need to survive girl, it's all about survival she thought to herself, and you will. Paddy persisted in his slurred drunken voice.

'He's an angry, dangerous boy, your pretty boy. You should be careful. You know what he did to poor Dingo. And he's not the first bloke he's belted senseless.'

'Yes, I know,' Maysa replied in a calm, steady voice. 'He is very dangerous, especially with people he doesn't like or trust.' She finished the sentence with a knowing smile. 'Tom, Paddy is home,' Maysa yelled out loudly as she stared with conviction into Paddy's eyes.

Tom arrived in time to see Paddy crossing the room toward his bedroom and Maysa standing uncomfortably in the door.

'You ok?' Tom inquired with concern.

'Sure . . . yes I am.' Maysa replied, looking after Paddy with and angry, distasteful look. 'Yes, I am fine. See you in the morning.' She kissed Tom on the cheek again and walked off.

Tom watched her until she entered the gate to the homestead garden, then looked at Paddy's bedroom door for a while, wondering what had just transpired.

CHAPTER TWENTY

Maysa happily decided to stay on at the station after long discussions with Len and Irene seeking assurance that they had a meaningful position for her. Of course, Tom was relieved and happy that she was staying on and had expressed as much with her. Bob had been notified, and although he feigned annoyance at the need to find a new cooks assistant, he was quietly pleased. He didn't want to have to deal with this problem again. When it came to the girl, if it wasn't Dingo, there'd be another no good for nothing ratbag causing him problems. He managed to take personal comfort in convincing himself that he had done an enormous service to Maysa, finding her this place to live and perhaps even a husband.

Tom went back to work immediately. He was sore and feeling sorry for himself, but there was no time for an able-bodied man to be lying about in bed in the middle of shearing. It was the last week with cut out expected late Friday morning, a long drinking session into the night for the shearers, and with them all leaving Saturday.

Saturday morning, Tom drove Maysa to the shed where she bid the shearers farewell. An array of utes, driven by blokes with sore heads, disappeared in clouds of red dust, bound for their next shed. Maysa left Bob with a long letter for her brother and a thank you kiss on his blotchy red cheek.

Work began straight away for Maysa. Immediately after lunch on Saturday, she rode with Tom and Paddy out on the final shearing muster. They returned a mob of four hundred ewes and lambs to their paddock, a couple of miles from the shearing shed. It was 3 or 4 hours work in the hot sun and a very long time in the saddle for a new rider. It was a baptism of fire for her backside and legs. The ride was actually slow and easy, with the ewes knowing their way to their paddock. Still, the lambs sent the ewes into a regular state of disarray as they ran about the mob playing. After half an hour in the heat, the mob finally settled into a steady walking pace. The horses and dogs followed on as though they were all heading home together as a group. Angel was a calm and steady horse and an easy ride for a beginner. With her head hung low, apart from the occasional swishing of her tail, the only real movement from Angel was a rhythmic rolling from side to side as she walked. Maysa sat in the saddle, occasionally adjusting her seat to ease the rubbing of her trousers on her inner leg and her aching backside. She could have fallen asleep, but for the constant desire to glance at Tom, who rode beside her. Paddy rode on the other side of the mob, also in silence, occasionally spitting in the dust and taking a swig from his water bottle.

The next few days were not dissimilar for Maysa. She worked her time between the house with Irene and the paddocks, with Len, Paddy and Tom whenever there was a stock job on. She quickly fell into a routine of hard work that made her tired and happy. She slept as she had never slept before. The spare time she had was spent with Tom. Their difficulty was not taking advantage of Len and Irene and the special project they had made of Tom and Maysa. They had to remind each other they were paid hands on the property, with an obligation above all else, to earn their keep. Fortunately, they each had a strong work ethic. They got enormous pleasure out of their accomplishments, particularly anything they achieved together. The days became weeks and the weeks slid behind them, forming their first memories and stories. It was the most peaceful and happy time Maysa could remember.

For Tom, the dreams of Milly had stopped, the nagging guilt he felt at letting her down no longer tore at his insides when he was idle. He felt a level of contentment he had never felt. It was different from his youth when he had an urgency for growth and change. It was different from the last couple of years when his peace was torn apart by anger, resentment and guilt. He could now sense a future beyond the next week and the following season. He imagined himself with Maysa and taking her to meet his parents. He could see reconciliation with his parents. He began to think of home and the future that eventually would be his. He began to imagine Maysa as part of that future.

It was six weeks after shearing, and the dipping was due to start. The sheep were to be run through a plunge dip. It was a concrete race, filled with water, where a sheep could be completely submerged in a concoction of chemicals that would kill lice and keep blowflies away for a while. Lice were a significant threat for the graziers. They spread like wildfire through sheep mobs and had a major impact on a fleece. The sheep would lose condition, and the fibres would be weakened or tender as it was called, causing the fibre to break in manufacture. In many cases, the affected sheep would shed their fleece. Lousy or lice-ridden sheep couldn't be sent to market. This was a critical process. The mustering began. It reminded Maysa of shearing time. Mob after mob were brought to the yards and forced into the dip by shouting stockmen and barking dogs. Reluctant sheep leapt out into the race, hoping to avoid the plunge but ended up completely submerged. Those sheep who did walk quietly into the race were rewarded with their heads being forced under the surface by stockman with a pole.

The days were long for Maysa, helping prepare meals and working with the men. Her job was chiefly mustering on Angel which she loved, and she had quickly become a competent rider. Banjo was always by her side. His love for working sheep had returned. She worked with Tom or Paddy and sometimes Len.

It was the weekend, and after a week of hard work, on Saturday morning everyone slept in. Breakfast wouldn't be before 8:00am. Eating each day with Len and Irene, Maysa had never had so much food. Eggs, chops and toast with cups of tea were common. She was always surprised by her ability to maintain her figure. Still, all of the hard, physical work wore off anything she ate. She often thought about her one moment with Tom, when she undressed for him, standing half-naked before his adoring eyes. There hadn't been another opportunity to be with Tom in such an intimate way since that night. She was under the microscope of the doting Irene and determined not to jeopardise the relationship. And then there was always the dark and brooding Paddy. He seemed to be there, around every corner, or in the distance just loitering when she was with Tom. They had been back to the river for several picnics, but their intimacy was constrained to long but affectionate embraces and passionate kisses. Tom, like all young men, couldn't help but search for ingenious ways to innocently stumble too far into Maysa's very personal space, but she was strong and determined. She had seen and recognised the value in what she had here with the Pattersons. She was sure of Tom's love, and time was moving so quickly that she knew that sooner rather than later, she and Tom would be together in the most intimate way.

'Maysa, are you off to walk with Tom while he does his chores this morning?'

'Yes, I was going and see him after breakfast, unless you want me to do something else?' Maysa replied to Irene.

'No, not at all dear. You go and see him, of course. But could you both please come in for morning tea today? There are a couple of things Len, and I would like to talk to you about. So, if you come in about 10:45, I will have some fruit scones and tea ready for you both.' Irene winked at Maysa.

'Yes, we'll be here.' Maysa was intrigued but a little disappointed. She was looking forward to a whole morning with Tom alone and deep down she liked to be the one who baked his fruit scones. Silly, she thought, but she knew how he loved them, and she cooked them well. She enjoyed looking after him, it was in these moments she could pretend to herself she was his wife. Regardless, she couldn't fight the intrigue. She and Tom were only ever summoned to the house for social reasons or to discuss upcoming farm jobs that required forward planning. Often Paddy was also there for work planning, which was mostly awkward and not particularly social. But Irene was giving nothing away, which was unusual. Suddenly, Maysa remembered something an efficient lady in an office had once said to her father. They had arrived unexpectedly wanting to speak with her boss. She thought she'd try it on Irene.

'Can I tell Tom what this is about?'

Irene smiled, laughed a little and replied.

'No, best not 'ey. See you at morning tea.' With that, Irene turned on her heel and strode away, looking pleased with herself.

CHAPTER TWENTY-ONE

Tom was loading bales of hay on a truck at the hay shed when he felt two hands on his waist, gently tickling him. Soft breasts pressed against his back, and warm breath on his neck preceded a gentle kiss.

'Is that you, Paddy?' Tom asked matter-of-factly.

'No, it's not.' Maysa slapped his arm, and he swung around smiling.

'Hey, sorry, May. That's what Paddy usually does.' Maysa leant fully against Tom, who fell back against the truck and took her in his arms, kissing her and tasting her sugary tongue, sweet with tea and breakfast.

'That's how you'd like me to touch you, isn't it Spooney.'

Tom and Maysa both got a shock as they looked to see Paddy walk past carrying two tin buckets, cigarette in mouth and looking at them both distastefully.

'He has to work occasionally, you know, between playing with you, Girlie.'

'She has a name, Paddy. You need me to remind you? And you can mind yer bloody business. If you've got a problem, go speak with the Pattersons 'ey.' Tom played his trump card.

'Yeah might do that. Sure Irene'd like to know about the night the girlie patched yer up after you beat up me good friend Dingo. Yer got some good close nursin' that nigh I bet.' Tom stood up, shrugging Maysa aside. Paddy smiled, discoloured teeth shadowed by smoke tendrils. He held his stare. Maysa grabbed Tom's arm.

'Tom, no. Come on.'

'Good thing one of yer can control their bloody temper, ain't it.' Paddy walked on, looking like he'd had a win.

'I never get a moment's rest from that monkey. I'd beat him senseless if it wasn't a waste of time and effort.'

'Well, it is. He's not worth it. He will get his. One day when he least expects it, something will jump up and bite him hard.'

'A snake biting a snake.' Tom replied venomously.

Tom smiled and pulled Maysa back into his arms and kissed her passionately.

After a moment, Maysa spoke softly, looking up into Tom's eyes.

'We have been summoned to the big house for morning tea with the Pattersons. I asked what it was about and Irene wouldn't tell me.'

There was a clank of tin, and seconds later they saw Paddy walking away from the shed abruptly.

'Shit, he was standing there listening to us.

There's something bloody wrong with that bloke. He worries me. You stay away from him, alright? If he makes another smart remark about you, I'm going to punch his teeth so bloody far down his throat, he'll be eating his breakfast through his arse.' Tom was angry.

'Tom, that's disgusting.' Maysa smiled, a little shocked. 'Please, don't speak like that. Don't waste a punch on him.' Maysa stroked Tom's arms until the tension eased from his body. 'Now, what do you think the Pattersons want to talk to us about? It's exciting, isn't it?'

'Yeah, guess so.' Tom was as cranky as a young boy scolded. Maysa kissed his chin and then his neck. His mood melted away, and he smiled.

'So why does Paddy call you Spooney?'

Tom looked angry again. 'No bloody idea. He does a good job of trying to get three feet up my nose.'

'Mr Tom, your language is very unpleasant today.' Maysa mocked. 'Please try and tidy it up before we meet with the Pattersons.'

Len and Irene were seated at the kitchen table when Maysa walked through the door, smiling enthusiastically and followed by Tom looking a little sheepish.

'Come in and sit down. Tom, tea? Maysa? Scones for both of you I trust?'

They sat together opposite Irene. Len sat at the end of the table. He folded a newspaper he'd been reading and threw it onto a chair laden with papers and magazines.

'How are you both?' Len asked, looking a little nervous, darting glances at Irene who was looking like the cat that stole the cream.

'Yeah, good thanks, Len. What's this all about?' Tom leaned forward on his elbows, with a tea in one hand and reached for a scone. He took a big bite that left cream on his lips and the tip of his nose. Maysa laughed at him before trying to wipe his face with a serviette.

'Good scones, Irene. Real good.' Tom mumbled through a mouthful.

'Not as good as mine.' Maysa replied, and they all smiled in good spirit.

'I expect you're wondering why we've asked you to come up for morning tea, are you?' Irene asked.

'Not at all, actually.' Tom feigned indifference then added, 'I'll just finish my scone, and I'll be off.'

'Be quiet, Tom. Of course, we are fascinated. 'Maysa answered Irene, and with a hand on Tom's arm, she stopped his silly behaviour.

Watching them, you could be forgiven for thinking they were a couple with far more history. They'd already adopted the typical roles of a married couple.

'Well, Tom,' Irene directed her speech at Tom in a firm tone. 'Maysa has been here on the station for more than 6 weeks now, and you two have been stepping out for most of that time really. Len and I felt . . .' Len coughed into his teacup. Tom and Maysa looked at him, and Irene glared at him. Looking sheepish he returned to a scone over-loaded with whipped cream., '. . . Len and I felt that it was high time your parents met Maysa.'

Tom finally stopped chewing his food, sat his teacup down and stared at Irene.

'It's been some time since you've seen your parents. What with shearing and everything else that's been going on. It's been a long time since Len and I have seen them as well. They're our best friends, not just our neighbours, Tom. They're your mum and dad.'

'Well, yes. You're probably right.' Tom answered, still a little shocked. It had been less than pleasant when Tom had last spent any considerable time with his parents. However, he had worked a lot out of his system since then, particularly since Maysa had arrived. His anger and indifference were far less prominent, and he could now imagine introducing Maysa to his parents and healing wounds. Maysa would definitely heal wounds. She had a way of soothing the crankiest soul.

'Yes, you're probably right. I will get in touch with them soon and organise to go and visit them over the next few weeks or so.'

Maysa was intrigued. She watched all this with fascination. She couldn't help but think of Len and Irene as Tom's parents. Although he lived in a separate house, he virtually had the run of the property and was welcome at the homestead anytime. The only odd part of this whole situation at the Patterson's was the relationship between them and the almost estranged nephew, Paddy, whom she didn't like at all. Why did Tom get treated like a son and Paddy the nephew, as just a worker? Of course, it was the connection with their beloved daughter. And what of Tom's real parents? He spoke little of them. She knew they had a property somewhere nearby, but knew nothing of it. She knew that Tom and his parents had a strained relationship after Milly's death and that he didn't like to talk about it. She hadn't pursued this with Tom. They had little enough time together as it was, without opening up wounds. There would be time enough to learn about the past if they could forge a future together. A future that she only allowed herself to daydream about. Her often unfortunate childhood led her to keep herself in check. She was fascinated at the prospect of meeting Tom's parents sometime soon and pleased that he wanted to take her to meet them. Would his mother like her, or even love her eventually? Would she take her into her arms as quickly as Irene had? Sometimes she pinched herself to be sure all of this was really happening.

'Good, it's settled then.' Irene announced triumphantly. 'In fact, Tom, you'll be pleased to know that your parents are coming here this evening for a barbeque and it goes without saying that both you and Maysa are invited.' Tom almost spat his tea out on the table. Len rubbed his forehead firmly. He'd been looking at the table for most of the conversation, he drew circles in the flour from the scones.

'Stop that, Len. You're making a mess.' Irene slapped his hand gently. He sat still, looking guilty by association with this scheme.

Maysa sat frozen. It was just hours until she'd meet Tom's parents. For weeks she had lived in a bubble, surrounded by these wonderful people who had accepted and loved her before they even knew her. She felt comfortable that she had proven them right in their judgment, and she was winning their respect and love based on her own merits. Their immediate and close embrace had created a veil of security. She had not been conscious of that until this moment. Now she needed to stand on her own two feet. She would meet these people in just a few hours and be required to demonstrate to them she was worthy of their wonderful son. All of a sudden, the enormity of everything that had transpired over the last couple of months hit Maysa. Her confidence was shaken. She looked to Tom for assurance, but he was shaking himself out of the shock and needed a moment to balance himself first. Just a couple of months earlier, Maysa had lost her father and then had to say goodbye to her brother. She'd left the relative safety and familiarity she had in her home in Melbourne and travelled nearly a thousand miles to start what was turning out to be a new life. She had fallen in love; it was the last thing she'd ever imagined. She'd just meant to survive. She'd been brutally attacked at the shearers camp, and she was still nervous and wary. She'd made a new family and found a new home and all in a matter of weeks. Suddenly all of this hit her like a freight train. She began to wonder whether she had lost her senses.

'Goodness me,' Irene laughed. 'Maysa darling, you're quite pale. I've given you a fright. I'm sorry dear.' She reached across the table and stroked Maysa's hand. Tom shaken back to his senses, looked at Maysa and awkwardly put an arm around her.

'Irene, just give the poor girl a moment to take this all in.' Len finally spoke up in a protective fatherly tone.

'Maysa darling, they will love you like Len and I do. How could they not?' Irene smiled affectionately at Maysa. Finally overwhelmed by this all, Maysa shed a tear and Irene squeezed her hand with a mother's touch.

'I'm sorry.' Maysa whispered as she composed herself quickly. 'This has all happened so quickly. I am just a little bit overwhelmed. But it is good . . . good. Thank you.' Suddenly she realised that she and Tom had not really spoken much about the future. Regardless, it seemed to be implied and ultimately out of their control.

'Come on, Boy, we better get things tidied up a

bit and get some wood up for the barbeque. Tidy up the lawns a bit before we have to freshen up.' Len stood up and beckoned Tom to leave with him.

'Yes Maysa, we have some cooking to do, some tidying up and then we need to organise a dress for you.' Irene stood up and took an apron off a hook and passed it to Maysa.

Tom and Maysa felt like they were swimming in a current that was moving so fast they could barely lock their hands together. Irene's enthusiasm and intent were clear, and she was strong and determined. They began to realise they hardly knew each other. They were nervous but equally as excited.

'Where're you off to, Spooney?' Paddy leant on the kitchen table smoking, drinking a beer and thumbing through a magazine when Tom walked out of the bathroom freshly showered and dressed for the barbeque.

'Well frankly, it's none of yer bloody business. But since I am a gentleman, unlike yerself, I'll tell you.' Tom couldn't think of a reason why he shouldn't tell Paddy. He got a particular pleasure out of knowing how much it would irritate Paddy to know that he and Maysa would be dining with his uncle yet again. 'My mum and dad are over for dinner with Irene and Len. Maysa and I are joining them.'

Paddy's face was a picture of disinterest, but

Tom saw something deep in his eyes. 'Well good on yer, Spooney.'

Tom smiled and waved goodbye to Paddy, who drew a long drag on his cigarette and let it slowly coil out of his mouth and nose like a charmed snake. The door shut behind Tom.

'Fuck you and fuck that bitch. Here we go again.' Paddy mumbled angrily to himself and into the neck of an open beer bottle. Shoving the chair out from behind him, he walked off to his room and lay on his bed. He lay there watching the fan spin on the ceiling. His stomach was tight and aching, and his head thumped lightly. He lay there and thought. He remembered. He imagined. He got angrier. Then he was aroused. He went to a drawer and found her underwear, buried deep under his clothes in a box.

CHAPTER TWENTY-TWO

Tom was walking up the back path of the homestead when Maysa appeared carrying a tray with glasses, plates and cutlery. She was followed by Irene giving running advice and orders and motioning Maysa in the direction of the outdoor table and chairs. Tom stopped. As always, he was taken aback by Maysa's beauty. Every time he saw her, it was like the first time he laid eyes on her. She was dressed for dinner, and she looked stunning. She wore a cotton floral dress, with white shoes that showed off the olive skin of her legs, and a white belt that accentuated her figure. Her hair was tied back with a broad ribbon. She was the product of Irene's hard work and officious instructions.

'Don't stand there gawking. Len's inside. He needs a hand with the drinks and getting the meat out to the barbeque. Come on, they'll be here at any moment.' Irene was in overdrive. With the mention of the guests, Maysa stopped and drew breath. Tom watched her, and he felt for her. Of course, he wasn't overly nervous about seeing his parents. It had been some time since he'd seen them, but he had patched up relations with his father. At least to the extent they could be civil and talk about simple and general things. There was a deep love and respect between the two of them. It was silent and invisible and would take a little to surface again, given all that had occurred in recent times.

Maysa and Irene had spread a tablecloth and were setting the table when they heard a vehicle approaching. It was late afternoon and still light. They could see the dust first, then the dogs began barking and pulling at their chains. A few minutes later, a utility pulled up at the back fence of the homestead with all the familiarity of a good friend. Irene and Len both strode down the path to the gate. Maysa stood back in the garden and watched as Tom began to walk toward the gate. She stood very still, almost frozen on the spot, clutching her hands together tightly.

Seeing the ute, and actually looking forward to seeing his parents, Tom had for a split second, forgotten Maysa. He stopped and chastised himself. He turned around, and there was Maysa, standing nervously by herself near the outdoor table. He strode back to her, feeling silly.

'I'm sorry, please forgive me. I'm not thinking straight.'

'No, don't be silly, Tom. Please go and see your mum and dad. They will be so excited to see you. And after so long.'

'Come on.' Tom smiled. 'I think we both know

they are here to see you as much, if not more than me. Maysa, this is the country. They're sticky beaks first and then my parents second. Mum and Irene are very close. Closer than you realise. Almost like sisters. How do you really think I ended up here?'

Maysa walked side by side with Tom down the path, wishing he would hold her hand, but in his shy country way, his hand was wedged firmly in his pocket. Maysa watched as Tom's mother stepped out of the ute.

Maysa's first impression was of an attractive and tastefully dressed lady. She wore stylish clothes, and what seemed likely to be very expensive jewellery, but she looked warm and kind as she affectionately hugged Irene. Tom's father was now coming around the front of the ute smiling. He was Tom, older, but just as handsome. He was tall like Tom, fit and aging well. He strode toward Len, and they shook hands vigorously, clearly happy to see each other. He then turned to Irene and grasping her shoulders in his big weathered hands, he kissed her cheek affectionately, while Len hugged Tom's mother. Then everyone stopped, and they all turned around as one to face Tom and Maysa. Maysa flushed with embarrassment and wished she could control her reddening face. She stepped back involuntarily from Tom, leaving him front and centre. Irene strode forward and stood next to Maysa with an arm around her shoulder. Tom's mother stepped forward toward Tom.

'Tom, darling' She took his face in her hands. 'You look so well.' She kissed his cheek and squeezed his forearm.

'I am. I am well. Thanks mum. It's good to see you.'

Tom's mother turned to Maysa, and after an awkward moment's silence, Irene spoke up.

'So, I'll introduce Maysa, will I Tom?'

Tom looked embarrassed and began to mumble, but his mother stepped forward and put her hand forward to Maysa, who quickly accepted the offering. As Maysa was starting to realise, these country women were strong and confident. They stood alongside and not behind their men, and often in front.

'Maysa, this is Mrs Sutherland.'

'Oh Irene, don't be silly. Hello Maysa, I am Elise, Tom's mum. I'm really pleased to meet you. Irene has told me so much about you. It's so nice, at last, to put a face to the name.' Elise addressed Maysa warmly. 'And this is Tom's father, Edward.'

'Hello Elise'. Maysa replied shyly. 'I'm very pleased to meet you too. Tom has told me all about you as well.' As she said it, Maysa realised she really knew almost nothing of Tom's parents at all.

'I'm Ed.' Tom's father stepped forward and also shook Maysa's hand, but more gently than Len's. Ed turned to Tom and smiled broadly and warmly and shook his hand. 'It's good to see you, Boy.'

'Good to see you too, dad.' Tom looked like a young boy, really pleased to be with his parents and to have them meeting a girlfriend. Maysa smiled affectionately, sensing the importance of the greeting between Tom and his father.

Everyone stood around for a moment smiling and relieved, no one speaking until it all seemed a bit odd. Finally, Len clapped his hands enthusiastically and announced, 'Right, let's get a beer then.' As he began to stride off, Irene called after him.

'You'll get the ladies a drink first please Len.'

'Yes, dear.' Len replied begrudgingly and turned on his heel and headed toward the kitchen.

'Come Elise. Maysa, we have some food to bring out so you can help me if you don't mind please?' The ladies walked off together. Maysa was firmly wedged between them and being managed by a couple of seasoned campaigners. Tom and his father walked off slowly toward the barbeque, exchanging comments about the properties, pasture and weather. Tom looked over his shoulder at Maysa just as she looked back at him and they smiled at each other as they were posted into their roles for the evening.

The evening went well with lots of questions, stories, and wisdom shared. Tom and Maysa were hardly called upon to comment until the evening was well underway.

'So, Tom, when are you going to bring this charming young lady over to see the station?' Ed asked Tom as they shared a beer while staring at the flames of the barbeque fire, mesmerised.

'Well, soon, I guess. Now you that and mum have met her. I guess if all goes well tonight and mum likes her, I will bring her over to see my home soon. What do you think?'

'What do I think? About your plan? Or do I like her?

'Well both I guess. It's important to me that you and mum like her, of course.'

'Do you, Boy? Do you like her?'

'Haven't been able to think of much else since I first laid eyes on her, to be honest.'

'Well, can't say's I blame yer, Boy. She sure is a damn good-looking girl, isn't she?' Tom smiled at his dad.

'Listen, Boy, what comes first is how you feel about her. Then hopefully, and I know we will, the rest of us will like her just as much. No doubt we'll all fall for her as well mate.' Ed gave Tom an encouraging smile. 'You know how close mum and Irene are, and you know they trust each other like sisters. Well, Irene goes on and on about Maysa. Mum and I laughed. We think Irene wants to adopt her. To be honest, and I am sorry to say this, we both wanted to meet her to see if all this could be true.' Then more gently. 'We wanted to be sure that it wasn't just Irene latching on to her because she still desperately missed Milly.' Tom acknow-ledged his father with a nod, and they sat in silence a moment longer.

'But I reckon Irene might be on the money. You've done well, Boy. Really well. Don't bugger it up now, will you.' Ed laughed and gave Tom a gentle slap on the back.

'Mmm . . . Milly . . . sometimes, Dad I . . .' Tom Spoke hesitantly, but Ed interrupted Tom before he could finish.

'Tommy, you did everything you could and everything anyone would expect of you mate. Something died inside of us all when we lost her. And I know something died inside of you. And mum and I have felt for you. But mate, what you had, belonged to Milly and you. It was nothing anyone else could or would ever share, or even expect to. It's still there though, and it belongs just to you. She was a wonderful girl, and I am betting she's watching over you now. She probably sent Maysa for you.' In a rare show of affection, Ed put his arm around his son's shoulders. 'It's time, my boy, to move on and feel ok. You don't have to say goodbye or forget her, but you do have to feel alright to move on.'

'Thanks, Dad. Listen . . . I am sorry for all the bloody trouble I caused.'

'Mate, please. We want you back soon, and we don't need to talk sorry or anything like that. We're family.'

Ed extended a hand, and he and Tom shook hands and held the grip as long as they could, before getting uncomfortable. The handshake wasn't lost on the others. They'd all watched the physical aspects of the exchange from a distance. Their relief was as palpable as was Tom and Ed's.

'Maysa, let's take those boys a beer ey? I am sure they could do with a top-up.' Elise offered a hand to Maysa who took it happily. Len and Irene remained seated in a pair of old squatter's chairs watching this all play out before them.

'See, my dear? It is just as I said it would be.' Irene spoke to Len while watching her best friend and her 'adopted' daughter.

'Pleased with yourself, I'm betting?' Len laughed quietly. 'Well done, Luv. Good job.' He took her hand. 'But you know, you're pushing this fast, and you know what that means. We might lose Tom, sooner rather than later. I am used to having him around now. He's going to have to go home soon though. Ed's got a few years on me, and he will want to start the handover soon.'

'Have you spoken with Ed lately about the arrangements?'

'No, not for a while. I think we both felt we needed to get Tom really settled first and back to himself, then we could get our ideas straight and drag him into the whole deal. It's gonna take a few years to get it all together. But it's a good thing, and the right thing to do. It'll be the biggest station in these parts by a country mile. And now . . . I feel like we have a daughter again to contribute to the deal, as funny as that sounds.'

'Len, is it silly? Sometimes I think it's stupid of

me. We hardly know her really, but I feel like I love her like a daughter already.'

'I agree, Luv. She's a Godsend.'

'The poor thing must be totally overwhelmed. We must be careful to be mindful of how she feels. We can't assume this is what she wants, although she is clearly head over heels for Tom. Do you know what she asked me the other day?'

'What?'

'What's a Spooney? She said Paddy calls Tom 'Spooney' all the time. Oh Len, how are we going to deal with him in all of this?'

'So, what did you tell her. Did you tell her what a Spooney was?'

'No, I didn't. I said I am not sure what he means. I lied through my teeth to the poor girl. And it's just as well. It seems Tom's told her nothing of any substance about where he comes from. He's told her his parents have a property somewhere over that way,' and Irene motioned with her arm off into the dark night. 'She has the impression he's off a small property, a small farm or something.'

'Well, Luv. It's not a bad thing she if she falls in love with him without knowing anything about him. It shows how genuine she is.' Len paused, and they both watched Maysa and Elise organising beers. 'Paddy, yes he's a problem. He's a strange lad. Bit nasty by nature isn't he. It's no bloody wonder though, with all he's been through. I can't help but feel responsible. I'm his uncle, blood, and it means something, to me at least. I don't know what he expects here. Even if he was entitled to all this, he'd never make a fist of it. He just doesn't have it. He's a good stockman, but that's it. Just a good stockman. And on top of that, he can be downright bloody rude and unpleasant. Even to me, at times. I don't know where it comes from. Anyway, let's not think about him tonight ey?'

'Here, Maysa. One for your man and one for mine.' Elise handed Maysa a beer for Tom, and Maysa smiled. They paused a moment just looking at each other expectantly, each waiting for the other to speak.

'Elise, everyone has been so kind to me. I, . . . I don't know how I can ever repay Irene and Len. Everything has happened so quickly.'

'What is it dear? Is it Tom? Is everything ok? You both look very happy.'

'That's just it. I am so happy, and I feel so lucky that I can't think straight. I am being swept along on this happy cloud. I hope I am doing the right thing.'

'How do you feel about my boy?'

There was a long pause before Maysa had summed up the courage to speak.

'I don't know whether to be embarrassed to say this but . . . I love him. I love him more than anything or anyone I have ever known or loved. I am like a silly little girl. I think about him all day. I daydream about him and me.' Elise was watching and smiling as Maysa spoke animatedly. 'Am I talking too much?'

'Not at all, Dear. Please go on. There is nothing a mother likes to hear more than how much her boy is loved.'

'There's not much more to tell. This is silly, but I see how wonderful Irene and Len are and how much they have and how generous they are. Sometimes I daydream that Tom and I might have a little cottage of our own somewhere, by the river. Tom loves the river.'

'Well dear, if you work hard together, as a team like Len and Irene, or Ed and I, then I am sure one day you and Tom could have a cottage of sorts.' Elise smiled to herself. She knows nothing, she thought.

'Come on then, before these spoilt boys complain.' Elise and Maysa joined Tom and Ed and discussed plans for Tom and Maysa to visit the next weekend after chores on Saturday and to stay over until Sunday rather than drive back in the dark.

After some time, Irene and Len joined the party, and Len beckoned Tom and Ed away for a quiet chat. They chatted confidentially for some time while the ladies spent more time getting to know each other.

Eventually, Len wrapped up the conversation.

'Well Ed, we'll need up to five years before Irene and I will want to genuinely slow down. If you're winding down now, then I think we're right to begin the transition as soon as possible. Your six hundred and eighty thousand acres and my two hundred will give us a fair old station. What do you say, Tom?'

'I just can't get my head around it all just yet, but it's what I always wanted and what I dreamt of. I am sure I can make you both very proud. And at the same time, maybe a little cash.' Tom grinned.

The three men shook hands enthusiastically as both Elise and Irene watched on knowingly.

Maysa watched the men talking animatedly and shaking hands in a congratulatory fashion, although she had no idea what they were celebrating and wasn't consciously aware of the scene. She was so overwhelmed by everything that she didn't think any more of this than anything else in the last six weeks.

The night ended soon after with Ed and Elise driving off into the pitch-black. Len and Irene said their goodnights to Tom and Maysa who stood in the garden after everyone had left.

Tom took Maysa's hands in his.

'So, did you like my mum and dad?'

'They were wonderful, of course. Now I know how you will turn out. You are just like your dad, and your mum is so pretty and stylish. I was a bit scared at first. I felt very plain next to her, but she is so lovely and warm.'

'You could never be called plain!' Tom stared at Maysa. 'We'd better go. I guess it's getting late, and dipping starts this week. Tomorrow I'll have to start mustering.'

'Then I will come with you, of course.'

Tom pulled Maysa toward him. Her soft warmth press against him. He kissed her gently.

'Quick, please come with me for a moment. It's too bright here.' Tom led Maysa away from the light of the kitchen windows. In the darkness between an old garden shed and a large shrub, Tom swung Maysa into his arms. She returned his kiss with passion, buoyed by a sense of her right to be in his arms. It had been an evening where she had been accepted and welcomed, and this gave her a sense of ownership over Tom. There was no disguising of his desire as he kissed her passionately. Her arms around his neck, his hands slid from the small of her back, reaching hungrily for her bottom. She became conscious of his arousal as he pushed himself against her, and she moaned involuntarily, as he caressed her. He reached for her dress and gently edged it up and slid his hand under it, feeling the bare flesh of her leg, warm, smooth and soft. She moaned again, and he shivered in anticipation.

'Oh, God . . . Tom, you must stop. I can't control myself. Soon, I promise. But not here, not now. Please.' Tom sighed, not able to hide his frustration, and held her in a tight embrace. After a few moments, he seemed to recover his senses and get

228

his desperate urges under control. She couldn't help but wonder how long she could keep him at bay, let alone keep her strength.

'I love you, Maysa,' he whispered in her ear.

'I love you more than anything,' she whispered in return.

CHAPTER TWENTY-THREE

Over the next week, all energy was focussed on dipping. Large mobs of sheep were brought into the yards each day and run through the plunge dip. Everyone worked hard. The mustering pace was even faster than shearing with a thousand sheep a day being dipped. Maysa worked hard alongside the rest of the team, as hard as anyone and possibly harder. She was up early with Irene, making breakfast, morning tea and preparing for lunch, then off on Angel with the boys mustering. Typically, she would ride out a few paddocks to meet the boys as they came in from an earlier start and help them with the challenges of the last paddocks and yards. Everyone was on deck to push the mobs through the dip as quickly as they could. It was a huge job and lots of hard work. By Friday night, everyone was exhausted, and tempers were stretched to their limits.

Standing in the yards watching the last of a large mob walk out into the paddock, Len announced to the crew, 'Right, Paddy, you and I will take them out past the river tomorrow. Let's get into it early, ey? It'll take a few hours, and I want to be done by lunchtime.'

'What about him?' Paddy looked bitterly at Tom.

'What about him, Paddy?' Len was tired and wasn't hiding his irritation.

'Why isn't he helping? Doesn't he work bloody Saturdays now?'

Tom watched on in angry silence. Maysa standing some distance away could hear the discussion but was pretending not to be aware of it.

Len drew a long breath.

'Listen, Paddy. I don't know what's eating you, Boy, but I make the decisions around here and what I say goes. You'll help me, alright? Tom's off home for the weekend, not that it's any of your business, but it's not a secret either. Now Tom and Maysa will be off tomorrow morning, so he won't have time to help. You satisfied now?'

Tom was ropable. What he was doing was none of Paddy's business, and more so, it was none of his business that Maysa was going with him. Paddy shrugged his shoulders as though he didn't care and walked away, trying to leave the impression he didn't know what the fuss was all about. He mounted his horse, looked back over his shoulder at Tom and then kicked the horse too hard into a canter while pulling back on the reins at the same time. The horse thrashed its head about, biting at the bit and trying to respond to the conflicting directions.

'Jesus, he's a rough bastard Len. I am sorry, I know he's your nephew and all, but somethings not quite right with him.'

'I know. I know, Tom. But I have to try and help him along. He had it bloody rough as a kid. It's no wonder he's an angry bastard. Hopefully, he'll settle down one day.'

After they returned from the yards, Tom said goodnight to Maysa at the back gate. They were both dusty and dirty. Irene wanted Maysa inside to talk about her weekend to come, and Tom was dog tired and couldn't wait to wash up, eat and get to bed. He walked through the door into the stockman's cottage, and Paddy was standing at the kitchen sink.

'Hey Tom.'

'Hey what?' Tom replied suspiciously and impatiently.

'Listen,' Paddy continued, 'I'm sorry about before, ok? I know I was outta line. I'm just bloody worn out like everyone and the thought of gettin' on the horse again tomorrow and yellin' at the dogs just gives me the shits. But I shouldn't a taken it out on you.'

Now Tom was utterly suspicious.

'Yeah righto, don't worry about it.'

'Here, have a beer. I got a couple of steaks out of the cooler and I'll whack on some veggies to go with 'em while you take a shower mate.' Tom couldn't believe what he was hearing. In all the time he'd lived with Paddy, he had hardly ever had a friendly word from him. There were plenty of non-emotional exchanges. There was only essential communication, and nothing more. This was out of character, but Len's words rang in his head. He knew the poor bastard had a rough time as a youngster and he felt he should accept the olive branch, however poisoned the chalice might turn out to be.

'Alright, good on yer. Give us half an hour, and I'll be ready.'

Tom showered and changed. When he got back to the kitchen, Paddy was serving the steak and had poured a couple of beers.

'Here yer go, mate. Get that into yer.'

'Yeah, don't mind if I do. Looks pretty bloody good actually. You'll make someone a good wife one day if you keep this up.'

Paddy laughed and drained half a glass of beer. He looked at Tom and smiled a queer smile as though he was not really amused, but rather being polite.

'Good yer getting on home for the weekend. Been a fair while I guess?'

'Yeah, been a few months. Too long.'

'Yeah, good to sort these family things out ey? Bloody hard work when the family gets up each other's arse. So yer takin the girl with yer ey? That's a bit of a sign, isn't it?'

'Maysa? Yes.' Tom felt the usual hackles coming up on the back of his neck.

'Yeah, Maysa. Yeah, sorry mate, that's what I meant. She's a bit of alright, ain't she?'

'Yes, she is.' Tom's tone was sharpening with suspicion. Tom could sense Paddy ducking and weaving, trying to regain the friendly edge he'd just had. Tom was trying to be patient, being pleasant wasn't Paddy's forte.

'So, what's on over there? Got a lot to catch up on, I guess. How's yer mum and dad going? Yer dad must be getting on to slowing down a bit, is he? I thought I heard a couple of years ago he was thinking about winding down as soon as you were ready to take over. Been a rough couple of years, but I guess things are settling down a bit now.' Tom chewed on his steak, which had suddenly lost its appeal and listened while he watched Paddy's face carefully. Where's this going, he thought.

'Yeah, guess so.' Tom gave him nothing but an abrupt answer.

'Len'll miss yer when yer go back home I guess, but we'll manage. Expect he'll put on a new young-ster to take up the slack.'

'Mmm . . . Probably.' Tom was enjoying this now. This was the hardest he'd seen Paddy work. He knew he was driving him crazy, not answering anything. 'You know, I'll probably keep my finger in the pie over here. Len's got a few years in him yet. I can still learn a lot from Len. Besides, I think he values me.'

Tom looked at Paddy, swigging his beer hard

now and starting to flush. He was clearly working hard to maintain his composure. Now Tom knew where this was heading, he couldn't help himself.

'Besides, Maysa, she's almost family over here now. She's already like a daughter to Len and Irene.' Tom had no idea what he'd just done, all in the name of a bit of vengeful fun.

Paddy worked hard to try and draw what information he could from Tom, but he was getting very little. Not a muscle moved on his face as he listened carefully. The tension in his neck was at bursting point. He was looking directly at Tom but seeing well beyond him. Memories flashed through his mind – screams and whimpers, pleading, blood, torn clothing, bare flesh, torn flesh.

'You all right, mate? You look a bit pale all of a sudden.'

'Yeah, yeah, sure. Just feeling a bit off-colour. What were you saying?' Paddy refocused on Tom. This was exactly what he wanted and needed to know. In fact, he already knew it, he just had to have it confirmed.

'Nothing really. Anyway, I might hit the sack, mate. I'm buggered, and Maysa and I've got a big weekend coming up. Thanks for the tucker 'ey.'

Tom got up and left the table. Paddy remained, sitting there staring straight ahead, in a kind of trance, deathly still.

CHAPTER TWENTY-FOUR

There was a knock on the stockman's cottage door shortly after lunch the next day. Tom and Maysa had long since left for Tom's parents. Paddy opened the door, and Len stood there with Sergeant Penfold from town. Sergeant Penfold was six foot four, a big barrelled chest and built like a brick shithouse as the local boys described him. He could pick up a drunk by the belt and throw him clean out of the pub door into the street, and catch his arse with a polished leather boot before he hit the ground. Penfold was tough but fair. He was a staunch Catholic with three daughters and a strong sense of family. Cases relating to children or sexual assaults were always managed with extra vigour. It was well known, and accepted, that if you dealt in the wrong sort of crime in his town, you got two sentences. Penfold would administer the first sentence, which lasted a couple of hours in the cell. The second, the lighter of the two, was in the magistrate's court a few weeks later when the bruises had had time to subside. He was well respected by the locals.

'Hey Paddy, there's been some strife in town.

The Sarge wants to talk to us about it. You got a minute?'

'Yeah sure, how yer going Sarge? What's the news?'

'Well, a couple of incidents to tell you about. See if you got any ideas. A couple of weeks back, one of the local girls was beat up pretty bad and sexually assaulted.'

The Sergeant paused for effect, and Paddy was careful to display his indifference to the news, but not to appear completely uncaring. It was a common technique that police officers used so often they were not even aware they were doing it. Let 'em stew on it a minute. Their eyes will tell the story if there is one. Paddy had enough experience personally and enough friends who'd had run-ins with the law to know and anticipate these little policing nuances. He was confident he'd give nothing away to the Sergeant.

Len broke the silence.

'Jesus, that's no good, Barry. There's a bit of it goes on, isn't there? In town, I mean.' Len was always particularly sensitive to any reports of these assaults, his awareness far more heightened, given Milly's case.

'Yeah Len, there is. Unfortunately, it's quite often, but usually, we know who did it and pretty quick. More often than not, it's someone related, an angry or drunk boyfriend or husband, or even worse, a father or uncle. Bloody horrible stuff.' Penfold paused again for a moment. Paddy thought

237

of his own father and how he'd treated his mother, and he knew Penfold knew the intimate details and was probably sensitive to Paddy's feelings. Penfold continued. 'Anyway, we don't have too many clues yet. I am just getting around and seeing a few people on the properties to see if anyone's heard anything. Regardless, you fellas are connected to this one.' Len looked shocked. Paddy remained unemotional, almost cold.

'But this one is a bit unusual Len.' He looked back at Paddy. Paddy was aware the analysis continued, and he consciously relaxed his face and particularly his eyes. 'It was two blokes that assaulted the girl. One's too bloody many, but two. Real bad stuff. When we find him, he'll get a floggin' he can't imagine before we hand him over to the magistrate.'

'Hang on Barry, you said two blokes. But now yer saying when we find him. Just one.' Len pressed Penfold.

'Yeah, well that's the interesting thing. We've got one of em already.'

'Well that's a good start, shouldn't be hard to get the other one then.' Len added positively.

'Well, he ain't much use Len. We dragged him out of the river a couple of days ago. And you know who it was?' The sergeant paused again looking at both Len and Paddy in turn.

'It was that bloody Dingo. He was roughed up a bit by the water, and the fish had started chewin' on him, but he was recognisable for sure. He's down the morgue now. Poor girl got taken in to identify him. No worries. Even bloated and chewed on, she knew it was him. We figured it might have been, given her description.'

Len was clearly stunned by the news. His jaw dropped. Paddy did his best to look surprised. Although he wasn't surprised, they'd found the body.

'Christ, so what was he doing in the river? Do you know how he died?' Len asked after gathering his thoughts.

'Well, we know he had a skin full of grog during the afternoon, and he had a bump on his forehead. So either he fell over, bumped his head and rolled into the river, unlikely . . . or his mate did him in. Either way, it sounds rough, but we won't be missing him. It's usually not a bad way to finish a case, to be honest. Especially after the strife out here with the girl.'

'What about the other fella, how did the girl describe him then? Len pushed Penfold along. Paddy took a long deep breath through his nostrils, keeping himself steady and maintaining a concerned look on his face. In truth, at that moment, he was very concerned.

'Well, that's where we draw a bloody blank. All we know was, he was a well-dressed fella, moleskins, good shirt and boots, smelt of drink, obviously been giving the grog a nudge. But no one remembers seeing a bloke like that with Dingo down the pub during that afternoon. And she never saw his face. She got a bit of a look at his clothes, but it was dark, and the poor girl was scared and beaten half unconscious. She's probably blocked the bloody terror out.' Penfold looked at Paddy for a moment, who was still motionless and hadn't spoken. Penfold squinted as if still assessing Paddy.

'In fact, Paddy, a couple of fellas said they'd seen you drive into town that day and have a couple of beers with Dingo, then leave a couple of hours before him. So, I figured I'd come out here and just ask if you'd seen anything or knew of anything to give us a clue. Did he tell you he was meeting anyone, mention any mates? I believe there had been a bit of trouble out here, Len. With a girl . . . and Dingo that is.'

'Yea, that's right Barry, but we dealt with it. Bob came in quick smart and moved him on. Paddy drove him into town. But that was quite a few weeks ago.' Paddy could see Len was shocked to hear he'd had a drink with Dingo. He was trying to remain carefully focussed on the conversation. Still, he couldn't help be distracted by the thought of the conversation he would inevitably face in explaining his actions to Len.

'He was a bit knocked around, I understand.'

'Dingo?'

'Yeah, Dingo, he had copped a bit of a belting I hear.'

For the first time since Penfold had started talking, Paddy started to cheer up and could sense his opportunity. He chimed in quickly.

'Yeah, Tom. Tom gave him a right old floggin'. In fact, they had to pull him off him for fear he'd do him some real harm. Bloody good thing though. Fair enough. I'd have done it myself if I'd got their first.'

Penfold straightened up, interested now. Paddy could see the intuitive cogs of the policeman grinding into action. He knew Tom. Yes, he knew him to be a good young man from a good family, but he also knew he had a temper, and after a couple of grogs, he'd had to pull Tom into the station more than a few times after he delivered a few locals a good belting over the last couple of years. Penfold knew it all, and Paddy knew he would have to discount the family and any good behaviour as he considered Tom as a suspect. He was trouble for Penfold and everyone else ever since his girlfriend Milly had died. Paddy was well aware that more than once, Penfold had put Tom in a cell for a night until he calmed down and dried out.

Gauging Penfold's interest and seeing the look of alarm and distress on his uncle's face, Paddy knew he'd achieved all he needed to. Regardless, he couldn't help himself.

'Geez, I'm not suggesting Tom would ever do anyone in. No way. Never, Sarge, he's a good bloke. Wouldn't harm a fly. Only givin' Dingo what he deserved.'

'And what was that?' Penfold asked.

'Shit, shouldn't have opened me big mouth, should I?'

Len broke in firmly obviously trying to slow Paddy down which may or may not have helped Tom's case.

'Listen, Barry, yes there was a bit of trouble. But it was nothing more than you often get when you get a bunch of bloody larrikin shearers, all jammed in a couple of huts together. They'd been at it for weeks, living in each other's pockets, with a gut full o' grog and nothing to do in their spare time. Bloody Dingo got well ahead of himself and tried it on with the cook's helper, Maysa. She's a bloody good kid. She didn't deserve it, not that any sheila deserves that sorta treatment. Anyway, we were all bloody annoyed, mad as hell actually and Tom took exception to it and just gave Dingo a bit of a going over. But he got as good as he gave, no doubt about it. Dingo fought dirty, and Tom was cut up, he needed sewing up afterwards.'

'Yeah, you see,' Paddy felt he needed to hammer in another nail, 'the girl, she's Tom's girl, been on with her since the first day they met. In fact, she and Tom are over at Tom's parents' place now. He's introducing her to his parents right now and showing her the big station. Like to be a fly on the wall over there, ey Len? So you couldn't blame him being real angry with Dingo. Really angry.'

Paddy had had the effect he wanted, Penfold was hooked. Penfold was watching Paddy closely. Paddy hoped he hadn't been too enthusiastic. He needed to be careful Penfold didn't suspect there was anything between him and Tom. Len was visibly annoyed with the rapid flow of information coming from Paddy that was obvious, and Paddy felt that could only help. Overall, Paddy was pleased. He felt he'd given Penfold just enough information to fire up his interest, but without sounding like he was deliberately trying to put Tom in.

'Well, I guess I better have a talk with Tom when he gets back. When's he back Len?'

'Late Sunday I reckon Barry.'

'Ok, tell him to be around Monday, will you? I'll be out in the morning.'

'Righto then. You best come out to the yards, Barry. We're dipping at the moment, and he'll be at the yards.'

'Thanks Len. Listen, it's just routine mate, I don't think there's anything in it. But I have to follow it up, or I wouldn't be doing my job. There are plenty of well-dressed young fellas coming and going through town.' And as an afterthought, he added. 'Besides, could have been some monkey who borrowed some good clothes for the day.'

CHAPTER TWENTY-FIVE

Earlier that morning and shortly after 9:00 am, Tom had driven the ute up to the back gate. He got out and strode up the path to the back door where Maysa was coming out with Irene, followed by Len carrying a bag for her.

'Morning.' Tom said cheerily.

'Morning,' the others chorused in return.

'So, ah, you got enough luggage there, Maysa?' Tom enquired with an exaggerated note of sarcasm. Len was carrying a large bag that could hold enough clothing for a week. In fact, Maysa had insisted it was way too much, and she felt a little silly carrying it all, but Irene would have none of it. '*You never know what you'll need until you get there, and the last thing you want is to be caught short, especially this weekend.*' Maysa had conceded and packed everything as she had been told. Tom backtracked to the ute where he undid the canvas cover. Taking the bag from Len, he threw it into the ute next to his bag and reattached the tarp to keep the dust off.

'Len, can you throw the dogs a bit of meat

for me, last thing. They'll be right until tomorrow then.'

'Sure, Tommy. You two have a good and safe trip 'ey, and say g'day to your folks for us.'

Everyone said goodbye and Irene gave Maysa a kiss on the cheek and wished her good luck.

'Don't forget dipping Monday morning. I expect you back Sunday night ready to muster Monday morning, alright?' Tom waved a confirmation at Len as he drove away.

A few moments later, Tom and Maysa were heading along the front drive of the Patterson's station. Red dust billowed out behind the ute. It was a clear day, heating up quickly. Tom had the window open with an elbow out, trying to stay cool. Maysa was excited and watching everything as they drove along together, including Tom, regularly. He was conscious of each time she looked at him, but he kept his eyes on the road. He pointed out a mob of kangaroos as they fled across the track in front of them. An old buck, bringing up the rear of the mob, stopped and watched them defiantly. No more than 50 yards away. Tom beeped the horn, and the buck turned and bounded off behind the mob.

A few miles on, Tom pointed out a small group of wild pigs, black, white and mottled in colour. There were at least eight of them. They rooted around, churning up the dirt with their snouts, seemingly in a feeding frenzy until they were interrupted by the sound of the ute. They stopped, rigid, watched the ute for a second, then took off for the lick of their lives. Maysa took in all of this scene while Tom commented on what a nuisance the pigs were. There were endless birds, white and black cockatoos, galahs, crows and kookaburras sitting in the sun peacefully. Tom pointed them all out as they drove along and provided bits and pieces of information on each. Maysa marvelled at everything he had to say and just enjoying watching him speaking about this country which he clearly loved.

After about twenty minutes, and a few cattle grids, Tom announced they were at the end of the drive and turning onto the road. To Maysa, it just looked like more of the same. It was fenced only on one side so the stock could graze the long paddock. The long paddock, as Tom explained, was an Australian expression for the road and the pasture it afforded travelling stock. It was particularly important in times of drought.

'How far is it to your parent's house?'

'Well, we actually live next door, so not too far.' He smiled.

'Ok, so how far is it? How long will it take?'

'It's about seventy miles door to door, which is a good couple of hours drive, all going well.' Maysa was amazed. She was trying to compute how it could take two hours to drive to your neighbour's home, although she conceded the going was a bit slow. The road was badly corrugated for long stretches. Sometimes when they were not expecting the corrugations, the ute would shudder sideways across the road. It made Maysa reach for the door handle and Tom's arm, to brace herself. As much as it was uncomfortable, it seemed to amused Tom. Maysa couldn't help but suspect he hit each run of corrugations at full speed just to get her reaction.

Finally, after a long hour on the road, Tom announced the front gate was getting near, probably just a couple of miles away. He slowed the ute down, and it disappeared for a moment in the red dust that caught up with them.

'What are we doing?' Maysa enquired.

'Well.' Tom replied slowly and in a measured fashion. 'I should tell you a few things about my home and family before we get there, so you know what to expect. He paused and watched Maysa closely. 'It's just that it might not be as you expect. I don't know what you've pictured. I haven't told you too much.'

'You've told me very little at all to be truthful. But that's ok. I didn't want to push you. I know it's been a difficult couple of years for you. I felt you should tell me things in your own time. I'll be happy when you're ready to tell me. I'll be happy to listen all day, all week and forever.' Maysa unpacked a thermos with cold cordial and poured some into enamel mugs for her and Tom.

'Let's get out and stretch our legs a bit 'ey.' Tom suggested, and he stepped out onto the dusty road. Maysa followed him carefully, stepping through

247

the dust, a little disappointed her shoes would be so dusty before arriving. Tom walked around to the passenger side of the ute and leant against the door and took a drink. Maysa stepped up close to him. He smelt her perfume even in competition with the eucalyptus and dust. He leant toward her, and she stretched up on her tiptoes to kiss him. He kissed her and then just stared at her for a moment.

'God, you are so beautiful. I hope all this is what you really want. Because I've fallen madly in love with you. I want to be with you forever.'

Maysa, still looking back into his eyes, replied softly.

'Tom, I love you more than anything. Be sure of that. If we had to live in the desert, or on a snow-capped mountain, I would want to be by your side.' She kissed him again.

'Well, I guess I better tell you a few things.' He drew a deep breath, preparing to begin.

'First things first 'ey? Spooney, that mug Paddy keeps calling me Spooney. He's a rude bugger, isn't he? You don't know what a Spooney is, do you?'

'No, but I figured it was a bit rude, or annoying at least since you look annoyed every time he says it.'

'Well, yes. It gets up my nose. I guess I shouldn't care less.'

'So, what does it mean?'

'It comes from the saying, born with a silver

spoon in your mouth. I guess the easiest way to explain it is this, some people eat their food with a tin spoon and some people eat their food with a silver spoon if they're lucky and they can afford it . . . that is. He reckons I got my food given to me on a silver spoon because we could afford the good cutlery. Do you get it?'

'Yes, you had better cutlery than some people.' Maysa paused before suggesting, 'I think perhaps your mother's jewellery doesn't just look beautiful, but it is also expensive.'

'Well, we do all right. My family does alright. But it's been a lot of hard work for generations of Sutherlands. We didn't get where we are now just sitting on our backsides.'

'Yes, I understand, of course, Tom. So, what are you telling me? Are your parents as wealthy as the Pattersons?' Maysa smiled gently at Tom to coax him through this, although she didn't understand his hesitation. She was quietly excited with the fact he was from a wealthy family, but she dared not show her enthusiasm. She fell in love with him as a stockman with a horse and two dogs, and she would love him if he drove her to a bark hut by the river right now. Perhaps that may have been easier.

'The Pattersons are Mum and Dad's best and oldest friends. Both families have lived side by side for generations. My parent's property, Sutherland Downs . . . well it is more than three times bigger than the Patterson's.' He paused for a moment to let Maysa take this in. She looked stunned. She thought the Patterson's property was so big you could never find where it ended in most directions. He had not given any suggestion that he came from this sort of wealth. Suddenly, she felt terrified, tiny and worth nothing. A person with nothing to give in comparison, nothing at all. She felt overwhelmed by what she was being led into and couldn't help but ask herself why her.

'It's important to me that you know that all this wealth is not important, it's not everything. It's not to me, and not to my family.' Right now, this was cold comfort for Maysa. Her life with her father and brother had been hard. They barely scraped by, but they were happy. Then she was thrust into much tougher conditions in the shearers camp. She was able to accept this and to work hard, and she understood and accepted her position. It was about survival. And then, she was dragged into the Patterson's family and smothered with love and attention at the same time as falling in love with the quiet and reserved but angry man standing before her. It was the most incredible thing that had ever happened to her, and it was more than enough. She was almost terrified by how good it was, for fear of losing what she'd found. Now he was telling her he was from one of the wealthiest pastoralist families in New South Wales. She was suddenly more than a little terrified. This was another world, a wonderful world, but a different world in which she was far from comfortable. A world where she was far from confident she belonged or ever could belong. Maybe this was all too much, all just a silly pipe dream. Maybe she really shouldn't be here. Overcome by what she was hearing, she shed a tear through a strained smile.

'Hey, Maysa, hey. It's ok.' Tom spoke gently. 'You've met my parents. They are good people, and they thought you were wonderful. Why do you think they invited us up home so quickly? They don't have strange or unreasonable expectations. They just want me to be happy, and they want you to be happy. You'll see.' Tom took Maysa in his arms and held her for some time.

'I'm sorry, Tom. All of a sudden, I'm very, very nervous. Now I don't really understand why you are working at the Patterson's. I know you argued with your family, but that seems long ago now. You should return home to your family, surely. I really don't understand anything that is going on. It seems I hardly know you.'

'Well, there is more to it. I'm sorry. You see, and I know this will be hard, but given I stand to inherit the station and . . .'

'Wait!' Maysa interjected. 'Tom, not just you, surely. You have a brother and a sister. Surely you will all have part of such a big station.'

'The power in this property is in not splitting it up. It's always been the way. The firstborn boy gets the property. But don't worry, if and when my brother and sister want to come back, they

251

will be looked after very well. You'll meet my Aunts and Uncles this weekend. They all live on the property with their families, and they all live well. This station takes a big and strong family to run it. That's always been the success of the Sutherlands.'

Maysa looked shocked and took a moment to compose herself.

'I'm sorry, please keep going.'

'Well, as I've told you, the Patterson's son, Jeffrey, he's never coming back to their station. He's looked after as well. But it's not for him. He'd go mad with loneliness and boredom. But Milly, she was strong and capable as any bloke, and she was set to take over their property at some stage, and that would have been when she married. When she married me. That is.' Tom stopped again. Maysa was trying to receive and understand all of this information and its implications as quickly as she could.

'Are you ok? I hope I haven't upset you, talking about Milly and marriage. That's a lot to take in. I know. But you should know everything.'

'I'm fine, really. Go on, Tom. So, you were going to live on the Patterson's station with Milly? What about your parent's station?'

'Well, the thing is, the plan was always to join the two properties together. Our station was originally about six different properties. A few small ones and a few very big ones. One of the properties, my family's property, was over three hundred thousand acres. My parents, grandparents and great grandparents all acquired other properties along the way making Sutherland Downs the big station it is today. It became obvious there wasn't a boy at the Patterson's to take over. That didn't make any difference. Milly was strong, and a better stockman than most blokes out here anyway. Milly and I had always seemed destined to be together from a young age, it just made sense to join the properties together. Milly and I would eventually take over the lot. And you know that Irene and mum are like sisters. They wouldn't have wanted anything else.'

Maysa stepped backward, hands on hips, she paced back and forward in front of Tom slowly.

'So how big would the station have been, Tom? More than a million acres?'

'No, no, don't be silly. A bit less than nine hundred thousand actually. It's a bit hard to imagine, isn't it?'

Tom poured more drinks and Maysa took a swig from her cup as though it was a neat brandy. After a while, Tom began again. 'Thing is, it's not what it would have been, it is still what it will be. The other night at the barbecue, we were talking through the plans again for the first time in a couple of years. Everyone is excited again.'

'But how does it work now?' Maysa asked.

'It'll be a slow process. Maybe take four or five years depending on how good the seasons are and how much cash there is to spare. Len and Irene would stay on of course, for as long as they want, or forever for that matter. My family would buy out their station over time. One of the other reasons I came to work on the Patterson's station was to get to know the property over a few years. It takes a long time to really know a place like that. Years in fact. How it behaves across the seasons, how it behaves across the years. I have a lot to learn from Len. That's why I am staying on. I was always going to have to do that at some stage, it just happened sooner than we thought and for slightly different reasons.'

Tom opened the ute door and threw his and Maysa's enamel mugs onto the floor between the seats.

'We better get going ey? You'll see it all soon enough.' He opened the door for Maysa and shell shocked, she sat down in the ute.

'Oh, and by the way, one more thing.' Tom looked a little sheepish. 'My brother and sister are home this weekend as well. It's a big welcoming party.'

CHAPTER TWENTY-SIX

Tom steered the ute back onto the dusty road and sped up quickly, only to pull up a couple of miles on and turn right, through a stand of old gums. It had obscured the entrance to the property until they were driving through it. Impressive rock walls had been constructed amongst the gums, and a large sign read Sutherland Downs. They were funnelled in between the walls and over a cattle grid. The country was similar to that of the Patterson's station, with paddocks that stretched as far as the eye could see and sheep spread out and grazing. Maysa looked out into the paddocks and allowed herself to imagine for a moment that she would marry Tom and that her children would inherit this property, this land. She was immediately overwhelmed again with the enormity of this prospect. She shook the thoughts from her mind and turned to focus on Tom, hoping the butterflies in her stomach would settle again. He looked different. He looked somehow taller and stronger although he was just sitting in his ute, driving along the track, just as he was an hour ago. As he reached down to change gears, she placed her hand over his wrist. He turned and smiled at her looking happy.

Tom explained they had a thirty-minute drive from the road to the homestead. Maysa was pleased to delay the arrival as long as she could. She gripped Tom's wrist tighter as they travelled along, and he felt her nervousness. He looked sideways at her. They gave each other a reassuring smile, each trying to hide how anxious they actually were.

As they drove on, Tom found himself staring at Maysa, mesmerized as usual. Suddenly, there was a terrible crash, and they were both thrown forward in their seats.

'Shit!' Tom cursed as he jammed his foot down on the breaks and the ute skidded to a halt in the middle of the track.

'What was that, Tom?'

'Dunno, hang on.'

The impact was not enough to do anything other than give them both a fright and remind Tom to concentrate on the road. They'd hit a pig, a sizeable boar. The rest of the group he was with, including a sow and her piglets, hurried away through the coarse tussocks not pausing to look back. Tom looked through the rear window of the ute and through the dust-coating, could just make out the black and pink mottled animal thrashing about on the road. He opened his door, and Maysa went to follow. He stopped her with a hand signal, cautioning her to wait.

256

'Wait here until I see if it's safe. These pigs are as tough as nails and dangerous.'

By the time Tom stepped out of the ute, the pig was lying flat out on its side, and he could see it must have been dead. There was blood pouring from its leg, staining the dust. The leg was badly damaged by the impact. The bone, high in its leg, protruded out through the skin. The muscle was shredded and exposed. The pig was a terrible mess.

Tom leaned into the ute window.

'Thankfully, it's dead. It's a bloody mess too. It's safe out here, but you're better off staying in the ute, to be honest. It's pretty grizzly.'

'Nonsense. If I am going to live out here, I need to be strong like Irene. What do you need to do with it?'. 'Gotta drag the poor bastard off the road a few yards. Just enough that no one hits it in a car or anything. Other than that, nothing. The pigs and wild dogs will clean it up in a day. Not to mention the crows. They'll be on it before we're a hundred yards down the track.'

Tom walked toward the pig tentatively. Maysa walked nervously behind Tom, her hand on his shoulder for reassurance. She smiled to herself, thinking, this was their snake walk. Tom stood next to the pig, looking it over, preparing to drag it off the track with Maysa close behind him. He gave it a gentle kick in the soft fleshy belly. There was no response, and he and Maysa both visibly relaxed.

Maysa looked closely at the animal lying

motionless in the dust in a pool of its own blood. Even dead, the animal looked terrifying. Its snout was covered in dirt and blood, with coarse hairs sprouting out through the muddy mask. Sharp tusks protruded at least three inches out of its mouth, forcing its upper lip into a permanent snarl. They looked sharp enough to skewer you. Its piggy eyes were shut, and Maysa was pleased of that much. The pig's neck was so broad it was hard to tell where its head finished, and its body began, and its hide was a mass of black and pink patches.

'Is it dead?'

'Yes, it is. Ok, I'm going to drag it off the road.' With that, Tom leant down and took hold of the pigs badly broken leg and began to pull it toward the side of the road. There was a terrible shriek, like a woman being choked while she screamed, and the pig burst into life. It frightened the hell out of Tom, but he held on to the leg for grim death. Maysa froze.

'Get back!' Tom shrieked at Maysa, but still, she was frozen to the spot in horror. 'For Christ sake, get back! Get back on the ute.'

Finally, Maysa shook herself free of her fright and began to back up toward the ute. The pig, on three legs, was unbalanced and lurching sideways. It was spinning Tom on the spot as though he were in a hammer throw, with a hefty and over-sized hammer. The pig gathered momentum as it swung around thrashing in the dust. Seeing Maysa through its beady and bloodied eyes, it pulled forward hard and dragged Tom behind it. Despite a desperate effort to hold the old sow away from Maysa, Tom lost his footing and slipped in the dust falling flat on his face. The pig lunged toward Maysa who had turned and was running back toward the ute. It caught up with Maysa just as she was about to leap on the back of the ute. With a wild swing of its head, it sliced her dress like a razor just below the knee. Maysa screamed as she got up on the back of the ute. She turned to see the pig rounding on Tom. Tom was scrambling to his feet as the pig reached him. Given their shape, pigs are not particularly flexible, and they are not good at ducking and weaving. Tom knew this from experience, and he instinctively leapt sideways at the last moment of the charge. The pig twisted all it could, just grazing Tom, before careering past and driving itself face-first into the dirt as its front legs collapsed under it. Tom made the back of the ute in half a dozen huge steps. Maysa sat terrified, her dress dusty and shredded.

'Are you ok?' Tom asked breathlessly, and without thinking, he lifted Maysa's dress to check her leg for any wounds. The horror of the attack and the adrenaline pumping around his body only heightened his awareness of her beauty. He was taken aback by her long slender legs, always covered, but the skin was a rich, smooth olive in colour.

'What about you?' Her voice was shaky and laced with concern.

He looked down at his leg.

'Bugger it.' he cursed again.

'What? What is it?' Maysa moved to see what Tom was looking at. His pants, like Maysa's dress, were sliced, as though with a razor-sharp knife, and were stained with blood. Tom looked back at the pig that had managed to drag itself off the track about thirty yards away and was finally spent. Although he wasn't in a hurry to check, he was sure it had made its last stand, and the lifeblood was finally drained from its body.

'I'll have to get this cleaned up quickly. They're bloody filthy these pigs. It'll infect in no time if I don't. Hopefully, it's just a scratch.'

Tom and Maysa climbed down from the ute, each keeping an eye on the pig in the distance to make sure it didn't stir. Tom bent down to try and pull his trouser leg up to inspect the damage, but it was too difficult to pull it up over his injured calf which was now stinging. He started undoing his belt and then the zip to his trousers.

'What are you doing?' Maysa looked as horrified as she had when the pig first charged.

'I've gotta drop these, sorry, and get a look at the damage. I promise I've got my undies on.' Maysa put her hand to her forehead, to cover her eyes, rubbing her forehead as though she was trying to soothe a headache.

'Tom, what will everyone think? What would they think if they drove along now? We are both covered in dust. My beautiful dress is torn to shreds, and your pants around your ankles.' Tom was listening as he loosened his trousers.

He looked at Maysa, and he started to laugh. He laughed hard and loud as all the tension of the pig attack, the family meeting and the last couple of years all caught up with him in one big rush. He laughed so hard tears streamed down his face. He stood up to look at Maysa who was looking at him in amazement. She was starting to laugh as well. Tom was laughing so hard, he let go of his trousers to wipe the tears from his eyes, and they dropped to the ground. He was left facing Maysa with his pants around his ankles. Maysa erupted into peels of laughter. As she laughed, her emotions caught up with her at last. Tom looked at her, and it slowly dawned on him through the hilarity that she was now crying and he was shocked. He shuffled forward and took her in his arms.

'Hey, whatever's wrong? I thought you were laughing. It was so funny.'

'I was, I am just overwhelmed by all of this. And I wanted so desperately to make a good impression, and now I look like a wreck and what will your parents, and your brother and sister think of me?'

'Listen, I don't care what anyone thinks.' Tom held Maysa's face gently in his hands. He kissed her salty tear-drenched lips.

'My mum and dad have already met you. They know how wonderful you are. Everyone will understand when they hear about our adventure, and they'll just be pleased we're both safe, that's all. Besides, my brother and sister are coming in after us, so they probably won't be here yet anyway, and you'll have time to clean up.' Tom kissed Maysa again. They were a peculiar sight, standing in the hot sun on a dusty track, Maysa's dress shredded with a strip dragging in the dust, Tom's pants around his ankles, and tears all round.

'If this is as bad as it gets, then life will be ok'. He hugged her tight.

They turned their attention to Tom's leg. He had a bad scratch, not quite a cut, just below the calf muscle and it bled much more than it really should have. Suddenly they both became aware of the sound of an engine and startled, they turned to see another vehicle closing in on them quickly.

'Christ, quick!' Tom reefed his trousers up in one quick movement. Maysa instinctively stood between him and the approaching vehicle whilst he buckled and buttoned himself up.

'Who is it? Do you think they saw you had your pants down? Oh, I hope not.'

'I think you're going to meet my brother and sister a bit sooner than we thought.'

The car pulled up, and a younger version of Tom, dressed in an army uniform stepped out of the vehicle. Tom recovered his demeanour quickly.

'Ah, Private Sutherland, I presume?' Tom stepped forward, still buckling his belt and took his brother's hand, enthusiastically. Tom's sister, Sarah, stepped out of the passenger side of the car and smiled broadly at Tom and then at Maysa. Alistair stepped forward and addressed Maysa.

'Hi, I'm Alistair. I am the one with the brains and style.' He looked sideways at his dishevelled older brother. 'You must be Maysa. I'm really pleased to meet you. And Tom, always good to see you. And with your trousers up too.'

'And I'm Sarah. I'm really excited to meet you, Maysa.' Tom's sister smiled enthusiastically, almost laughing with excitement.

Alistair was dressed in Jungle Greens and had just returned from Cadet camp with the school. Sarah was dressed in casual slacks and a T-shirt and was the perfect blend of both her parents. There was no mistaking she was Tom's sister. Both were strong and confident individuals, and the three of them were visibly pleased to see each other.

'So, can I explain why my pants were around my ankles, please?'

'Tom, . . . no!' Sarah chimed in. 'Remember, I am only sixteen,' and she laughed.

Tom turned to Maysa.

'See, what'd I tell you? I said she was cheeky.' Maysa smiled, unsure how to take all of this. But as usual, she hadn't had to open her mouth and had little hope of competing anyway. Tom pointed at the pig, lying dead thirty yards away.

'See that? There's your reason for my pants around my ankles.'

'Good God, Tom. This is too much, man.' Alistair replied in a very uppity accent. Maysa smiled away, blissfully unaware of the innuendo in the exchange.

'Ok, ok you two. That's enough. Please, you've only just met Maysa. Can we be bloody serious for just a minute?' Tom relayed the incident with the pig in detail. He and Alistair walked back to look at the pig which was now stiff as a board. Alistair kicked it regardless of Tom's caution. Like a tyre on a car for sale, every dead animal needed kicking when you were a young man. They strolled back and inspected the little bit of damage to the front fender of the ute. Sarah and Maysa went through Maysa's version of the story and mourned the condition of her pretty dress and resolved to mend it together as soon as it was washed and ironed. After five minutes, the pairs split up. Tom and Alistair in the front vehicle and Sarah driving Maysa in the second vehicle.

It seemed like an eternity since Maysa had spent any time with a girl close to her own age and she was relishing the time. It was also an opportunity to ask lots of questions about Tom.

The short trip to the homestead was quick and very relaxing, with Maysa and Sarah forming an instant rapport. With a common interest in Tom, there was a lot to discuss, and it was clear they were going to be the best of friends. Maysa was engrossed in easy conversation with Sarah when Sarah stopped her mid-sentence, 'Look Maysa, here is the homestead. Here's home.' It was hardly a homestead.

For half a mile, they had been driving along a laneway flanked by imposing conifers that tried in vain to replicate an English estate in this harsh Australian environment. Now they had come out into an open area which revealed an old two-story brick homestead. It was perfectly situated amongst a well-manicured but rambling garden of English shrubs, dominated by roses in a variety of colours. A very large pond, almost a small lake, out to the left of the building was shaded by trees, and its dark colour indicated its depth. It doubled as a garden feature and the source of water for the garden. It also supported the rainwater reserves in drought times.

The two vehicles came to rest on the circular driveway near the front garden gate, and the young group all got out of the two cars with Tom quickly moving to Maysa's side. An old gentleman, in working clothes, was hunched over a garden bed, feeding rose cuttings into a wheelbarrow. He stopped, stood up, stretched out his bent back and smiled broadly.

'G'day you lot, nice to have you home.'

'Who's that?' Maysa asked Tom quietly.

'It's Douglas, the gardener.'

'G'day Dougie. How are you?' Tom yelled out enthusiastically as he strode over to shake the old man's bony and arthritic hand.

'You have a gardener?' Maysa asked Sarah in a shocked tone. Sarah laid a friendly hand on Maysa's shoulder.

'Of course. We have servants galore.' Sarah announced matter-of-factly, pausing for a moment to enjoy Maysa's face. 'I'm just kidding.' She laughed at Maysa.

'Old Doug was a jackaroo for my grandfather. He retired to work in our garden which he always loved. He's like part of the family now. Mum and Dad care for him. We do have a lady who cooks for us and does some cleaning. It just depends on what needs to be done. And we also have one of the very junior jackaroos come in and help in the garden with the heavier work for Doug, and he chops wood and that sort of stuff. So that's it, I guess. Roughly three, otherwise we do it all ourselves.'

The homestead stood on three acres of a fenced-off garden within a ten acre paddock. The garden rambled comfortably and casually between large trees and expanses of lawn that seemed to flourish even in this harsh environment. The homestead rose majestically from within the shrubbery. It had red brick walls with white pointed lintels over the windows and doors, and white balustrades on the expansive verandas that provided shelter from the scorching sun. A full-length verandah, closed in by flywire wrapped around the lower story. The second story provided views of the garden and the property in every direction through a myriad of windows. This imposing structure was softened by English trees heavy in leaf.

Tom came back quickly to Maysa and retrieved the bags from the ute, throwing his across his shoulder and carrying hers by the handle.

'So Maysa, you staying for a month?' Alistair asked jokingly, eying the large suitcase Tom carried for her.

'Irene packed it for her. What d'yer reckon?' Tom laughed as well, and Maysa felt embarrassed and self-conscious.

Tom strode forward and opened an old wrought iron gate that led from the drive into the main garden. A white pebble path flanked by English box hedge guided the way to the front entrance of the homestead. Halfway along the path, it encircled a statue, a concrete female figure standing amongst a lily pond with orange fish that Maysa saw darting from lily to lily as they passed.

As the group strode along the path, Tom's parents appeared on the verandah at the front steps, smiling, waving and calling welcome. Sarah led the party, followed by Alistair, then Tom, and Maysa walking shyly behind Tom, entirely overwhelmed. Tom's mother embraced Sarah, and they all stood as if in a queue waiting their turn. She passed Sarah onto Tom's father then continued along the line. When finally she came to Maysa, she embraced her with all the love and enthusiasm she had done with Sarah. She took Maysa, holding an arm in each hand.

'It's just lovely to see you, dear. You're very welcome in our home. How was the drive?'

With that, Elise held Maysa back to look at her and caught sight of her dress. Both women were immediately embarrassed, and Elise looked away as though she hadn't noticed the torn shred hanging from Maysa's hem. Maysa flushed red with embarrassment. Sarah, watching everything was immediately at Maysa's side.

'God Mum, Dad, you should hear what happened to Tom and Maysa.' Sarah spoke rapidly, adding excitement to the story with wild gesticulations.

'There was a pig, and Tom ran it over and got out to kick it, and it chased him, and ripped Maysa's dress and tore his leg and then it ran off and died, so Tom took his pants down and then we came along.' Sarah took a moment to catch her breath then burst out laughing and wrapped Maysa in an affectionate hug.

'My goodness, perhaps you'll let Tom and Maysa tell the story, Sarah. I hope you're ok Maysa, there's never a dull moment around here is there?' Elise restored a little order to the moment.

Tom's dad took a bag from Tom and lent toward Tom and spoke in confidence, close to his ear.

'Most of that seemed ok, Boy, but you might need to explain why you dropped your trousers. If I dropped my trousers every time something got a bit tense around here, the police'd lock me up.' They laughed and walked off into the house. Tom checked over his shoulder, but as he suspected, when it came to Maysa, he was now rendered obsolete. Maysa was completely swallowed into the embraces and chatter of his mother and sister.

Tom and his brother strode through the open front door, almost oblivious to Maysa and the ladies behind them laughing, talking and kidding each other along. Elise led Maysa up the stairs and across the timber verandah to a large timber door with stain-glassed window panels and an ornate polished brass knob. She took her through into the darker interior of the front entrance hall. Tom was there, waiting for Maysa and smiling as she came in. Like the Patterson's homestead, the hall was decorated with photographs of generations of the Sutherland family. The hall was eight feet wide, and the ceilings were twelve feet high with pressed tin ceilings. Very large and ornate mahogany buffets, decorated with precious china and silver, flanked the hallway. And there, among the photos, Maysa spied Tom as a child. She stopped to look, and Elise and Sarah joined her.

'Ah, what a beautiful little boy he was, Maysa.' Elise cooed.

'Yes, shame he grew up to be so ugly.' Alistair contributed from a distance.

'He is so handsome.' Maysa murmured to herself louder than she expected, staring at the photo. Elise and Sarah smiled at each other and then looked back at Maysa affectionately.

CHAPTER TWENTY-SEVEN

The afternoon passed by happily. Tom showed Maysa through the garden, walking around the picturesque pond and surrounds and showing points of interest in the distance. Maysa's level of excitement and anticipation, only kept in check by her anxiety, was growing steadily. Her fascination with Tom and his family was all-consuming.

The evening came, and Tom's aunts and uncles arrived as expected. There was Ed's brother Peter, and his wife Angela, and Ed's sister Sarah, after whom Tom's sister was named, and her husband, Rob. Both couples lived on the property in substantial homesteads and were paid as employees but took a share of profit from the Station. They also ran their own significant herds of cattle and flocks of sheep to supplement their income, ensuring they lived in the style to which they had been accustomed as part of the Sutherland family. This was how the family had existed for generations as it expanded and prospered.

Tom stood in the garden talking with Doug and Rob, discussing the shearing season and all the farming news concerning the Patterson's property. All of the gentlemen were privy to the plans and had been for some time. They each shared the family entrepreneurial outlook and were keen to see this transaction take place sooner rather than later. It would be the most significant development of their generation. They all stood to prosper from this transaction, so they were keen to meet this Maysa. To meet the woman who had stolen their nephew's heart so quickly and so dramatically. She was partly responsible for the rebirth of the plans that had been sadly shelved for so long.

The men, standing near the fire, were talking and drinking animatedly when Maysa finally appeared, accompanied by Tom's sister, Sarah. As usual, the men, those who hadn't yet met Maysa, were visibly taken aback by her beauty. Tom sensing the reaction, proudly stepped forward and grasped Maysa's hand and introduced her enthusiastically to his uncles, before pouring her a glass of wine. Two tables had been set in the garden, with table cloths, silver cutlery, good china and crystal glasses. Roast pork and vegetables were served with apple sauce and followed by a dessert of chocolate pudding. There was much discussion throughout the meal, and lots of embarrassing stories told, particularly about Tom. Not the least was a recount of the days encounter with the pig which they all hoped wasn't their present meal. Everyone had had plenty to drink, driven along by a series of toasts to numerous achievements, some serious and some just another excuse to empty a glass.

When the meal was over, Tom offered Maysa a stroll about the lake and garden in the moonlight. It was a beautiful cool evening, not a breath of breeze to chill them. The stars shone brightly above, and a three-quarter moonlit the garden and sent light leaping from the lake, shimmering and dancing. Tom looked at Maysa in the moonlight. He couldn't imagine anything more beautiful. For the first time in a long time, his thoughts were filled with the future, with dreams and ideas. He walked Maysa around the edge of the lake and pointed to the ripples on the surface made by fish and insects. Music from an old gramophone carried across the lake along with voices of the family, talking and laughing. Insects hummed quietly, as if deliberately in concert with the music, supported by the deep base of bullfrogs amongst the reeds at the edge of the lake.

Finding a secluded spot, out of sight of the rest of the party, Tom stopped, and holding Maysa's hand, they looked back across the lake at the family.

'Well, that's my family. What do you think?'

'I think they are completely wonderful, that's what I think.'

With that, Tom stepped in behind Maysa and putting his arms around her waist, pulled her close. She laid back against him and leant her head back to rest against his chest. They continued to look out across the lake together. He leant down and kissed her neck. She snaked an arm around his neck and twirled the hair on the back of his head with her fingers as he kissed her.

'I love you,' he whispered as he kissed her, as much to himself as to her.

'I love you, too,' she whispered in return as she craned her head back further, opening up more of her neck to his kisses. The music, chatting and laughter seemed only to increase in volume the more intense their feelings became. Tom ran his hands from her stomach slowly up over her ribs, which were pushed out and accentuated with the arching of her back. He cupped her breasts in his hands. Maysa turned her face to kiss Tom, and she took the full force of his passion on her lips. Her mouth tasted of wine and dessert as his tongue explored. She moaned quietly at the sensation. He broke the kiss momentarily to tell her in a hoarse voice, 'I want you and need you now. God, I need you.'

She grabbed a handful of his hair roughly and pulled his face back to hers and answered his words with her kiss.

'You have me. I am yours.' The world beyond them disappeared.

CHAPTER TWENTY-EIGHT

Paddy stood in his bedroom, leaning on the window sill, drawing on a cigarette. His stomach ached around about the solar plexus, and he had a dull thumping headache. He stared out into the paddocks and across at the Patterson homestead, watching the lights through the living room window. He thought about his dreams, to be the owner of this property, not just to be welcome at the homestead on rare and only official occasions. He would pick and choose who came through that front door, and the back door for that matter. Perhaps he would take a wife. Someone to cook and clean for him and whatever else he needed, whenever he felt the urge. And then he thought of his mother and pictured her lying in the corner of the kitchen, bruised and battered, with tears streaming down her face. He felt the helplessness of when his father shoved him aside, almost knocking him over, walking drunkenly from the kitchen and leaving his mother lying there. And then he felt the betrayal of his uncle, his mother's brother. He cared nothing for her. And he never treated him like anything more than

274

a paid worker and looked down upon him. He spat out the window and upended a long bottle of beer. He held the bottle up toward the ceiling and drained it to the last bit of froth. A fuzzy wave engulfed his head, and for a moment, the headache subsided. He threw the bottle out the window, and it smashed on a rock.

'Shit.' Mumbling, he walked away from the window to get another bottle from the refrigerator. He leaned on the refrigerator door staring inside. There was beer, half a loaf of bread and a leg of lamb that looked like a dog had gnawed at it. He took another bottle of beer from the fridge and the leg of lamb and pushed the door shut with his foot. He threw the lamb down on the table and opened the beer and took a long swig. Holding the meat in one hand and the beer bottle in the other, he continued eating and drinking. He decided to walk back to his room for another smoke and back to his perch at the window. His bitter mood wasn't easing. The front door had been left slightly ajar, and after having smelt the meat, one of the dogs ventured into the cottage. It followed on Paddy's heels. In its eagerness, it got in front of him, looking up at the lamb, wagging its tail. He kicked it hard in the chest.

'Fuck off you mangy bastard, or I'll shoot you.' The dog shrieked in pain and then whimpered off, escaping outside.

As he passed by Tom's room, Paddy hesitated

and tried hard to build some rational thoughts through the haze of anger and alcohol.

'You can fuck off too, Spooney.' With that, Paddy swung the lamb bone into Tom's door, leaving a smear of fat on the timber. The door slowly opened, squeaking on its aging hinges and Paddy hesitated, looking through the door. He walked tentatively inside the room.

The floorboards creaked, and he stood still for a moment as though waiting to see if someone had heard. Realising that was impossible and that Tom was miles away, he relaxed and looked about the room. He walked over to the bedside table and opened the one drawer. He rifled through the contents carelessly. There were a few coins, a couple of notebooks with jottings about stock, handkerchiefs, pencils, nothing of any interest. Paddy sat down on the bed, staring at the wall. There was something big going on, and he needed to know what and at the same time, he needed to know how to derail it. He took another long swig from the beer bottle and shuffled his feet in agitation. His heel caught something under the bed. He placed the beer bottle down on the bedside table then got down on his hands and knees and peered under the bed.

There was an old khaki kit bag, a pair of old riding boots, a pair of dirty socks and a small metal box. He dragged the box out from under the bed. It had a lock but wasn't locked. He sat back on the bed, took another long swig from the beer bottle, wiped his mouth with his shirt sleeve and opened the box. It was full of letters and documents. He couldn't believe his luck.

'Bloody idiot.' He began reading through the documents. There were bills, legal documents, and a couple of documents relating to the trouble Tom had had with the police before he moved onto the property with Len and Irene. There was a bundle of envelopes held together with an elastic band. These were addressed to Tom, and when Paddy turned them over, he found they were all from Milly. Paddy sighed, he felt a mixture of emotions including regret, anger and arousal. He opened one of the letters excitedly, like a child ripping open a chocolate bar, and began reading. It was a recount of all the things happening on the farm, day to day activities, the weather, visitors, stock movements and finally a declaration of love forever.

'Boring shit.' Paddy mumbled again and took another drink. He placed the letter back in its envelope, disappointed, although he wasn't really sure what he was looking for. He took a moment to sit and think. He could still clearly hear her pleading, the screams, the blood, the thud of rock on flesh and then the stony silence. He thought about her underwear that he'd taken and hidden carefully in his room for all this time. His arousal began to consume his thoughts. Then he thought of the girl just a couple of weeks ago. She wasn't as good looking as Milly, not by a mile, but she served her purpose. And then there was Dingo, on his knees, still battered and bruised from his run-in with Tom, pleading to him. He'd even started to cry which disgusted Paddy. He'd given him his last supper, good food, beer and one of the local girls, and now his time was up. The rock had made a bloody mess of Dingo's face, and Paddy had gotten blood all over his shirt and pants. It wasn't quite enough though, so he'd helped it along by wrapping his arms around Dingo's bloodied body as he'd thrown it into the water. Just the shallows though and near a group of trees where he knew it would resurface and be found within days. Later he'd felt pleased with himself as he put the bloodied clothing into a bag, washed in the river and changed before opening a bottle of beer and driving back out to the station.

One last shuffle of papers in the box returned the result he had hoped for. He found a large piece of paper, map size. It was a map of the area with both the Patterson's and the Sutherland's properties marked on it. All of the various homesteads were marked and the occupants listed. Someone had taken a red pencil and had marked an outline of the properties right around both, showing them as one huge property. In the corner, they had written the size in acres of each property with a plus sign. They then added them together, writing, *Combined Land Holding – 880,000 acres.* Where the Sutherland homestead was marked, the words *Tom and Milly* were written, suggesting they would live there. But also, on the Patterson's homestead, they had been written again, *Tom and Milly ??*, with a couple of question marks following.

Paddy stared in disbelief. They were going to combine the two properties and that Spooney and his dead bitch girlfriend were going get the lot. Of course, there was no sign of his name anywhere on this document. Well, he thought, I fixed her. But now this bloody new one.

Paddy folded the map and replaced it in the box, put the box on the floor and kicked it under the bed. He stood up, grabbed his beer, sculled what was left and walked into his bedroom. He opened the door to his wardrobe, pushed the clothing aside and dragged a box out onto the floor.

'Least I've got the brains to lock mine,' he mumbled to himself as he fumbled with the key and the lock, in his drunken stupor. He opened the lid and pulled a canvas bag from the box and put it on the floor beside him. He opened the bag and looked inside at the bloodied shirt. He'd stolen this shirt from Tom's washing a few weeks earlier as part of his plan. Tom always wore these shirts into town, he had several. For that matter, so did half the men in the district. He had decided to ditch the pants as it was more of a risk, making sure they could not be tied back to him. He took the canvas bag into Tom's room, knelt down beside the bed and dragged out the kit bag and pushed the canvas bag deep into it and then placed it back under the bed.

'That'll do that. Good luck, Spooney. Yer gonna

279

need it now.' He smiled to himself and went back to his room.

Back with the box in his own room, he pulled out two more pieces of clothing. One had belonged to Milly and one to the girl from Saturday night. His heart began racing as he held the sordid souvenirs, one in each hand.

CHAPTER TWENTY-NINE

Shortly after lunch on Sunday, Tom and Maysa bid their farewells to the family at the Sutherland property. They were both exhausted from what had been an emotionally tiring, but very positive weekend. They drove for some time in silence until eventually, Tom asked Maysa what she was thinking about. She told him she'd had a wonderful weekend and she'd already fallen in love with his family, particularly his sister, Sarah who she missed already. Tom smiled to himself as he navigated the ute along the dusty, rutted road, daydreaming. He hardly noticed a pair of emus running alongside the ute. They persisted with the race until they realised their efforts to outrun the vehicle were in vain, and they ducked away into the scrub. 'So, what are you thinking about Tom? What's that grin on your face?'

'Last night, actually.' Tom thought of Maysa and the moment the moonlight reflected off the pond and onto her olive skin.

'Hey, watch where you're going.' Maysa barked at Tom, as the ute veered to the side of the road and hit a shallow gutter.

'Sorry, just a little bit distracted by the memory of a beautiful woman.'

'Ok, ok, you're forgiven this once. But I won't be very beautiful if you crash this car every time you take me out in it. Now concentrate!'

'Who said I was thinking of you?'

Maysa responded by punching Tom playfully on the arm.

'How are you feeling about everything you heard over the weekend?'

'I'm still overwhelmed Tom, even more now. We've only known each other for a very short time. There is no doubt in my mind of how much I love you. I think about you, and us, all day long. But this is a huge thing. Everyone is talking as though we will be married and take over the whole property and look after the whole family. I am only just starting to learn about life on the farm, and about you.' The words were pouring from Maysa, and she was clearly stressed. 'What are you thinking?' she asked.

Tom pulled the ute over to the edge of the road and turned to face Maysa.

'I've never been surer of anything in my whole life.' He lent across and gathered Maysa in his arms and kissed her passionately. Then he cupped her face in his hands.

'You will be amazing. I know what it takes and so does everyone else here and we all think you'll be amazing. In fact, you are amazing. Oh and also, I can't stop thinking about you all day, every day either.' Tom gave a cheeky smile, and Maysa gave him another slap on the arm.

'I'll throw a bucket of cold water on you in a moment.'

'They're all just a little over-excited, that's all. They can finally see the future for the property and for the family, and those two things are everything, the whole world to, my family. Don't worry, in the end, we are still in the country, and things move along slow and steady out here. This is all going to take some time. A long time. There will be plenty of time and space for us to both to get used to this and get comfortable. For now, though, we just need to get back. Len wants to plan out this week. There is a lot of stock to move around. We've got some long days ahead of us. I hope you're up to it.'

'I am, of course, but I am getting saddle sore just thinking about it.'

'Well, I could give your backside a rub if it would make you feel better. It'd certainly make me feel good.'

Maysa slapped Tom's arm again as he pulled the ute back on to the road.

'Things move slow out here Tom, and so do I, so you need to try and relax.' They both laughed, although Tom not so genuinely.

CHAPTER THIRTY

Len and Irene heard the dogs barking first, then the ute pull up outside the back gate. They stole a knowing glance at each other.

'Let's get them settled in first and then we can fill them in on everything including tomorrow morning.' Irene nodded her agreement with Len as they walked out into the backyard and down the path to the gate. They greeted Tom and Maysa as they were getting out of the ute.

'Hello, you two.' Irene smiled and waved. Maysa smiled back, happy to see Irene.

'Hello, Irene. It's good to see you and to be home.' The home reference wasn't lost on Irene as she strode forward and took Maysa in her arms and hugged her. Of course, she already knew the weekend had been a huge success after a long telephone call with Elise.

Tom unloaded Maysa's suitcase, and Len took it from him.

'Settle yourself in Tom, then come up for some arvo tea, mate. We have a few things to talk about.

See you shortly.' Len waved Tom off and took Maysa's things inside.

Tom unloaded his belongings at the stockman's cottage. Looking about, he was frustrated by the mess, empty beer bottles in the sink, plates and cutlery strewn across the table. Regardless, he was relieved that Paddy wasn't home and that the glow of the weekend that he was still basking in wouldn't be abruptly stifled out by seeing Paddy.

He returned to the homestead a short while later to discuss the plans for the next week of mustering and dipping. They all gathered in the kitchen and Len gestured for them to sit down.

'You look a bit serious, Len. It's just dipping. I am sure we can handle it. What's the plan?'

Len looked at Tom, and there was an awkward pause, while he took a long sip of his tea.

'You better prepare yourselves.' Len addressed Tom and Maysa, who were sitting close together. 'There's been some big trouble in town in the last couple of days.' Len took another sip on his tea as he collected his thoughts. 'A girl was assaulted. Sexually assaulted.'

Maysa was shocked. She visibly stiffened, and Tom reached for her hand.

'Apparently, it was two blokes that did it.'

Tom looked at Maysa again and knew she'd be thinking of Darkie and Dingo. He could feel that barely controlled rage, bubbling in the pit of his stomach, as he thought of Dingo, the fight, of Maysa's bruised face, and of Darkie's words, *he's got something over me.*

Reading their minds, Len began again quickly. They've got one of them. It was Dingo. He turned up dead in the river.' He gave Tom and Maysa a moment to comprehend the news and deal with their shock. 'The victim . . . the girl . . . she identified him.'

Maysa covered her face to hide her tears. Tom could see she was utterly overwhelmed. There was never joy or pleasure in vengeance. There'd be some relief he was gone, that the threat was gone, the fear, and he felt that relief for Maysa.

'What about Darkie?'

'Darkie's long gone, Tom. He's up north in another team. It wasn't him.'

'So who then? Who was it?'

'They don't know yet. That's the problem. Here's the thing, they're looking for a well-dressed, well to do type. The poor girl never got a look at his face. Just said he was a well-dressed farmer type. Jackeroo or whatever. Moleskins, a good shirt, and so on.'

Len gave everyone time to think about this and take in the news that had been an enormous shock.

'Tom, Sargent Penfold, will be out here tomorrow to talk to you in the morning.'

'Me? Why?' Tom was visibly stunned. 'What's he want to talk to me about?'

'Well, before I tell you this, I need you to just

stay calm.' Maysa grasped Tom's arm. 'You promise, mate?'

'Yeah, of course.' Tom was working hard to control his agitation.

'Penfold was out here yesterday, and he was just asking if we knew anything or had heard anything, given Dingo had been working out here recently. He'd heard just a little about the incident with Maysa, not much. Seemed to know there had been some trouble and Dingo had been kicked off the contract. Obviously, he'd been noticed in town, drinking and carrying on for a bit.'

'Ok, but what's that got to do with me?'

'Well, now this is where you need to stay calm. Bloody Paddy spilt the beans about the blue you and Dingo had. He told him you'd given Dingo a good hiding and then told him you and Maysa were an item. Of course, he told Penfold you'd never do that, never . . .' Len hesitated. 'Never kill a bloke . . . but the damage was done by then.'

'Jesus bloody Christ.' Tom banged his fist on the table. Teacups rattled as both the women jumped. 'Never kill a bloody bloke! Well, there is always a first time, and Paddy might be him.'

'Listen mate, you need to get yourself under control. I think you better get your kit and bunk down here with us tonight, away from Paddy. Penfold'll be here tomorrow, and the last thing we need is for you to have belted Paddy stupid in a rage while we're trying to claim you're innocent.'

'But I am innocent.'

'We know that mate, and Penfold knows that too. But he has a job to do. He's locked you up a few times. You've got some history, and unfortunately, it's not that long ago. Just be sensible, and this will all be sorted in no time.'

Soon after, Len sent Tom to pick up whatever he needed to stay a night or two at the homestead. Len had deliberately sent a reluctant and bitter Paddy out earlier to move a couple of mobs around in preparation for the next day's work, mostly to keep him away from Tom.

Tom gathered together some work clothes, some toiletries and his boots. He looked around for his kit bag, which he knew was stashed under his bed. He knelt down to retrieve it and seeing it was half full decided to grab and empty old Gladstone bag instead. Moments later, he left the bag on the verandah while he fed his dogs who were tied up to their kennels. As he turned to walk back toward the verandah, he saw Paddy standing there, looking at his bag.

'You going somewhere?'

Tom had to breathe deep to control his temper and to steady his voice.

'Yeah, up to the homestead . . . to stay. I got a promotion, and we've got lots to talk about.'

As always, Paddy's face didn't betray his emotions, but as usual, Tom was sure he saw something in Paddy's eyes. Was it shock, anger or confusion? He couldn't tell. But he decided to put the boot in just a little more as he picked up his bag and wandered off.

'By the way. I heard you sorted things out for me with Penfold. Thanks for that.' They locked eyes as Tom stopped walking. 'You can be sure I won't forget it, mate.'

CHAPTER THIRTY-ONE

It was mid-morning, and dipping was underway at the yards when Sargent Penfold arrived. Everyone stopped for just a moment as his Land Rover pulled up, bringing with it the usual cloud of dust. Then work continued on, shouting, dogs barking, swearing, cursing and dust, always more dust.

'Morning everyone.' Penfold addressed the group as he climbed into the yards. He joined in, pushing the last of a mob through a gate, then leaning on a rail watching as they were pushed into the plunge dip.

'Morning, Barry.' Len shook Penfold's hand. 'Here to see Tom? I have filled him in as best as I could. No luck finding the other culprit yet?' Len called Tom over.

'No, nothing Len. This is just a formality. It wouldn't look good if I didn't tick this off. You know how it is.'

'Morning Sargent.' Tom looked uncomfortable and regretted knowing Penfold as well as he did. 'This is Maysa.'

'G'day, Tom. Hello Maysa. You can call me Barry.'

They exchanged a few pleasantries, weather, condition of the sheep, some local gossip. Finally, Penfold suggested he and Tom should head over to the stockman's cottage where they could sit down for a cuppa and have a bit of a chat. As an afterthought, he asked Maysa to join them so he could learn a bit more about her attack. Looking both disappointed with being excluded but also relieved, Paddy took his orders from Len and started pushing the mob towards the river. Len and Irene headed back to the homestead for an early lunch.

Back at the house, Penfold asked Len to take Maysa with him at first, while he talked to Tom. They sat at the kitchen table in the stockman's quarters, and the policeman told Tom all he knew.

'So that's it, Tom. We don't have a second suspect. And we can't be sure that his accomplice actually knocked him off anyway.'

'You don't actually think I would drive into town and kill him, do you? I know I've done some dumb things in the past and I know I've got a temper. But things are good now. I've settled down. I am feeling good for the first time in a long time. And then there's Maysa. That's not me, Barry. You know it's not.'

'I know Tom, I know. And if you hadn't flogged the shit out of Dingo recently, I wouldn't be sitting here now. I've no doubt he deserved it, but that's my job, not yours mate.'

'Well, I haven't been into town for a few weeks.

We've been too busy out here. Long days, early nights and mornings.'

'That's true. So Paddy could vouch for you being here each night a couple of weeks ago, at the time of the murder . . . I guess?' They looked at each other with a shared understanding. Paddy wasn't going to be any help to Tom. 'Can I take a look around Tom? Sorry mate, bloody embarrassing for me I can tell you. But I wouldn't be doing my job if I didn't.'

Tom showed Penfold through the cottage and finally to his bedroom.

'I know what sort of shirt our man was wearing. The girl described it well. Only about three hundred blokes in town with the same shirt, unfortunately. Regardless, I need to have a quick look at your clothes and through your drawers.'

'No problems, sorry it's a bit of a mess. Bachelor . . . you know how it is.'

'I do, I remember it well. Hopefully, things will change for you soon.'

Penfold opened the cupboard and flipped through the hanging clothes. He opened drawers and politely looked at the contents, moving things with a pencil and not touching anything. 'What's under the bed?'

'Just a box with some personal papers, letters and the like, and my kit bag. You want to see them?'

'Not really, but ok, just to be thorough.'

Tom opened the box with Milly's letters and

the maps of the properties. It was a little messier than he remembered. One letter was roughly stuffed into an envelope. He showed the contents of the box to Penfold, who raised an eyebrow when he saw the map and the collection of properties all outlined in red. Then Tom upended the kit bag on his bed. The last item to fall out was a blood-stained and torn shirt matching the one the girl had described and an embroidered woman's handkerchief. Both men stood motionless, staring at the shirt.

'That's not mine.' Tom spoke quietly. He was in shock.

'What's going on?' The silence was broken by Irene standing side by side with Maysa in the doorway holding a tray of scones.

'Nothing Irene. You better take the girl back up to the house. I'll speak to you shortly. Get Len for me please.' Penfold's tone was sharp and business-like.

It was thirty minutes later when Penfold emerged from the stockman's quarters with Tom in handcuffs. Len had pleaded, but Penfold insisted. 'If he loses his cool when we're on the road, we both know what he's like, We'll both end up dead.' Irene stood, arm around Maysa's shoulders in the homestead garden, watching through tears as Tom drove off with Penfold. Paddy had made it back to the machine shed at the homestead by this stage, after pushing the sheep and the dogs back to the river as hard as he possibly could.

He met Tom's eye as the Land Rover rattled past the shed. His face subtly shifted from feigned concern to a slight smile. Just enough for Tom to acknowledge it. Penfold, eyes forward, saw nothing.

CHAPTER THIRTY-TWO

'The best thing for it is hard work. It will take your mind of everything, even just for a couple of hours. I am sure Tom will be home soon. We just have to have faith.' Irene placed a cup of tea in front of Maysa, next to her uneaten breakfast.

After breakfast, they all headed to the yards. Paddy had mustered another mob of sheep, and they were ready to start dipping. They had a good few hours of work ahead of them and not having Tom made it a slower process. Irene was right, the work was a distraction for Maysa, and for the most part, she was able to block out her sadness and fear. Not for a moment did she believe Tom had done anything wrong, but she knew what it looked like and she had no answer for the shirt. It was compelling evidence. She hadn't had a chance to talk to Tom but for five minutes on the phone the evening before. There call had been cut off when Tom had been ushered back to his cell.

Once the dipping was complete for the morning,

everyone settled down for a quiet lunch and a break before the afternoons mustering began again.

'This afternoon I want you to go out and get the mob from the south-west paddock on Sutherland's boundary.' Len addressed Paddy. You need to bring them along the river, so they've got some shade and water. And, don't push 'em too hard, it's bloody hot. Just spell 'em along the way a bit, and they'll come in ok. I don't want 'em knocked up from the heat.' Paddy nodded and went on with his lunch. He seemed entirely unaffected by the turmoil that surrounded them. In fact, he was having difficulty hiding his buoyant mood.

'So that leaves us with two mobs to get back into their paddocks tonight. We are a bit caught out without Tom. Maysa, are you up to a ride? It will be a good couple of hours at least, but an easy ride.'

'By myself?'

'Well, not entirely. You'll have Banjo. You can take Billy and Barney with you as well. They seem to stick to you like glue when Tom's not around.'

'I guess so.' Maysa made little attempt to hide her uncertainty. Her usual bravado and confidence had taken a beating, and it was obvious to everyone.

'You sure that's a good idea?' Irene was concerned.

'She'll be fine. She'll just be walking Angel, and she can follow the fence line for most of the way. You can't get lost. You've been that general way a few times now. Paddy, once you've got the other mob in, you can head out and help with the last of the trip up through the trees and overs Sullivan's rise. I'll give you a good map, Maysa. You just take your time. The sheep are already buggered, they won't be moving fast. You could probably walk faster yourself.' Len looked to Paddy who smiled.

'Sure thing Len, that'll be fine.'

'Maysa, you ok with that?'

'Sure Len, I can do that.' Maysa forced a smile.

Paddy's heart raced. How could someone so bloody unlucky be so lucky? Again. He glanced carefully at Maysa. He was becoming aroused. She caught him looking, and he looked away as quickly as he could, then stood up to prepare his horse and dogs.

With lunch finished, Len spread a map of the relevant part of the property on the bonnet of his ute and began to explain the directions to Maysa. She recognised the river where she and Tom had spent their first afternoon together, and Len showed her the shallow crossing just downstream from their picnic spot. She was comfortable with the first half of the journey at least. Len had assured her the sheep knew their way back and that after a short while they would settle into the long walk. Maysa had seen how the sheep mobbed up and walked back to the paddocks from which they'd come on several occasions. On such a vast station, with so many sheep, she had already spent many hours mustering. At this time of year, it was part of daily life. The ride was a good slow hour past the river crossing. The last half mile was up a slight rise into some sparse scrub and through a gate into the destination paddock.

Angel was saddled, and the dogs were ready and excited for work. Len put the map in Maysa's saddlebag, along with a pocket knife and some matches. Irene had given her as many biscuits as she could jam into what space was left, and she had water. The sheep were let out of the yards, about five hundred in the mob. Len drove ahead to the first gate and Maysa settled in behind the mob who were keen to escape the yards. The dogs leapt into action. She thought for a moment about how she had watched for Tom during shearing as he came into the yards this same way with a new mob each day. And now, so soon after, she was doing the same work, taking the sheep back to their paddocks. But without Tom. How things had changed, and so quickly. And now, with so much uncertainty. As the last of the sheep scrambled through the gate, Len walked over to Maysa.

'OK, we'll see you in a few hours. You'll be right. You're very capable. Be good for you to have a bit of time to yourself. Don't worry about Tom. We'll have him back in no time. I just know it.' Len patted Angel on the neck. 'Look after her, Angel.'

'Thanks, Len. Here goes! See you soon.'

CHAPTER THIRTY-THREE

The sheep settled quickly into a slow and determined walk, heading back in the direction they'd come from. Maysa was completely relaxed on Angel, almost sleepy in the hot sun, being gently rocked by the rhythm of the horse's gait. Banjo strolled along behind Angel, occasionally glancing disparagingly at Billy and Barney. They remained enthusiastic in their sheepdog endeavours for a short while, before settling into a steady walk behind the mob. This was easy work. But for her worry about Tom, Maysa felt strangely at peace. It was almost meditative. At the shearer's quarters, she had been lonely a lot of the time, but not alone. At the homestead, she had been caught in a whirlwind of action with no time to relax and really think. At last, even just for a few hours, she was alone but far from lonely.

A good hour into the ride she reached the river and smiled to herself thinking about the picnic with Tom. She saw the bend in the river, the sandy beach and was grateful the sheep steered away from this special place and didn't trample it to dust as they had done much of the rest of the way. They crossed the river after a few false starts. The dogs got involved and were rewarded with a swim and being able to just lie in the shallows and let the cool water flow over them. Angel stood and drank and snorted with pleasure. But the sheep continued on, heading for their home, so Maysa followed and called the dogs along. She calculated she had another hour to an hour and a half to go. And with dark just a few hours away she'd have to keep moving. The return trip would be quicker. The heat would have eased a little, and the pace wouldn't be set by the mob.

Paddy managed to push the mob hard, out of their paddock and into the sheep yards. It was in complete contrast to the directions from Len. He was filled with a dangerous blend of nervousness, excitement and agitation. He had to keep his head together. This time was far more dangerous than the last. Someone just might put two and two together, but he was sure he'd covered his steps. He couldn't believe how lucky he was. Everything was falling into place.

This should have been over with years ago. When the Pattersons were destroyed, he was the one, he was there for them, two years ago when they needed someone. They needed him. The girl, Milly, she was taken care of. No one stood in the way of what was rightfully his, his grandfather's station. And then there was that upstart, bloody

Tom Sutherland. Without Milly, he was gone, why wouldn't he be? Nothing gave him more pleasure than the reports that Tom was falling apart and how he'd burnt every friendship, in fact, every acquaintance he had in town. He had no credit left with the local cops. It was just a matter of time, and he'd be locked up for good. But then, one day, like a bloody nightmare, he was back, not just visiting, but living under the same roof as him, and he was closer with the Pattersons than ever. But they were all on a tipping point. He knew they couldn't stand another tragedy. None of them. He had to finish them off and how easy this had been.

First, the girl appears. He was angry, and he was bitter. And then he began to see a plan, a few seeds germinating into a full blooming horror story. It all came together with hardly lifting a finger. He was watching this car crash as a spectator. Good old Dingo. He did the job on the girl. He fired up the boy into a frenzy and put him back in the eyes of the cops. And Dingo, he had a reputation, so, he actually just confirmed what everyone suspected. He was a dirty mongrel dog with an uncontrollable lust for the women. Who wouldn't suspect he'd be involved in another attack, and if he turned up dead, who wouldn't suspect Tom? So he took his chances. He had enjoyed the violent attack on the girl, that was just a bonus. And then Dingo, and the setup, putting Tom in the firing line. He could still see Dingo, on his knees, pleading for mercy in that very last moment, as he brought the rock down on his forehead. He felt nothing as he rolled the dead body into the water.

This next piece seemed too easy. The Spooney was in the lockup, 40 long miles of corrugated, potholed dirt road away. The girl was on a horse, by herself, in the middle of the scrub and no-one anywhere. Irene had asked Len, '*Are you sure she'll be ok?*' She'd done him a bloody favour. Sown the seeds of doubt in everyone's minds. But Len was too stupid to realise. She wouldn't be ok, would she? People fall off horses all the time, especially those who've only been riding a month or two. She got lost, she took the sheep down a wrong track. It took a long time to find the sheep, and when he did, he only found her horse. There was no sign of the girl, of her body. What's more, it was dark by the time he got back to the home-stead, and they'd struggle to find her in the daylight, let alone at night. This was all going to be too easy.

Around three-thirty, Paddy could see the dust of the mob drifting upward into the sky. He looked up and registered storm clouds building, dark bluish grey and ominous. Good, he thought. There was a God, after all. He knew the weather out here. It would be mostly dry lightning and a few heavy showers for a short time. Just enough to give back the moisture the sun had dragged out of the parched soil and vegetation over the last couple of weeks, and then, it would be gone again for a few more weeks.

The dogs noticed Paddy before Maysa did. A quick volley of barks from Billy and Barney, and suddenly he was there. Just materialized. In fact, he had held back and watched her from the edge of the scrub for a good fifteen minutes before trotting his horse up beside her. He made her uncomfortable, and she was immediately on guard. But there was a job to do and then she wanted to get home and get news about Tom. She was determined he wouldn't rattle her. Banjo was unmoved, hardly looked up and kept his place right beside Angel. It was almost as though he'd known Paddy was there all along.

'How yer going.' Paddy smiled as he reined in his horse next to hers.

'I'm fine thanks.'

'You've made good progress, any problems?'

'No, none. Not long to go now.'

'Not long at all.' Paddy smiled, a little too obviously.

Maysa thought Paddy's tone was a little queer, but he was always odd.

They rode on in silence for a little while longer.

'What do you think they'll do with your boyfriend then?'

'What do you mean?' Maysa replied defensively.

'Come on. I think we both know he did it, and even if he didn't, who's going to believe him?'

Paddy paused before going on. Maysa didn't take the bait. 'He was doing alright for a while, off the booze, stopped beating every second bloke half to death. In fact, the police probably put his file away to gather dust. Then you turned up, and here we go again. People getting bashed, then turning up dead. You've only got to do your sums. You were probably the worst thing that could have happened to him.' He paused. Again, Maysa didn't respond, she was fighting back a mixture of tears and rage. Paddy continued on in his matter of fact tone.

'Anyway, he won't be home any time soon. You can't have a murderer walking about loose can yer? And it will be a few weeks before they can get him in front of the magistrate.'

'He's not a murderer. And you know it. What is your problem?' Maysa spat her words at Paddy, which only served to excite him even more.

'Well, we'll see about that I guess, won't we?'

The silence was broken a few minutes later when Paddy announced, 'We need to steer the mob over that way round the edge of that scrub. The gates only about a mile up there now.'

'Are you sure?' Maysa was surprised and confused. 'I thought we had to make our way up through the scrub along the trail up the hill there. North East through the scrub, that's what Len told me, and that's where the sheep are headed. Besides, it's on the map.' There was a visible trail, vehicle tracks and battered scrub either side of the track. The stock had bulldozed their way through

304

in large mobs over the years and decades. It was all clearly visible in the direction that Maysa was pointing. The sheep had naturally started to head in that direction.

'Are you seriously questioning me?' Paddy's tone was a little threatening and Maysa felt uncertain. 'I've been working on this bloody property for years. Working for bloody nothing actually.' He was getting wound up now. 'This is my grandfather's property. Did you know that? My mother was entitled to her share of this place, and so am I. One day this place will be mine. So don't tell me what to do or where to go. You hear me?' The words struck Maysa like a blow to the stomach. She made no attempt to reply and kept her eyes to the front.

Paddy sent his dogs wide, and they turned the mob to the west and off the track to a smaller, less travelled path. Maysa wanted nothing more now than to be finished and on her way home to see Irene. Finally, the mob were filing through the gate and into the next paddock. From overhead, they looked like grains of sand pouring through an hourglass. The dogs weaved back and forward, keeping the sheep bunched up tight. The last of the sheep were through the gate. Off his horse, Paddy shut the gate and turned to see Maysa had already turned her horse for home and was trotting. He mounted his horse quickly and cantered to catch up to her.

'You could wait for me, girlie.'

'I am happy to ride alone. Thank you.'

'You reckon you can find your way back, do you?'

'I have a map.'

'Oh yeah. Of course.' He paused and let a few minutes pass.

'Listen, I want to say sorry. I have been a bit angry and stressed lately. A few things to sort out. I said some pretty stupid and insensitive things back there. I am not usually like this, honestly.'

'Ok.' Maysa was unsure, but relieved there wouldn't be any more aggression and hopefully minimal conversation.

'It's beautiful country, isn't it? A bit different to being in Melbourne, I guess. I've never been there myself. Too crowded for me, I reckon. I like being out here by myself, where nobody knows where you are, and what you're up to.'

'Yes, it is wonderful country. You are lucky to have grown up here.' Maysa smiled, relieved the tension had eased. She made no attempt to continue the conversation.

'Hey, can I take a quick look at the map? There are a couple of ways back to the homestead from here, and I am never quite sure which is the fastest. It looks like it's going to rain soon and so we'll have to get a move on.' On cue, lightning flashed to the east followed by a clap of thunder rolling in the distance. They both looked east to see the clouds had turned a deep purple-blue, and a shower had sprouted from the cloud line on the

306

horizon. Maysa hadn't seen rain since she had been on the station. The light dimmed, and the air-cooled noticeably as the storm closed in quickly.

Maysa reached into her saddlebag. She took out the folded map and handed it to Paddy. He unfolded it and looked at it for a moment. The horses were jittery, the weather unsettling them, but they stood still enough for Paddy to make a show of reading the map.

'Here, look at this.' He beckoned Maysa to his side to read the map. The two horses were side by side. Maysa was looking at the map, waiting to see what Paddy wanted to show her when she became aware he was smiling at her. She looked at him, unable to compute.

'What?' She almost whispered, and with uncertainty.

'The sheep. You put them in the wrong paddock.' Maysa was dumbstruck. Stunned, she said nothing.

'You've fucked this up, haven't you, you stupid bitch.' In an instant, Paddy had grabbed Maysa by the shirt at her throat. The horses took fright and pulled apart, both riders pulled on their reins. Paddy pulled Maysa toward him again so fast she lost balance and fell toward him, releasing one hand trying not to fall. He caught her and tried to kiss her, but the horses were scrambling now. He managed to kiss the side of her face as she turned away desperately. The dogs were excited and circling the horses. Bob barked. Maysa tried to pull away. Paddy pulled her toward him again then thrust her backward as hard as he could. It was too much. She lost her balance and fell backward off Angel, hitting the ground with a thump. Her foot was caught in the stirrup as Angel took flight and she was dragged just a few yards before the stirrup leather came loose off the saddle.

The pain in Maysa's arm seared from her wrist to her shoulder. Her ankle had been slightly twisted when she was pulled along by Angel. She was stunned and terrified and lay still just holding onto consciousness.

'Shit.' Paddy cursed as he watched Angel canter off into the bush. 'I'll have to chase you down, but you can wait five minutes.' Paddy mumbled to himself.

The storm clouds were rolling in right overhead now, and it was becoming prematurely dark. Paddy dismounted and stood looking at Maysa who lay, dead still, her eyes closed. It appeared as though she was already dead, and he looked disappointed. The lust in his eyes was unmistakable.

Maysa opened her eyes as Banjo licked her face. Looking up, she saw Paddy smiling and walking toward her, undoing his belt. She tried to drag herself away, but the pain was too much. She lay still, trembling, waiting for the inevitable.

'You can make this easy on yerself, or you can fight me. To be honest, I don't mind if you fight. It might be fun.' Paddy was by her side now and beginning to kneel down next to Maysa. Billy and Barney watched on excitedly like spectators at a pub brawl. Thunder clapped overhead, and even Paddy jumped. There was the sound of a horse cantering, and Paddy turned to see his horse disappearing into the rain as it began belting down. The first few huge drops splashed dust up off the baked red earth. Paddy turned back to Maysa and reached out to touch her when he felt a sudden jolt at his side followed by a mad shaking and then sharp pain. Banjo was attached. Attached to the soft flesh covering his kidneys. Growling and biting down hard. Paddy struck the dog as hard as he could and tried to climb to his feet. Banjo was stuck hard and doing his best to swing the prey around instinctively. Paddy punched at him. He was on his feet, and Banjo was entirely off the ground before he finally let go. Billy and Barney were barking and growling furiously. The rain was pelting down. Paddy lashed out trying to kick Banjo who ducked below the kick with ease and in the true style of a blue heeler, took Paddy around the ankle, breaking the skin and drawing blood.

'I should have shot you last time, you mongrel bastard.' Maysa just made out the words through the pouring rain.

Now even Billy and Barney were so worked up they joined the attack. It was short-lived. Paddy backed away. He looked at Maysa lying on the ground. She was injured. He watched for a moment as Banjo assumed his position as a guard, between

Maysa and Paddy, never taking his eyes off Paddy. Billy and Barney were sitting next to Maysa, trying to lick her. Paddy looked around and could just make out his horse in the distance and made off after it.

Maysa watched, stunned. She could hardly think. The whole attack had lasted only a few moments. She was in shock and desperately trying to get her thoughts together. Was he coming back? She had no choice. She had to stand up. She had to disappear. She looked around but couldn't see far with the rain. Her best chance was to move into the scrub, as far as she could. Her arm was feeling ok now. Perhaps it was just the adrenalin, but she managed to stand and begin to walk. Pain shot through her ankle as she limped slowly toward the scrub. She moved as quickly as she could and as far as she could. Dense, thorny bushes speared and tore her clothes, scratching her skin. The dogs followed, Banjo not far behind her and steady. What was only about fifteen minutes seemed like an hour when she finally had to stop and rest. She had moved up into the scrub and up a slight rise. She sat with her back against the trunk of a small scrubby bush. It prickled and scratched her back, but the pain was inconsequential compared to the pain in her shoulder and ankle. She could see the open area below the rise, although it was only a slight elevation. The rain was easing, yet the countryside continued to light up regularly with each sheet of lightning, and the thunder rolled on soon after each flash.

Maysa guessed it had been half an hour at least when she spotted movement down on the flat. Lighting struck, the sky lit up for a moment, and she could see a rider on a horse. A second strike just moments later, and she could make out the rider had changed directions and was heading toward home, leading a second horse. Leading Angel. For the first time since the attack, her muscles relaxed, and the shallow breathing eased. She closed her eyes for a moment. She woke sometime later. She wasn't sure how much later, except it was pitch black. There was enough cloud to extinguish any light from the stars. Banjo lay next to her with his head on her leg, and she reached down and patted him.

'Thank you.'

Billy and Barney sat nearby, watching her through sleepy eyes.

CHAPTER THIRTY-FOUR

It was after six o'clock when Paddy finally rode into the house paddock and right up to the back of the homestead. Len and Irene were at the back door when he arrived. He'd walked the horse as slowly as he could on the way back, to kill time and to make sure any thoughts of a search that evening were futile. He galloped the horses the last half a mile, so they looked exhausted when he arrived.

'Where the hell have you been.' Len yelled out across the yard as he strode down the garden path, followed closely by Irene.

Almost simultaneously, Len and Irene cried out.

'Where's Maysa?' as they registered the riderless Angel.

'I don't know.' Paddy made a good show of sounding frantic and out of breath. 'I rode out to catch up with her, and I couldn't find her. I figured she had taken the sheep into the paddock where you'd told her, so I rode in to check and thought I might see her. There was no sign of her, so I backtracked along the direction I would have thought she would come along looking for her.

There was no sign of her. I rode around every-where up on the rise looking for her. Finally, I figured she must have been on the way back to the homestead, and I started back. It was then, just before the storm, I saw the tracks of the mob. She'd turned and gone west into the Sutherland boundary paddock, instead of up and over Sullivan's through the scrub like you told her. I found the sheep soon after. They'd gone a fair way inside the gate. And then, a bit further on, I found Angel. She was stirred up. One stirrup was gone.' He finally drew breath. He surveyed the audience. This was going well. They were both shocked and upset, so he continued.

'I guess she must have come off the horse. Probably lightning or thunder. Angel probably took off. Maybe through the scrub. She wouldn't have stood a chance. She didn't have the experi-ence.'

There was another long pause, and Irene looked at Len.

'Doesn't have the experience, Paddy. Not didn't . . . She'll be ok, but we need to find her now.' Irene's voice was calm and deliberate and belied the terror she was feeling.

No more than fifteen minutes later, Paddy, Len and Neville were on their way in three vehicles. Under Paddy's direction, they headed off to the wrong paddock. The fastest way there by vehicle was not the way he and Maysa had taken the mob. The river crossing wasn't suitable. It took them thirty minutes to arrive at the gate to the paddock where they regrouped. Under Len's direction, they took off in three directions in search of Maysa.

It was after 10pm when Irene heard the vehicles returning, and she ran to the back gate to see Maysa. She ran from vehicle to vehicle in search of Maysa, but she was not with them. She hadn't been found.

'Kilarra Police, this is Shirley.'

'Shirley, it's Len Patterson, I need to speak with Barry please.'

'Ah, Len. How are you?'

'Alright Shirley, but I need to speak with Barry now!' Len was abrupt, almost panicky. Shirley had taken many of these calls over the years, she was never surprised or offended, and besides, as she looked at her watch, she realised how late it was. It wasn't a social call.

'I'm sorry, Len. He's not here. He's been called up to Brewarrina. There has been a big disturbance up there. A car crash in town and then a massive punch up. They needed some extra muscle. Is there something I can do to help?'

'What about the young constable?' Len had no faith in him. He was a nice young bloke, but he didn't know the country or the people yet.

'He's with Barry, but he'll be back tonight.'

'What about Barry?'

'Not until morning.'

'Shirley. A young girl out here's gone missing. Young Maysa.'

'I know who she is. Tom's been telling me about her.'

Shirley and Barry Penfold had been in town for twenty years. They were almost local. They'd been in town long enough to watch a generation of young kids grow up. Some of them left, some of them stayed in town and on the farms, and some of them inevitably got into trouble. She knew which ones were destined to visit her and Barry at the station. Tom wasn't one. Even at his worst, she still looked out for him. She never judged his behaviour given what he'd been through. She was pleased to see he was back on the straight and narrow and very disappointed when Barry had brought him in the previous night. She didn't believe Tom was guilty. Not for one minute, so she sat and ate with him and caught up on all the family news. Tom had told her all about Maysa. She worried about what his reaction would be when he heard this news.

'Len, I'll ring Brewarrina and get Barry back as soon as possible, but I'm sure it won't be before morning. What should I tell him?'

'There's nothing we can do tonight anyway Shirley. Just tell him she's missing. Probably a horse-riding fall, mustering. We've already been out and spent a few hours searching, but there is no sign. It's just so bloody dark with this cloud cover and too much scrub for a night search. This is a bloody nightmare we know all too well.'

'How's Irene coping?'

'She's ok. She's focused on organising everyone, which is a good distraction. But we can't let this go wrong. Not again. Never again. It'll finish her. It'll finish us both.' Shirley could hear the tremor in Len's voice.

'Ok. I better get on to Barry before it gets any later. I am sure he will be out first thing in the morning as early as he can.'

'Thanks, Shirley. Tell Barry I am going to ring the Sutherlands and get some extra men over here in the morning. Tom's dad and uncles. And Shirley, he needs to bring Tom with him. We need people who know the country, and that's Tom.'

'Got that Len. I'll let Barry tell Tom in the morning and save him a sleepless night. Take it easy now. I'll be thinking of you. I am sure you'll find her. Love to Irene.'

Len returned to the kitchen where Irene was fixing up Paddy and Nev with a plate of food each, to take back to their quarters. She offered to do their washing and to tidy up for them in the morning. They both declined the offer, but getting the look from Len, who was standing behind Irene, Nev graciously accepted. He'd been through the last search ending in tragedy, and he knew Irene needed to keep busy. Paddy was distracted and didn't seem to be interested or to care about anyone else. He excused himself as quickly as he could and returned to the stockman's quarters.

Paddy sat at the table, brooding, eating the meal Irene had prepared and drinking a beer, one and then another. He retired to his room to think things over and to plan his next move. This hadn't gone according to plan. It had all been going so well, and now it was all buggered up. He needed something more potent than beer. He pulled a bottle of scotch out of his bedside drawer and poured himself a long drink. He lay back on his bed and stared at the ceiling. He was hoping the girl was badly injured, hoping she wouldn't last the night. But if she was, how did she manage to disappear without a sign. She'd be soaking wet though, bloody cold. The cloud cover had gone, and it would be a pretty cold night now. Maybe she'd freeze to death. Maybe pigs, or wild dogs, something would find her. He shouldn't have given up so soon. He should have bashed the dog with a rock or a stick or something, and then he could have had her, then finished her off. He allowed himself to be distracted by a fantasy of taking the girl, out there, on the ground while she cried out and no one could hear her. He thought back to the girl in town a couple of weeks ago. He replayed the whole scene, and then he drifted into the past, thinking of Milly. Begging for mercy as he finished her off. Half naked. And then, Dingo. In the end, he was no better than her, crying as he killed him.

He was aroused now, and he couldn't sleep. He finished off the scotch and poured himself another. His mind was beginning to swim in murky water as the alcohol caught up. He took the box with his precious mementos from his cupboard. Sitting on the edge of his bed, he stared at the underwear he held in his hands from the two girls. And there was the bracelet as well. A delicate sterling silver bracelet, with a tiny heart charm. Not worth anything to anyone but Milly and Tom. A childish teenage gift from Tom that Milly cherished. Paddy knew that. He took great pleasure ripping it from her wrist during the attack and putting it in his pocket in front of her before continuing the assault. It meant a lot to him. He could still see her face as he took it.

Sometime later, Paddy woke, naked, lying on his bed, a mess. He felt sick and exhausted. He put his treasures back in the box and pushed them out of the way across the bed. Before he had soaked himself senseless in alcohol, he'd made his mind up to leave before dawn, before everyone else and find the girl and finish her off. He was the only one who knew approximately where she was, and she couldn't have gone too far. Between him and the dogs, he'd find her.

CHAPTER THIRTY-FIVE

As the first signs of the sunrise appeared, Len and Nev were mounting horses preparing to begin the search. Tom's mother, father and uncles had arrived early, and in three vehicles. They were also ready to head off. Irene stood, arm in arm, with Elise at the homestead gate. Irene would join the search as soon as Tom arrived with Barry Penfold and she could fill them in on the plan and the details as she knew them. Elise would remain at the house and coordinate as required.

'Where's bloody Paddy?' Len barked at Nev.

'I went to his cottage when he wasn't up the horse yards, and he'd gone already. Just left a note saying he wanted to get an early start, be out there at first light, so he's long gone.'

'Shit. Well, he could have done with coordinating with us, so we don't double up over the same ground. Anyway, least he is onto it. Let's get going then.' Len and Nev reined the horses round in the direction of the search area, waving to Irene and Elise. The vehicles followed on immediately after.

★　★　★

Tom was dead to the world when Penfold shook him. He'd had a rough sleep for the second night in a row at the police station. He had no idea how long he'd be in the cell. Barry had been out of town and had told him he just had to be patient and wait until he got back and he'd sort out some bail.

'Tom. Wake up.'

'Geezus Barry, what time is it? I feel like I only just got to sleep.' Tom looked up at the cell window, it was high on the wall, and he could see the sky. 'It's pitch black.'

'It's five, Boy. It'll be light soon enough. Get up quickly and get your clothes on. We are heading out to the Patterson's. I'll explain why on the way.'

'What's going on?' Tom was immediately frantic.

'In the car. Come on, I'll explain on the way.'

It was twenty minutes into the trip to the Patterson's when Penfold finally started telling Tom what was going on.

The words struck Tom like a sledgehammer.

'It's Maysa, she's missing.'

Tom could hardly form the words.

'When . . . how?'

As far as I know, last night. Probably a fall off a horse, mustering. Everyone will be out there again this morning, Len, your Dad and all the boys, your uncles too.

'She's been out there all night? In that storm?'

'I'm afraid so, Tom. But let's stay positive mate. She seems like a smart and capable young woman.

Let's focus on her being ok. She'll be cold and feeling sorry for herself, no doubt, but I bet she'll be ok.'

Tom was silent, staring ahead. His reaction was unnerving Penfold. It was almost as though he wasn't there. His body was, but his mind wasn't. Finally, he spoke quietly.

'This can't be happening again. It just can't.'

'Can I make you a cup of tea, Irene?' Elise offered.

'No, let me make it. You sit down. You've been awake for ages and travelling.'

'I have no doubt you've been awake half the night yourself. Ed and I hardly slept a wink. We have been worried sick all night. I'm so glad Tom is on his way, yet I am so worried as well. I hope he can keep it together. I can't believe this is happening . . . again.'

'This isn't happening again, Elise. It just can't. This girl is like a daughter to Len and I already. I can't lose her. I won't. Tom can't lose her.' Finally, the last twenty-four hours caught up with Irene, and she broke down. Elise took her in her arms as she cried for both the girls.

'Enough of this.' Irene wiped her eyes and drew a deep breath. 'I need to keep busy. Come on. I need to walk down to the stockman's quarters and pick up some dirty dishes. I made them dinner last night after the search, and they took it home with them. Shirley Penfold rang a short while ago. Barry and Tom will be another half hour at least.'

Irene led Elise to the Stockman's buildings. They collected Nev's plates from his smaller cottage a little further out than Paddy and Tom's. He'd washed his dishes and left them on the table for Irene. His quarters were neat and tidy and well organised. Then they moved on to the other building. The front door was slightly ajar as both women crossed the verandah and tentatively ventured inside. They were both taken aback by the mess and the smell of beer and stale food.

'This is disgusting!' Elise was unimpressed. 'Is this how my son lives?'

'Well, no. Obviously. He hasn't been here for a couple of days. This is Paddy. It's usually quite tidy, I can assure you. Tidy for a couple of young men of course. Take a look in there, that's Tom's room.' Irene pointed in the direction of Tom's room, and Elise pushed open the door to find it neat and tidy, with the bed made and nothing on the floor that should have been in cupboards and drawers.

'Take a look at this.' Irene called to Elise from Paddy's room. 'There's my dishes.' The plate and cutlery were on his bedside table, accompanied by what must have been a spirits glass. Casting an eye around, Irene noticed a couple of empty beer bottles under the window near some cigarette butts that had been dangerously extinguished beneath Paddy's feet on the timber floor.

'He's quite the pig, isn't he?' Elise remarked disdainfully.

'I think that's being polite. Look at that.' Irene pointed to the empty whiskey bottle on the bed. The blankets had been hastily pulled up to cover the mess. The bed looked like it hadn't been made in days, and the sheets hadn't been washed in who knows how long. Irene picked up the whiskey bottle gingerly, feeling the urge, however slight it was, to help Paddy, given he was out searching for Maysa. As she picked it up, it clinked against an object partially hidden under the blanket. As if avoiding something infectious, she grasped the blanket hesitantly between thumb and forefinger. She turned it back to reveal a battered old metal box. She stared at the box for a moment then looked at Elise, who was equally intrigued. They exchanged a silent agreement, and Irene opened the lid of the box. Paddy had left it unlocked in his drunken stupor and later still, in his hazy-headed hangover and urgency to leave and fix this sorry mess. They both stood silent and shocked. Inside there were two pairs of women's underpants and a folded paper.

Irene carefully took the paper out of the box and unfolded it. It was a map of the combined properties, outlined in red. On the map were the names of various members of the family. On the Sutherland's station, Tom and Milly had been written, obviously, some time ago, they both remembered when. In recent writing, on the Patterson's property, the names Tom and Maysa were written, now smudged by what was most likely spilt whiskey. Feeling ill, Irene lifted out the underwear that she recognised, as tears began to stream down her face. A glint caught Elise's eye, and slowly she reached into the box and took out the silver bracelet.

Elise spoke in a barely audible whisper. 'I was with Tom the day he bought this for Milly. I helped him choose it. He was so excited and nervous.'

Irene collapsed to her knees.

Back in the homestead, Elise helped Irene to lie down in her bedroom while they waited for Tom and Penfold to arrive. Elise paced back and forth in the kitchen planning and rehearsing what to tell Tom, or perhaps as importantly, what not to tell Tom.

Finally, Penfold's Land Rover pulled up to a halt at the back gate, and Elise heard the doors slam shut seconds later. Tom leapt from the vehicle followed closely by Penfold. Elise met them at the back door. She hugged Tom, then ushered them inside to the kitchen. A map was spread out on the table.

CHAPTER THIRTY-SIX

'I need to get going,' were Tom's first words, spoken with sharp urgency.

'You need to look at this first, Tom.' Elise pointed to the map. 'We need to show you the search area.'

'Where's Irene?'

'I'm here.' They turned to see Irene standing in the doorway. She looked older, smaller and exhausted. 'Len's saddled Bess for you, Tom. She's in the yard. He's put some food, first aid and things in your saddlebag, and a rope to tether her if you need to leave her and get into the scrub on foot.' Irene took over from Elise and quickly explained where Maysa had been directed to take the sheep. Then she ran through the information from Paddy saying the sheep were in the wrong paddock and then finally where Paddy said he had found Angel. As she relayed this last piece of Paddy's information, she didn't sound convinced. What they found wasn't one hundred per cent conclusive, but she and Elise were sure they knew the truth.

'Tom. Barry. There is more you need to know before you head off. Please, just sit for a minute.'

Elise began to say what Irene couldn't bear to speak aloud. She explained they had been at the stockmans' quarters to collect the dishes and what they found in Paddy's room. Tom was shocked and devastated. He'd been living under the same roof with Milly's killer for so long. He immediately had no doubt that Paddy was capable of such a crime. His anger was only eclipsed by his sense of urgency. He had wanted to leap out of Penfold's vehicle and go straight for his horse. He was only just persuaded to wait, and to hear the necessary detail of what had happened and to understand the search plan. Len had left instructions for Tom to search the scrub on Sullivan's rise in case Maysa had made it back that far. He hadn't been sure where Paddy had gone because he'd left early with no indication of his plan which had made Len curse him to the core. This only served to further convince this group that Paddy was guilty. Penfold was to join the searchers in the Sutherland's boundary paddock, bringing Irene to show him the way.

'Barry and I will head straight out and find Len and the boys and let them know about Paddy. Please be careful and find . . .'

'Don't worry about being careful, Tom.' Penfold interjected. 'Be sensible, Boy. It's no use to you or anyone else if we end up taking Paddy to town in a bag. If you find him, hold your tongue. Focus on getting what you need to find your girl. Let me deal with Paddy.'

Tom looked at Penfold, expressionless. The look gave away nothing. Tom had hardly spoken since Penfold told him the news on the way out. Tom was shutting down into pure focus. He could see one thing, and one thing only. It was Maysa. Everything else going on was background noise.

CHAPTER THIRTY-SEVEN

The sounds of birds welcoming the dawn roused Maysa from sleep. She woke, still shivering from cold and shock as the first rays of sunlight reached out to her through the scrubby trees and bush. The only warmth was Banjo lying against her thigh, and she gave him a thankful pat. Billy and Barney lay as close as they could whilst respecting Banjo's proprietorship over Maysa. They wagged their tails and kicked up just a little dust from the ground which was still damp from the previous night's storm. Maysa tried to stand, and pain shot through her leg, partly from the injury and partly from lying on the hard ground, motionless all night. She managed to walk a few steps before leaning against a tree to rest. She needed to think clearly and now, regardless of how she just wanted to panic and scream. She had no doubt people would be looking for her. How could she work out where she was, let alone where to walk to, to get back to the sheds or the homestead safely. And what if Paddy was still looking for her. Surely he must be. He would have to hide the evidence. She would need to stay in the scrub, undercover. She couldn't follow the sheep trail, even if she could find it. It was too open. She'd be seen but by the wrong person. She allowed herself just a moment for futile thoughts of Tom, desperately wishing he was with her.

She'd seen Tom draw maps of paddocks and properties in the dust with a stick and so she cleared a spot on the dirt and began, by memory, to scratch out the map Len had given her. The sun was clearly rising in the east now, and as it pushed well above the horizon, she was able to mark east and west on the red soil. She filled out the map, knowing that she'd travelled north with the sheep, only veering north-west at the last moment under Paddy's instructions. South from where she was, was the river. As anxious as she was, she thought for a moment of how proud Tom would be. The river meant water and shade, and she knew she could travel downstream and find the sheep crossing. She set herself a bearing based on a tall tree in the distance that she considered was in a southerly direction. It was tall enough she could see it each time the scrub broke open into small clearings.

The sun was rising as Paddy crossed the river at the sheep crossing. His head ached from the whiskey. His belly ached with a lack of food and nerves that promised to develop into an ulcer way too soon. He had a plan. Not much of a plan. But a plan none the less. He would return to where he'd pushed her off the horse then head into the scrub on foot. She couldn't have gone far, and his dogs would help track her down. Then he would finish this business.

Some twenty minutes later, he found the scuff marks where the horses had jostled against each other. Only he would recognise the marks for what they were. The storm had mostly washed away the evidence. He dismounted and began to lead his horse through the scrub when it got too dense, and they were making too much noise. He scanned about in the direction he believed she would have taken. He found broken branches and scuffed ground, but he was no tracker. The broken branches could have been from an animal careering through the bush during the storm. Backward and forward, he walked methodically and determined, to the south, then to the north and then deeper in. Sometime later, he was feeling sick to the stomach with fear and frustration when he noticed unusual markings in the soil, ten or fifteen feet away. As he approached, his heart raced. It was a map, scratched in the ground. It was partially obscured by footprints, probably a dog. Still, it was definitely a map, and it was clearly an attempt at copying Len's map that the girl had had with her before he'd taken it.

It was apparent now, she must have been here not long after dawn to be able to see what she was doing with the map and marking the directions, east and west. And the map showed the river crossing. She was much smarter and resilient than he'd given her credit for. He knew she would know where she was going if she could make the river, but she couldn't have gotten far on foot. And there was the odd footprint she'd left in the still damp soil. She'd leave those marks for another hour or so until the day heated up. He could follow those until the ground dried up, then she'd be much harder to find. He got back on his horse and began moving as quickly as possible, with no care for the noise now. He hoped his dogs would find her, or her dogs, and quickly. Then this whole bloody messy business would be over with at last.

'Go out.' Paddy directed the dogs as he pushed his horse urgently through the scrub at a steady trot, watching for footprints. The dogs cast out wide, as they always did, thinking they were looking for sheep. Running as fast as they could through the bush. It was barely five minutes later when Paddy heard a dog barking.

Tom reached the river crossing and cast an eye upstream to the trees where he and Maysa had first spent the day together. He thought of her that day, beautiful, in his arms, kissing her for the first time. He thought of her bruised face. The attack. How could this be happening again? It couldn't. Not this time. He kicked his horse into a canter and headed north along the sheep trail.

★   ★   ★

331

A mile away to the east, Paddy was closing in on Maysa.

For a moment, Tom fancied he heard a dog bark in the distance. He pulled Bess up to a halt and listened carefully, but there was nothing. Desperately wishful thinking, he supposed. He kicked Bess back into a canter and continued north.

Maysa felt a flood of adrenalin course through her body as she became aware of a quiet growl. Banjo was the first to become aware of the danger and responded defensively. Maysa recognised one of Paddy's dogs as it flashed through the bush up ahead. Billy barked, just once and Maysa quietly hushed him. His head sunk guiltily, and he hooked his tail up between his legs. She stood deadly still, against the trunk of a tree. Paddy's two dogs were first to arrive, and they excitedly barked when confronted by Tom's dogs. Moments later, she could hear the horse. Her heart sunk as she began to shake.

'Good morning.' Paddy's smile was lopsided, and his expression somewhere between evil and insanity. Maysa made no attempt to move, she felt frozen to the spot. Banjo continued to growl as Paddy picked up a substantial stick from the ground.

'You might wanna mind yer manners today Banjo, old boy, or it might just be yer last day.'

★　　★　　★

Tom continued north at a steady pace. He wanted to make a quick sweep of part of the paddock that Maysa should have taken the sheep to, before working his way back through the scrubby area as planned. In truth, he had no idea where to begin but hoped for a clue. He opened the gate and then headed north, yet instinctively he felt like he was getting further away from where he should be. He pulled Bess up and sat for a moment, trying to slow his racing mind and to think sensibly about what to do next. And there it was again. Much further away and carried on a light breeze. The sound of a dog barking, several times this time. Now it was a long way away. He began calling,

'Billy, Barney.'

Paddy moved slowly towards Maysa, watching her and watching Banjo out of the corner of his eye. He stood within arms distance of her now.

'Like I told you yesterday, you can make this easy or really hard. Makes no difference to me. I'm gonna enjoy it either way, and either way, I am gonna have you . . . now.' Maysa was terrified. She knew it was pointless, trying to outrun him. Pinned against the tree, Paddy reached out tentatively and put his hand on her chest, just below the throat. Banjo began snarling and growling, edging closer to Paddy. Maysa turned her face away from Paddy.

'Steady boy, it's ok, I'll be gentle.' Paddy slid his hand slowly down and over Maysa's breast and squeezed it gently. 'Mmm, nice. You like that, ey? I do.' Paddy squeezed Maysa's breast hard, and she flinched.

'Stop it. Please.' Maysa urged Paddy, but this only served to excite him further. He clenched her shirt at the throat and jerked it down, suddenly tearing the shirt, breaking buttons and pulling Maysa toward him. Banjo leapt and bit Paddy on the ankle again holding on with jaws of steel. Paddy let go of Maysa who backed away as quickly as she could. Paddy leant down to punch Banjo who let go of his ankle, avoiding the blow whilst trying to bite Paddy's hand. Paddy picked up the stick and swinging it hard, caught Banjo across the side of his head stunning him. He kicked Banjo hard in the ribs knocking the air out of him. Banjo sat still for just a moment, long enough for Paddy's dogs to swoop in. An almighty dog fight exploded. Biting, shaking, growling. With the dogs momentarily distracted Paddy went after Maysa who had escaped but had only made it a short distance, scrambling through the bush. He ran her down in a moment. Grabbing her arm, he turned her to face him, then pushed her backwards until she fell. He knelt down and then lay on her, all his weight on her, panting foul breath in her face. She could feel his arousal as he tried to kiss her, fumbling with clothes and fighting. Maysa had given in to the inevitability of the situation. She lay still for a moment, barely conscious of Paddy's fumbling fingers and began to drift, almost out of her body. Visions of Tom came to her, the river picnic, Milly, Tom's grief, Irene and Len, like parents now and Tom, always Tom.

Mustering her last reserves of strength, she decided she would not give in without a fight. She had to survive. She began punching and clawing at Paddy, leaving two bloodied scratches down the side of his face. But Paddy was too strong, driven by hatred and passion.

Just as Paddy began to overpower Maysa, Banjo was attached again. The dogs were barking furiously. The scene was chaotic as Paddy picked up a rock and slammed it down on Banjo finally beating him. Banjo fell limp and rolled on his side. The rock, stained with Banjo's blood lay next to his bleeding head. Maysa looked at Banjo and finally gave in, tears streamed down her face. She reached out to Banjo and stroked his face, deathly still. Paddy lifted himself off Maysa and knelt in front of her, bemused by her display of affection for the finally dead dog. He was relieved and excited as he realised the fight was over. She lay still, compliant, face turned to Banjo. Paddy undid his belt and pants and pushed them down.

'You want to pat something? Pat this.' He pushed his underwear down.

It wasn't until the very last second, he turned to see the bloodied rock in Maysa's hand that struck his face. A solid thump, then darkness. His limp body fell on her.

★   ★   ★

Tom was now riding steadily back in the direction of the barking dogs, but it was virtually impossible to pinpoint the location. He had hoped that Billy, Barney and mostly Banjo would still be with Maysa. He was certain Banjo would be. He had been found close by Milly when her body was found. And then there was silence, not a sound to follow. He stopped Bess, but he could hear nothing but his own heart beating in his chest. He continued on, walking slowly, hoping he would hear something, occasionally calling out for Maysa, Billy, and Barney.

Another fifteen minutes passed before Billy and Barney burst out of the bush enthusiastically. Tom leapt off Bess and squatted down and received the excited dogs as he had never done before.

Maysa was in such a state of shock. It took a moment to register that Paddy was lifeless. Was he dead? She couldn't help but hope so. With great effort, she pushed Paddy off herself and looked down and then quickly away, revolted by the sight of his partially clothed body. His face was badly scratched down one side from her fingernails and bruised on the other side by the rock. She wasn't sure whether the blood on his face was his or Banjo's. She took just a moment to kneel down and pat Banjo.

'Thank you, again,' she gently whispered as tears streamed down her face. She had to run, and she did. She barely recognised the pain in her injured leg as she made off through the scrub as quickly as she could. Billy and Barney trotted along with her.

Maysa was finally able to put some time and distance between her and Paddy. She was terrified he would materialise yet again and knew she couldn't fight him off anymore. She was scrambling through the scrub, scratched and bruised when she tripped and rolled down into a creek bed. It was dry except for the last signs of the previous night's storm.

If you're ever lost and want to find the river, follow the creek downstream. You'll get there in the end. Tom had enjoyed showing off his bushcraft to Maysa as they rode around the property together. She smiled to herself, remembering. But which direction? It was dry. She sat against the bank for a moment, feeling relatively hidden from view. And then, even in this heightened state of anxiety, she was able to think clearly. Much of the long tufted grass was bent and pointing in one direction, the direction of the water flow from the flash flood the previous evening. She set off in what she was sure would be the direction of the river. It was a few moments before she realised that Billy and Barney were gone. She couldn't backtrack in the direction she'd come from, and she couldn't call out. It was too risky, so she went on alone.

Maysa stumbled along in the creek bed as quickly as she could, occasionally stumbling and struggling, and being reminded of her twisted ankle by

337

searing pain. All the while, she was terrified she would see Paddy around the next corner, or perhaps his dogs, hunting her down on his deadly behalf.

Finally, her persistence and determination were rewarded when she noticed the creek bed beginning to show signs of moisture, sticky mud and occasional puddles. She scrambled out of the creek bed and up amongst the thorny scrub at its edge. She stood, under cover of the last of the scrub and there before her, was the river. Just beyond it, like a sort of paradise beckoning her, was their picnic spot. In all this vast endless space, she had arrived at this place so special to her and Tom. She stood and breathed a sigh of relief.

Maysa's respite was short-lived when she heard a distant barking dog. It was Paddy. It had to be. She knew he would just keep coming for her until one of them was finished, but she was determined it wouldn't be her. She stepped tentatively out of the cover of the scrub and moved quickly toward the river's edge. It was only about fifty metres to the other side and the picnic spot, and she knew her way home from there. She stepped nervously into the water. It was as threatening as Paddy. It was vastly different from what she had experienced with Tom. It was flowing far more quickly, and the bank gave way quickly to deep water. Looking across the river to the relative shallows, she pictured herself and Tom sitting in the water. It was shallow and ran slowly each time they picnicked. But not this time, and definitely not on this side of the river bend.

There was the barking again. Terrified, she stepped out and skidded down the river bottom until it was up to her waist, and then her feet were pulled out from under her by the current. She disappeared under the surface in an instant, vanished without a trace.

All Tom had to work on was the direction the dogs had come from. So he pushed into the bush on Bess. He cast the dogs out with an order, then back with a whistle, time and time again. And then, there through the trees, standing in a clearing was a horse. As he closed in, he could see it was Paddy's horse. And then there was Paddy, mounting his horse. He looked injured or groggy.

'Paddy.' Tom yelled.

Startled, Paddy looked around to see Tom emerging from the scrub. Feet in stirrups, he turned his horse to the scrub and kicked it hard. It leapt forward and took off, and so did Tom.

'Paddy, wait.' Tom was almost screaming as he surged forward on Bess.

A superior horseman, Tom closed in on Paddy quickly. Each time he broke into a clearing Paddy would push away, and Tom would lose a little ground. Finally, they broke into a large open space, and it was horse against horse. Tom felt nothing but hatred for Paddy now as the truth was so painfully clear. He unhitched his stockwhip as he rode and let it hang by his side as he stood in the stirrups at a gallop. He closed in on the exhausted Paddy, close enough now to see his scratched face and the look of terror in his eyes.

'Stop, NOW!' he screamed. But Paddy rode on.

The first crack of the whip landed right across Paddy's back with the end of the whip just catching the horse's rump and sending it pig-rooting at full speed. Paddy cried out in pain. He rode on. The second swing and the whip curled around Paddy's neck like a snake. Another cry in pain was short-lived as Tom yanked the whip backwards. Paddy let go of his reins, snatching at the whip and came off his horse, hitting the ground like a sack of wheat. Winded, he could hardly move. Tom was on him in an instant. He grabbed Paddy's shirt pulling him upward.

'Where is she?'

'I don't know what you're talking about.' Paddy spluttered.

Tom drove a fist into Paddy's face.

'Where is she? Tell me now.'

Spitting blood, Paddy smiled the smile of an insane man ready and resolved to meet his maker.

'I have no idea what you're talking about,' he spluttered.

The whip was still curled around Paddy's neck when Tom stood up, pulling at the whip and creating a leather noose. Paddy choked and coughed.

'Let's help you work this out then.' Tom strode off and dragged Paddy with the whip as though he weighed nothing. Paddy clawed at the whip as it crushed his throat. He stopped for a moment.

'Where's Maysa? Last chance.' Paddy couldn't talk now even if he tried. Tom dragged him again, another ten feet and Paddy began to blackout when Tom stopped again easing the pressure of the whip. Paddy gasped for breath and clutched his throat. Tom rolled him on his stomach and knelt on his back. It was a few moments before Paddy realised what the strange crawling sensation was. He was face-first on a bull ant nest, and the disturbance had driven them into a frenzy. They were quickly covering his face, trying to get in his nostrils, ears and down his shirt. He clenched his eyes shut. The ants began biting. Tom's hands were being bitten as he held Paddy down.

'Tom, please. Stop. You'll bloody kill me.' Paddy spat out ants as the bites kept coming.

'That's the idea. And it won't be an easy death.'

Tom became aware of a vehicle approaching. He looked up to see a ute, closely followed by a second and then horsemen. Len and the search party had also become aware of the dog barking and had finally caught up. The first vehicle was sounding its horn urgently now.

'Yer done now, Spooney.' In a stupor, Paddy tried to smile, before Tom lifted him one more time and slammed Paddy's head down on the bull ant nest.

'We'll see.' Tom whistled Bess, and she trotted

toward him, followed by the dogs. He mounted the horse as the vehicles pulled up and Paddy rolled himself off the ant nest.

'She must be in there.' Tom pointed to the scrub. 'I have to find her.' He rode off back in the direction from which they'd come.

The search party, including Penfold, got out of the vehicles. They called after Tom, but he wouldn't stop, and then he was gone.

CHAPTER THIRTY-EIGHT

Tom moved quickly, scanning about continually. He wasn't sure whether he was looking for Maysa moving, sitting still, hurt or ok. He couldn't bear to believe he was too late. He was frantic but determined to keep his head. He knew he was no use to her if he lost control. He backtracked to where he had seen Paddy at first and then scanned about the area looking for any sign of a clue. He circled the clearing where he'd found Paddy. Larger circles on each pass and more frustration, until finally, Bess shied, and Tom identified the cause of her fright. There, lying on the ground in front, was a dog. It was Banjo. Dead. Tom dismounted and knelt beside Banjo. He was long gone, no sign of a soul in his eyes. The glassy-eyed empty look of a dead animal, Tom had seen so many times before. The sight struck terror into Tom's heart. He scanned about and found a bearing for later, to come back and collect Milly's faithful companion, Maysa's friend.

On his horse again, Tom, with no sense of where to look or what he might find rode quickly back to the search party who were agreeing on next moves. Paddy had given them nothing, but his silence had confirmed his involvement. Penfold had cuffed Paddy and had him sitting in the front seat of his vehicle. Paddy was a sorry sight, scratched, bruised and covered in bites.

Len smoothed out an area of red dust and mapped out the paddock and the scrubland. Only Paddy could see the irony in that, as he watched on in pain from Penfold's vehicle. Those on a horse were sent to the east, north and south in the scrub. Vehicles would track the perimeter of the scrubby area, moving on foot in locations to cover as much ground as possible. Tom was sent south, around the scrub and as far as the river, and then back into the bush to backtrack north again. If anyone found anything, they'd have to fire a gun to alert the others. The horsemen could crack whips, which were often as loud as guns. Worst case, they could light a fire and heap it up with green leaves to make smoke. Everyone was to listen for signals and scan the horizon for signs of smoke.

Tom skirted the edge of the bushland heading toward the river crossing. There was no sign of anything. With a voice almost gone, he called as often as he could. But nothing. He made the river crossing. The water was up. The previous night's storm had been heavier upstream along the river, and they were seeing the signs of that now. He suddenly had a vision of the moment at the river so long ago when Maysa said to him '*I am ashamed to say, I can't even swim.*' For a brief moment, he hoped, if Maysa had made the river, she hadn't tried to cross it. He continued upstream with renewed urgency. As agreed, he would head back into the scrub somewhere just downstream from where he and Maysa had swum that wonderful day that suddenly seemed so long ago.

He could see their place, in the shade of the big old river gum, on the other side of the river not far ahead. It was time to head into the scrub and begin the relentless scanning back and forward.

'Maysa,' he cried out one last time. He sat still. Nothing. He turned Bess and started to walk into the scrub. But stopped. He'd imagined it. He knew he was desperate.

'Maysa!' He cried out again desperately. Then . . .

'Tom.' Ever so faintly, in the distance. There it was again.

'Maysa!' He yelled as loud as he could, excited and frantic.

'Tom.'

He kicked Bess into a trot, and stood up in his stirrups craning to see into the distance along the river bed. Just a flash, but he could see a hand waving. By the time he made it to Maysa, he couldn't contain his smile and nor could she. His relief exploded in tears as he leapt from the horse even before it stopped. He ran to her and took her in his arms, lifting her off the ground and squeezing her so hard she shrieked.

'Are you ok?'

'I am. I am now.' She held his face in her hands. 'I am so happy to see you.'

He gathered her into his arms, and she rested her head against his chest.

'Did he hurt you?' Tom whispered.

'He tried . . . He really tried. But no. No, he didn't.'

'Thank God.'

'Poor Banjo. He killed him.'

'I know. I'm so sorry. I found him.' Tom could feel Maysa crying.

'He was a hero, Tom.'

'I wish I could have protected you.'

'You did. It was the thought of you that kept me going when I was just about ready to give in. I really was.' Maysa paused for a moment. 'He's still out there, Tom. He was unconscious when I ran off.'

'No, no he's not. We got him. I got him.'

'No . . . oh no, you didn't . . .'

'No, I didn't. I did give him a bit of a belting, but he was already pretty beaten up by the time I got to him.' Tom took Maysa by the shoulders and held her back and looked at her. 'Did you do that? You did! You gave him a bloody good belting, didn't you?' He smiled.

'I did. In the end, I think he would have been sorry he attacked me. And poor Banjo of course.

346

Banjo attacked him over and over until . . .' Maysa burst into tears again.

'Yep. I reckon he was sorry. We make a dangerous pair, you and me. No one will ever cross us again.' They laughed and hugged.

'You're all wet. What happened? You didn't . . .'

'Let's just say, I am looking forward to those swimming lessons you promised me.'

Tom held Maysa to him. Her life was more precious to him than his own, and he vowed and knew he would never let anything happen to her ever again.

'Stand back.'

Tom cracked the stockwhip over and over with sheer joy.

CHAPTER THIRTY-NINE

Two months later.

'Here's to the happy couple.' With an arm around Irene, Len held a champagne glass high, as he toasted Tom and Maysa. 'Here here.' The gathering responded.

It was late in the afternoon, and the engagement party was well underway. All the Sutherland and Patterson clans were gathered at the Patterson homestead for the celebration. Tom held Maysa tight as he made a brief speech.

'One more gift, Maysa.' Tom's dad leapt forward and handed Tom a brand new Akubra hat which he presented to Maysa, much to the enjoyment of the crowd who cheered as he put it on her.

The crowd turned as they heard a vehicle approaching. Len looked at Tom and winked. The Holden ute pulled up amongst a cloud of dust. Maysa knew it immediately. It was Bob Jackson, and she was so happy to see him. Bob was out of the vehicle quickly and striding across to shake hands with Tom and to embrace Maysa.

'I am so happy for you both. Edi sends her best wishes. She is very pleased.'

'Thanks, Bob. It is so good to see you.' Maysa squeezed Bob's arm. 'Surely you didn't come all this way for the engagement party?'

'No. Of course not. I've come to take you to the next shed of course.' Everyone laughed. 'Seriously though, it is an engagement party after all, so I have a gift. Hold on a moment.' Bob returned to his ute that he'd parked in the shade of a tree and returned a moment later with a box that he handed to Tom. 'You hold this mate so your fiancé can open it up.'

Maysa smiled nervously, then carefully opened the lid of the box and a small head appeared. A little Blue Heeler puppy leapt up to the side of the box and licked Maysa's hand.

'He's your next Banjo.' Tom smiled at Maysa, who smiled back through tears as she lifted the puppy out of the box and held him in her arms as he tried desperately to lick her chin.

Everyone began to talk again and continue on with the happy celebrations. Maysa, the puppy in one arm, hooked her spare arm through Bob's and turned him toward the party.

'Let me get you a beer, Bob. Thank you so much. He is beautiful. I have missed Banjo terribly. I hadn't realised just what he meant to me. It was horrible. I guess you heard the story.'

'I did. He was a true hero. And nothing would

have made him happier than to know you were safe. I'm sure of it.'

'I will call him Uki, like ukulele, or eucalyptus.' Bob and Maysa laughed at the puppy's new name.

'So, Bob. What about Rick? I miss him so much. Do you have news of my baby brother? I am so anxious to hear about him. What's he doing?'

'Well . . . ask him yourself.' Maysa was shocked, as Bob turned her around slowly to face the garden gate again. There was Rick, standing with a kitbag at his feet, Akubra in hand and a smile from ear to ear.

The End